The Children's Pilgrimage

L. T. Meade

ESPRIOS DIGITAL PUBLISHING

The Children's Pilgrimage

FIRST PART.

"LOOKING FOR THE GUIDE."

"The night is dark, and I am far from home.
Lead Thou me on"

CHAPTER I.

"THREE ON A DOORSTEP."

In a poor part of London, but not in the very poorest part—two children sat on a certain autumn evening, side by side on a doorstep. The eldest might have been ten, the youngest eight. The eldest was a girl, the youngest a boy. Drawn up in front of these children, looking into their little faces with hungry, loving, pathetic eyes, lay a mongrel dog.

The three were alone, for the street in which they sat was a cul-de-sac —leading nowhere; and at this hour, on this Sunday evening, seemed quite deserted. The boy and girl were no East End waifs; they were clean; they looked respectable; and the doorstep which gave them a temporary resting-place belonged to no far-famed Stepney or Poplar. It stood in a little, old-fashioned, old-world court, back of Bloomsbury. They were a foreign-looking little pair—not in their dress, which was truly English in its clumsiness and want of picturesque coloring—but their faces were foreign. The contour was peculiar, the setting of the two pairs of eyes—un-Saxon. They sat very close together, a grave little couple. Presently the girl threw her arm round the boy's neck, the boy laid his head on her shoulder. In this position those who watched could have traced motherly lines round this little girl's firm mouth. She was a creature to defend and protect. The evening fell and the court grew dark, but the boy had found shelter on her breast, and the dog, coming close, laid his head on her lap.

After a time the boy raised his eyes, looked at her and spoke:

"Will it be soon, Cecile?"

"I think so, Maurice; I think it must be soon now."

The Children's Pilgrimage

"I'm so cold, Cecile, and it's getting so dark. "

"Never mind, darling, stepmother will soon wake now, and then you can come indoors and sit by the fire. "

The boy, with a slight impatient sigh, laid his head once more on her shoulder, and the grave trio sat on as before.

Presently a step was heard approaching inside the house—it came along the passage, the door was opened, and a gentleman in a plain black coat came out. He was a doctor and a young man. His smooth, almost boyish face looked so kind that it could not but be an index to a charitable heart.

He stopped before the children, looking at them with interest and pity.

"How is our stepmother, Dr. Austin? " asked Cecile, raising her head and speaking with alacrity.

"Your stepmother is very ill, my dear—very ill indeed. I stopped with her to write a letter which she wants me to post. Yes, she is very ill, but she is awake now; you may go upstairs; you won't disturb her. "

"Oh, come, Cecile, " said little Maurice, springing to his feet; "stepmother is awake, and we may get to the fire. I am so bitter cold. "

There was not a particle of anything but a kind of selfish longing for warmth and comfort on his little face. He ran along the passage holding out his hand to his sister, but Cecile drew back. She came out more into the light and looked straight up into the tall doctor's face:

"Is my stepmother going to be ill very long, Dr. Austin? "

"No, my dear; I don't expect her illness will last much longer. "

"Oh, then, she'll be quite well to-morrow. "

"Perhaps—in a sense—who knows! " said the doctor, jerking out his words and speaking queerly. He looked as if he wanted to say more, but finally nodding to the child, turned on his heel and walked away.

Cecile, satisfied with this answer, and reading no double meaning in it, followed her brother and the dog upstairs. She entered a tolerably comfortable sitting-room, where, on a sofa, lay a woman partly dressed. The woman's cheeks were crimson, and her large eyes, which were wide open, were very bright. Little Maurice had already found a seat and a hunch of bread and butter, and was enjoying both drawn up by a good fire, while the dog Toby crouched at his feet and snapped at morsels which he threw him. Cecile, scarcely glancing at the group by the fire, went straight up to the woman on the sofa:

"Stepmother, " she said, taking her hand in hers, "Dr. Austin says you'll be quite well to-morrow. "

The woman gazed hard and hungrily into the sweet eyes of the child; she held her small hand with almost feverish energy, but she did not speak, and when Maurice called out from the fire, "Cecile, I want some more bread and butter, " she motioned to her to go and attend to him.

All his small world did attend to Maurice at once, so Cecile ran to him, and after supplying him with milk and bread and butter, she took his hand to lead him to bed. There were only two years between the children, but Maurice seemed quite a baby, and Cecile a womanly creature.

When they got into the tiny bedroom, which they shared together, Cecile helped her little brother to undress, and tucked him up when he got into bed.

"Now, Toby, " she said, addressing the dog, whose watchful eyes had followed her every movement, "you must lie down by Maurice and keep him company; and good-night, Maurice, dear. "

"Won't you come to bed too, Cecile? "

"Presently, darling; but first I have to see to stepmother. Our stepmother is very ill, you know, Maurice. "

"Very ill, you know, " repeated Maurice sleepily, and without comprehending; then he shut his eyes, and Cecile went back into the sitting-room.

The sick woman had never stirred during the child's absence, now she turned round eagerly. The little girl went up to the sofa with a confident step. Though her stepmother was so ill now, she would be quite well to-morrow, so the doctor had said, and surely the best way to bring that desirable end about was to get her to have as much sleep as possible.

"Stepmother, " said Cecile softly, "'tis very late; may I bring in your night-dress and air it by the fire, and then may I help you to get into bed, stepmother dear? "

"No, Cecile, " replied the sick woman. "I'm not going to stir from this yere sofa to-night. "

"Oh, but then—but then you won't be quite well to-morrow, " said the child, tears springing to her eyes.

"Who said I'd be quite well to-morrow? " asked Cecile's stepmother.

"Dr. Austin, mother; I asked him, and he said, 'Yes, '—at least he said 'Perhaps, ' but I think he was very sure from his look. "

"Aye, child, aye; he was very sure, but he was not meaning what you were meaning. Well, never mind; but what was that you called me just now, Cecile? "

"I—I——" said Cecile, hesitating and coloring.

"Aye, like enough 'twas a slip of your tongue. But you said, 'Mother'; you said it without the 'step' added on. You don't know — not that it matters now—but you won't never know how that 'stepmother' hardened my heart against you and Maurice, child. "

"'Twas our father, " said Cecile; "he couldn't forget our own mother, and he asked us not to say 'Mother, ' and me and Maurice, we could think of no other way. It wasn't that we—that I—didn't love. "

"Aye, child, you're a tender little thing; I'm not blaming you, and maybe I couldn't have borne the word from your lips, for I didn't love you, Cecile—neither you nor Maurice—I had none of the mother about me for either of you little kids. Aye, you were right enough; your father, Maurice D'Albert, never forgot his Rosalie, as he called her. I always thought as Frenchmen were fickle, but he worn't not fickle enough for me. Well, Cecile, I'm no way sleepy, and I've a deal to say, and no one but you to say it to; I'm more strong now than I have been for the day, so I'd better say my say while I have any strength left. You build up the fire, and then come back to me, child. Build it up big, for I'm not going to bed to-night."

CHAPTER II.

A SOLEMN PROMISE.

When Cecile had built up the fire, she made a cup of tea and brought it to her stepmother. Mrs. D'Albert drank it off greedily; afterward she seemed refreshed and she made Cecile put another pillow under her head and draw her higher on the sofa.

"You're a good, tender-hearted child, Cecile, " she said to the little creature, who was watching her every movement with a kind of trembling eagerness. Cecile's sensitive face flushed at the words of praise, and she came very close to the sofa. "Yes, you're a good child, " repeated Mrs. D'Albert; "you're yer father's own child, and he was very good, though he was a foreigner. For myself I don't much care for good people, but when you're dying, I don't deny as they're something of a comfort. Good people are to be depended on, and you're good, Cecile. "

But there was only one sentence in these words which Cecile took in.

"When you're dying, " she repeated, and every vestige of color forsook her lips.

"Yes, my dear, when you're dying. I'm dying, Cecile; that was what the doctor meant when he said I'd he quite well; he meant as I'd lie straight and stiff, and have my eyes shut, and be put in a long box and be buried, that was what he meant, Cecile. But look here now, you're not to cry about it—not at present, I mean; you may as much as you like by and by, but not now. I'm not crying, and 'tis a deal worse for me; but there ain't no time for tears, they only weaken and do no good, and I has a deal to say. Don't you dare shed a tear now, Cecile; I can't a-bear the sight of tears; you may cry by and by, but now you has got to listen to me. "

"I won't cry, " said Cecile; she made a great effort set her lips firm, and looked hard at her stepmother.

"That's a good, brave girl. Now I can talk in comfort. I want to talk all I can to you to-night, my dear, for to-morrow I may have the weakness back again, and besides your Aunt Lydia will be here! "

"Who's my Aunt Lydia? " asked Cecile.

"She ain't rightly your aunt at all, she's my sister; but she's the person as will have to take care of you and Maurice after I'm dead. "

"Oh! " said Cecile; her little face fell, and a bright color came into her cheeks.

"She's my own sister, " continued Mrs. D'Albert, "but I don't like her much. She's a good woman enough; not up to yer father's standard, but still fair enough. But she's hard—she is hard ef you like. I don't profess to have any violent love for you two little tots, but I'd sooner not leave you to the care o' Aunt Lydia ef I could help it. "

"Don't leave us to her care; do find some one kind—some one as 'ull be kind to me, and Maurice, and Toby—do help it, stepmother, " said Cecile.

"I *can't* help it, child; and there's no use bothering a dying woman who's short of breath. You and Maurice have got to go to my sister, your Aunt Lydia, and ef you'll take a word of advice by and by, Cecile, from one as 'ull be in her grave, you'll not step-aunt her—she's short of temper, Aunt Lydia is. Yes, " continued the sick woman, speaking fast, and gasping for breath a little, "you have got to go to my sister Lydia. I have sent her word, and she'll come tomorrow—but—never mind that now. I ha' something else I must say to you, Cecile. "

"Yes, stepmother. "

"I ha' no one else to say it to, so you listen werry hard. I'm going to put a great trust on you, little mite as you are—a great, great trust; you has got to do something solemn, and to promise something solemn too, Cecile. "

"Yes, " said Cecile, opening her blue eyes wide.

"Aye, you may well say yes, and open yer eyes big; you're going to get some'ut on yer shoulders as 'ull make a woman of yer. You mayn't like it, I don't suppose as you will; but for all that you ha' got to promise, because I won't die easy, else. Cecile, " suddenly bending forward, and grasping the child's arm almost cruelly, "I can't die at *all* till you promise me this solemn and grave, as though it were yer very last breath. "

"I will promise, stepmother, " said Cecile. "I'll promise solemn, and I'll keep it solemn; don't you be fretted, now as you're a-dying. I don't mind ef it is hard. Father often give me hard things to do, and I did 'em. Father said I wor werry dependable, " continued the little creature gravely.

To her surprise, her stepmother bent forward and and kissed her. The kiss she gave was warm, intense, passionate; such a kiss as Cecile had never before received from those lips.

"You're a good child, " she said eagerly; "yes, you're a very good child; you promise me solemn and true, then I'll die easy and comforted. Yes, I'll die easy, even though Lovedy ain't with me, even though I'll never lay my eyes on my Lovedy again. "

"Who's Lovedy? " asked Cecile.

"Aye, child, we're coming to Lovedy, 'tis about Lovedy you've got to promise. Lovedy, she's my daughter, Cecile; she ain't no step-child, but my own, my werry own, bone of my bone, flesh of my flesh. "

"I never knew as you had a daughter of yer werry own, " said Cecile.

"But I had, Cecile. I had as true a child to me as you were to yer father. My own, my own, my darling! Oh, my bonnie one, 'tis bitter, bitter to die with her far, far away! Not for four years now have I seen my girl. Oh, if I could see her face once again! "

Here the poor woman, who was opening up her life-story to the astonished and frightened child, lost her self-control, and sobbed hysterically. Cecile fetched water, and gave it to her, and in a few moments she became calm.

"There now, my dear, sit down and listen. I'll soon be getting weak, and I must tell everything tonight. Years ago, Cecile, afore ever I met yer father, I was married. My husband was a sailor, and he died at sea. But we had one child, one beautiful, bonnie English girl; nothing foreign about her, bless her! She was big and tall, and fair as a lily, and her hair, it was that golden that when the sun shone on it it almost dazzled you. I never seed such hair as my Lovedy's, never,

never; it all fell in curls long below her waist. I *was* that proud of it I spent hours dressing it and washing it, and keeping it like any lady's. Then her eyes, they were just two bits of the blue sky in her head, and her little teeth were like white pearls, and her lips were always smiling. She had an old-world English name taken from my mother, but surely it fitted her, for to look at her was to love her.

"Well, my dear, my girl and me, we lived together till she was near fifteen, and never a cloud between us. We were very poor; we lived by my machining and what Lovedy could do to help me. There was never a cloud between us, until one day I met yer father. I don't say as yer father loved me much, for his heart was in the grave with your mother, but he wanted someone to care for you two, and he thought me a tidy, notable body, and so he asked me to marry him and he seemed well off, and I thought it 'ud be a good thing for Lovedy. Besides, I had a real fancy for him; so I promised. I never even guessed as my girl 'ud mind, and I went home to our one shabby little room, quite light-hearted like, to tell her. But oh, Cecile, I little knew my Lovedy! Though I had reared her I did not know her nature. My news seemed to change her all over.

"From being so sweet and gentle, she seemed to have the very devil woke up in her. First soft, and trembling and crying, she went down on her knees and begged me to give yer father up; but I liked him, and I felt angered with her for taking on what I called foolish, and I wouldn't yield; and I told her she was real silly, and I was ashamed of her. They were the bitterest words I ever flung at her, and they seemed to freeze up her whole heart. She got up off her knees and walked away with her pretty head in the air, and wouldn't speak to me for the evening; and the next day she come to me quick and haughty like, and said that if I gave her a stepfather she would not live with me; she would go to her Aunt Fanny, and her Aunt Fanny would take her to Paris, and there she would see life. Fanny was my youngest sister, and she was married to a traveler for one of the big shops, and often went about with her husband and had a gay time. She had no children of her own, and I knew she envied me my Lovedy beyond words.

"I was so hurt with Lovedy for saying she would leave me for her Aunt Fanny, that I said, bitter and sharp, she might do as she liked, and that I did not care.

"Then she turned very red and went away and sat down and wrote a letter, and I knew she had made up her mind to leave me. Still I wasn't really frightened. I said to myself, I'll pretend to let her have her own way, and she'll come round fast enough; and I began to get ready for my wedding, and took no heed of Lovedy. The night before I was married she came to me again. She was white as a sheet, and all the hardness had gone out of her.

"'Mother, mother, mother, ' she said, and she put her dear, bonnie arms round me and clasped me tight to her. 'Mother, give him up, for Lovedy's sake; it will break my heart, mother. Mother, I am jealous; I must have you altogether or not at all. Stay at home with your own Lovedy, for pity's sake, for pity's sake. '

"Of course I soothed her and petted her, and I think—I do think now—that she, poor darling, had a kind of notion I was going to yield, and that night she slept in my arms.

"The next morning I put on my neat new dress and bonnet, and went into her room.

"'Lovedy, will you come to church to see your mother married? '

"I never forgot—never, never, the look she gave me. She went white as marble, and her eyes blazed at me and then grew hard, and she put her head down on her hands, and, do all in my power, I could not get a word out of her.

"Well, Cecile, yer father and I were married, and when we came back Lovedy was gone. There was just a little bit of a note, all blotted with tears, on the table. Cecile, I have got that little note, and you must put it in my coffin. These words were writ on it by my poor girl: "'Mother, you had no pity, so your Lovedy is gone. Good-by, mother. '

"Yes, Cecile, that was the note, and what it said was true. My Lovedy was gone. She had disappeared, and so had her Aunt Fanny, and never, never from that hour have I heard one single word of Lovedy. "

Mrs. D'Albert paused here. The telling of her tale seemed to have changed her. In talking of her child the hard look had left her face, an expression almost beautiful in its love and longing filled her poor

The Children's Pilgrimage

dim eyes, and when Cecile, in her sympathy, slipped her little hand into hers, she did not resist the pressure.

"Yes, Cecile, " she continued, turning to the little girl, "I lost Lovedy—more surely than if she was dead, was she torn from me. I never got one clew to her. Yer father did all he could for me; he was more than kind, he did pity me, and he made every inquiry for my girl and advertised for her, but her aunt had taken her out of England, and I never heard—I never heard of my Lovedy from the day I married yer father, Cecile. It changed me, child; it changed me most bitter. I grew hard, and I never could love you nor Maurice, no, nor even yer good father, very much after that. I always looked upon you three as the people who took by bonnie girl away. It was unfair of me. Now, as I'm dying, I'll allow as it was real unfair, but the pain and hunger in my heart was most awful to bear. You'll forgive me for never loving you, when you think of all the pain I had to bear, Cecile. "

"Yes, poor stepmother, " answered the little girl, stooping down and kissing her hand. "And, oh! " continued Cecile with fervor, "I wish—I wish I could find Lovedy for you again. "

"Why, Cecile, that's just what you've got to do, " said her stepmother; "you've got to look for Lovedy: you're a very young girl; you're only a child; but you've got to go on looking, *always — always* until you find her. The finding of my Lovedy is to be yer life-work, Cecile. I don't want you to begin now, not till you're older and have got more sense; but you has to keep it firm in yer head, and in two or three years' time you must begin. You must go on looking until you find my Lovedy. That is what you have to promise me before I die. "

"Yes, stepmother. "

"Look me full in the face, Cecile, and make the promise as solemn as though it were yer werry last breath—look me in the face, Cecile, and say after me, 'I promise to find Lovedy again. '"

"I promise to find Lovedy again, " repeated Cecile.

"Now kiss me, child. "

Cecile did so.

The Children's Pilgrimage

"That kiss is a seal, " continued her stepmother; "ef you break yer promise, you'll remember as you kissed the lips of her who is dead, and the feel 'ull haunt you, and you'll never know a moment's happiness. But you're a good girl, Cecile—a good, dependable child, and I'm not afeared for you. And now, my dear, you has made the promise, and I has got to give you directions. Cecile, did you ever wonder why your stepmother worked so hard? "

"I thought we must be very poor, " said Cecile.

"No, my dear, yer father had that little bit of money coming in from France every year. It will come in for four or five years more, and it will be enough to pay Aunt Lydia for taking care on you both. No, Cecile, I did not work for myself, nor for you and Maurice—I worked for Lovedy. All that beautiful church embroidery as I sat up so late at night over, the money I got for it was for my girl; every lily I worked, and every passion-flower, and every leaf, took a little drop of my heart's blood, I think; but 'twas done for her. Now, Cecile, put yer hand under my pillow—there's a purse there. "

Cecile drew out an old, worn Russia-leather purse.

"Lovedy 'ud recognize that purse, " said her mother, "it belonged to her own father. She and I always kept our little earnings in it, in the old happy days. Now open the purse, Cecile; you must know what is inside it. "

Cecile pressed the spring and took out a little bundle of notes.

"There, child, you open them—see, there are four notes—four Bank of England notes for ten pounds each—that's forty pounds—forty pounds as her mother earned for my girl. You give her those notes in the old purse, Cecile. You give them into her own hands, and you say, 'Your mother sent you those. Your mother is dead, but she broke her heart for you, she never forgot your voice when you said for pity's sake, and she asks you now for pity's sake to forgive her. ' That's the message as you has to take to Lovedy, Cecile. "

"Yes, stepmother, I'll take her that message—very faithful; very, very faithful, stepmother. "

"And now put yer hand into the purse again, Cecile; there's more money in the purse—see! there's fifteen pounds all in gold. I had that

The Children's Pilgrimage

money all in gold, for I knew as it 'ud be easier for you—that fifteen pounds is for you, Cecile, to spend in looking for Lovedy; you must not waste it, and you must spend it on nothing else. I guess you'll have to go to France to find my Lovedy; but ef you're very careful, that money ought to last till you find her. "

"There'll be heaps and heaps of money here, " said Cecile, looking at the little pile of gold with almost awe.

"Yes, child, but there won't, not unless you're *very* saving, and ask all sensible questions about how to go and how best to find Lovedy. You must walk as much as you can, Cecile, and live very plain, for you may have to go a power of miles—yes, a power, before you find my girl; and ef you're starving, you must not touch those four notes of money, only the fifteen pounds. Remember, only that; and when you get to the little villages away in France, you may go to the inns and ask there ef an English girl wor ever seen about the place. You describe her, Cecile—tall, a tall, fair English girl, with hair like the sun; you say as her name is Lovedy—Lovedy Joy. You must get a deal o' sense to do this business proper, Cecile; but ef you has sense and patience, why you will find my girl. "

"There's only one thing, stepmother, " said Cecile; "I'll do everything as you tells me, every single thing; I'll be as careful as possible, and I'll save every penny; but I can't go to look for your Lovedy without Maurice, for I promised father afore ever I promised you as I'd never lose sight on Maurice till he grew up, and it 'ud be too long to put off looking for Lovedy till Maurice was grown up, stepmother. "

"I suppose it would, " answered Cecile's stepmother; "'tis a pity, for he'll spend some of the money. But there, it can't be helped, and you'll do your best. I'll trust you to do yer werry best, Cecile. "

"My werry, werry best, " said Cecile earnestly.

"Well, child, there's only one thing more. All this as I'm telling you is a secret, a solemn, solemn secret. Ef yer Aunt Lydia gets wind on it, or ef she ever even guesses as you have all that money, everything 'ull be ruined. Yer aunt is hard and saving, and she do hanker sore for money, she always did—did Lydia, and not all the stories you could tell her 'ud make her leave you that money; she 'ud take it away, she 'ud be quite cruel enough to take the money away that I worked myself into my grave to save, and then it 'ud be all up with Lovedy. No, Cecile, you must take the purse o' money away with you this very night, hide it in yer dress, or anywhere, for Aunt Lydia may be here early in the morning, and the weakness may be on me then. Yes, Cecile, you has charge on that money, fifty-five pounds in all; fifteen pounds for you to spend, and forty to give to Lovedy. Wherever you go, you must hide it so safe that no one 'ull ever guess as a poor little girl like you has money, for anyone might rob you, child; but the one as I'm fearing the most is yer Aunt Lydia. "

CHAPTER III.

"NEVER A MOMENT TO GET READY. "

To all these directions Cecile listened, and she there and then took the old worn purse with its precious contents away with her, and went into the bedroom which she shared with her brother, and taking out her needle and thread she made a neat, strong bag for the purse, and this bag she sewed securely into the lining of her frock-body. She showed her stepmother what she had done, who smiled and seemed satisfied.

For the rest of that night Cecile sat on by the sofa where Mrs. D'Albert lay. Now that the excitement of telling her tale had passed, the dreaded weakness had come back to the poor woman. Her voice, so strong and full of interest when speaking of Lovedy, had sunk to a mere whisper. She liked, however, to have her little stepdaughter close to her, and even held her hand in hers. That little hand now was a link between her and her lost girl, and as such, for the first time she really loved Cecile.

As for the child herself, she was too excited far to sleep. The sorrow so loving a heart must have felt at the prospect of her stepmother's approaching death was not just now realized; she was absorbed in the thought of the tale she had heard, of the promise she had made.

Cecile was grave and womanly far beyond her years, and she knew well that she had taken no light thing on her young shoulders. To shirk this duty would not be possible to a nature such as hers. No, she must go through with it; she had registered a vow, and she must fulfill it. Her little face, always slightly careworn, looked now almost pathetic under its load of care.

"Yes, poor stepmother, " she kept saying to herself, "I will find Lovedy—I will find Lovedy or die. "

Then she tried to imagine the joyful moment when her quest would be crowned with success, when she would see herself face to face with the handsome, willful girl, whom she yet must utterly fail to understand; for it would have been completely impossible for Cecile herself, under any circumstances, to treat her father as Lovedy had treated her poor mother.

"I could never, never go away like that, and let father's heart break, " thought Cecile, her lips growing white at the bare idea of such suffering for one she loved. But then it came to her with a sense of relief that perhaps Lovedy's Aunt Fanny was the guilty person, and that she herself was quite innocent; her aunt, who was powerful and strong, had been unkind, and had not allowed her to write. When this thought came to Cecile, she gave a sigh of relief. It would be so much nicer to find Lovedy, if she was not so hard-hearted as her story seemed to show.

All that night Mrs. D'Albert lay with her eyes closed, but not asleep. When the first dawn came in through the shutters she turned to the watching child:

"Cecile, " she said, "the day has broke, and this is the day the doctor says as perhaps I'll die. "

"Shall I open the shutters wide? " asked Cecile.

"No, my dear. No, no! The light 'ull come quite fast enough. Cecile, ain't it a queer thing to be going to die, and not to be a bit ready to die? "

"Ain't you ready, stepmother? " asked the little girl.

"No, child, how could I be ready? I never had no time. I never had a moment to get ready, Cecile. "

"Never a moment to get ready, " repeated Cecile. "I should have thought you had lots of time. You aren't at all a young woman, are you, stepmother? You must have been a very long time alive. "

"Yes, dear; it would seem long to you. But it ain't long really. It seems very short to look back on. I ain't forty yet, Cecile; and that's counted no age as lives go; but I never for all that had a moment. When I wor very young I married; and afore I married, I had only time for play and pleasure; and then afterward Lovedy came, and her father died, and I had to think on my grief, and how to bring up Lovedy. I had no time to remember about dying during those years, Cecile; and since my Lovedy left me, I have not had one instant to do anything but mourn for her, and think on her, and work for her. You see, Cecile, I never did have a moment, even though I seems old to you. "

The Children's Pilgrimage

"No, stepmother, I see you never did have no time, " repeated Cecile gravely.

"But it ain't nice to think on now, " repeated Mrs. D'Albert, in a fretful, anxious key. "I ha' got to go, and I ain't ready to go, that's the puzzle. "

"Perhaps it don't take so very long to get ready, " answered the child, in a perplexed voice.

"Cecile, " said Mrs. D'Albert, "you're a very wise little girl. Think deep now, and answer me this: Do you believe as God 'ull be very angry with a poor woman who had never, no never a moment of time to get ready to die? "

"Stepmother, " answered Cecile solemnly, "I don't know nothink about God. Father didn't know, nor my own mother; and you say you never had no time to know, stepmother. Only once—once——"

"Well, child, go on. Once? "

"Once me and Maurice were in the streets, and Toby was with us, and we had walked a long way and were tired, and we sat down on a doorstep to rest; and a girl come up, and she looked tired too, and she had some crochet in her hand; and she took out her crochet and began to work. And presently—jest as if she could not help it—she sang. This wor what she sang. I never forgot the words:

"'I am so glad that Jesus loves me;
Jesus loves even me. '

"The girl had such a nice voice, stepmother, and she sang out so bold, and seemed so happy, that I couldn't help asking her what it meant. I said, 'Please, English girl, I'm only a little French girl, and I don't know all the English words; and please, who's Jesus, kind little English girl? '

"'Oh! *don't* you know about Jesus? ' she said at once. 'Why, Jesus is— Jesus is——Oh! I don't know how to tell you; but He's good, He's beautiful, He's dear. Jesus loves everybody. "

"'Jesus loves everybody? ' I said.

The Children's Pilgrimage

"'Yes. Don't the hymn say so? Jesus loves even me!'"

"'Oh! but I suppose 'tis because you're very, *very* good, little English girl,' I said.

"But the English girl said, 'No, that wasn't a bit of it. She wasn't good, though she did try to be. But Jesus loved everybody, whether they were good or not, ef only they'd believe it.'

"That's all she told me, stepmother; but she just said one thing more, 'Oh, what a comfort to think Jesus loves one when one remembers about dying.'"

While Cecile was telling her little tale, Mrs. D'Albert had closed her eyes; now she opened them.

"Are you sure that is all you know, child, just 'Jesus loves everybody?' It do seem nice to hear that. Cecile, could you jest say a bit of a prayer?"

"I can only say, 'Our Father,'" answered Cecile.

"Well, then, go on your knees and say it earnest; say it werry earnest, Cecile."

Cecile did so, and when her voice had ceased, Mrs. D'Albert opened her eyes, clasped her hands together, and spoke:

"Jesus," she said, "Lord Jesus, I'm dreadful, bitter sorry as I never took no time to get ready to die. Jesus, can you love even me?"

There was no answer in words, but a new and satisfied look came into the poor, hungry eyes; a moment later, and the sick and dying woman had dropped asleep.

CHAPTER IV.

TOBY.

Quite early in that same long morning, before little Maurice had even opened his sleepy eyes, the woman whom Mrs. D'Albert called Aunt Lydia arrived. She was a large, stout woman with a face made very red and rough from constant exposure to the weather. She did not live in London, but worked as housekeeper on a farm down in Kent. This woman was not the least like Mrs. D'Albert, who was pale, and rather refined in her expression. Aunt Lydia had never been married, and her life seemed to have hardened her, for not only was her face rough and coarse in texture, but her voice, and also, it is to be regretted, her mind appeared to partake of the same quality. She came noisily into the quiet room where Cecile had been tending her stepmother; she spoke in a loud tone, and appeared quite unconcerned at the very manifest danger of the sister she had come to see; she also instantly took the management of everything, and ordered Cecile out of the room.

"There is no use in having children like *that* about, " she said in a tone of great contempt; and although her stepmother looked after her longingly, Cecile was obliged to leave the room and go to comfort and pet Maurice.

The poor little girl's own heart was very heavy; she dreaded this harsh new voice and face that had come into her life. It did not matter very greatly for herself, Cecile thought, but Maurice— Maurice was very tender, very young, very unused to unkindness. Was it possible that Aunt Lydia would be unkind to little Maurice? How he would look at her with wonder in his big brown eyes, bigger and browner than English eyes are wont to be, and try hard to understand what it all meant, what the new tone and the new words could possibly signify; for Mrs. D'Albert, though she never professed to love the children, had always been just to them, she had never given them harsh treatment or rude words. It is true Cecile's heart, which was very big, had hungered for more than her stepmother had ever offered; but Maurice had felt no want, he had Cecile to love him, Toby to pet him; and Mrs. D'Albert always gave him the warmest corner by the hearth, the nicest bits to eat, the best of everything her poor and struggling home afforded. Maurice was rather a spoiled little boy; even Cecile, much as she loved him, felt that he was rather spoiled; all the harder now would be the changed life.

But Cecile had something else just at present to make her anxious and unhappy. She was a shrewd and clever child; she had not been tossed about the world for nothing, and she could read character with tolerable accuracy. Without putting her thoughts into regular words, she yet had read in that hard new face a grasping love of power, an eager greed for gold, and an unscrupulous nature which would not hesitate to possess itself of what it could. Cecile trembled as she felt that little bag of gold lying near her heart—suppose, oh! suppose it got into Aunt Lydia's hands. Cecile felt that if this happened, if in this way she was unfaithful to the vow she had made, she should die.

"There are somethings as 'ud break any heart, " she said to herself, "and not to find Lovedy when I promised faithful, faithful to Lovedy's mother as I would find her; why, that 'ud break my heart. Father said once, when people had broken hearts they *died*, so I 'ud die. "

She began to consider already with great anxiety how she could hide this precious money.

In the midst of her thoughts Maurice awoke, and Toby shook himself and came round and looked into her face.

Toby was Maurice's own special property. He was Maurice's dog, and he always stayed with him, slept on his bed at night, remained by his side all day; but he had, for all his attachment for his little master, looks for Cecile which he never bestowed upon Maurice. For Maurice the expression in his brown eyes was simply protecting, simply loving; but for Cecile that gaze seemed to partake of a higher nature. For Cecile the big loving eyes grew pathetic, grew watchful, grew anxious. When sitting very close to Maurice, apparently absorbed in Maurice, he often rolled them softly round to the little girl. Those eyes spoke volumes. They seemed to say, "You and I have the care of this little baby boy. It is a great anxiety, a great responsibility for us, but we are equal to the task. He is a dear little fellow, but only a baby; you and I, Cecile, are his grown-up protectors. " Toby gamboled with Maurice, but with Cecile he never attempted to play. His every movement, every glance, seemed to say —"*We* don't care for this nonsense, I only do it to amuse the child. "

The Children's Pilgrimage

On this particular morning Toby read at a glance the new anxiety in Cecile's face. Instantly this anxiety was communicated to his own. He hung his head, his eyes became clouded, and he looked quite an old dog when he returned to Maurice's side.

When Maurice was dressed, Cecile conducted him as quietly as she could down the stairs and out through the hall to the old-world and deserted little court. The sun was shining here this morning. It was a nice autumn morning, and the little court looked rather bright. Maurice quite clapped his hands, and instantly began to run about and called to Toby to gambol with him. Toby glanced at Cecile, who nodded in reply, and then she ran upstairs to try and find some breakfast which she could bring into the court for all three. She had to go into the little sitting-room where her stepmother lay breathing loud and hard, and with her eyes shut. There was a look of great pain on her face, and Cecile, with a rush of sorrow, felt that she had looked much happier when she alone had been caring for her. Aunt Lydia, however, must be a good nurse, for she had made the room look quite like a sickroom. She had drawn down the blinds and placed a little table with bottles by the sofa, and she herself was bustling about, with a very busy and important air. She was not quiet, however, as Cecile had been, and her voice, which was reduced to a whisper pitch, had an irritating effect, as all voices so pitched have.

Cecile, securing a loaf of bread and a jug of milk, ran downstairs, and she, Maurice, and Toby had their breakfast in truly picnic fashion. Afterward the children and dog stayed out in the court for the rest of the day. The little court faced south, and the sun stayed on it for many hours, so that Maurice was not cold, and every hour or so Cecile crept upstairs and listened outside the sitting-room door. There was always that hard breathing within, but otherwise no sound. At last the sun went off the court, and Maurice got cold and cried, and then Cecile, as softly as she had brought him out, took him back to their little bedroom. Having had no sleep the night before, she was very weary now, and she lay down on the bed, and before she had time to think about it was fast asleep.

From this sleep she was awakened by a hand touching her, a light being flashed in her eyes, and Aunt Lydia's strong, deep voice bidding her get up and come with her at once.

Cecile followed her without a word into the next room.

The dying woman was sitting up on a sofa, supported by pillows, and her breathing came quicker and louder than ever.

"Cecile, " she gasped, "Cecile, say that bit—bit of a hymn once again. "

> "I am so glad Jesus loves me,
>   Even me. "

repeated the child instantly.

"Even me, " echoed the dying woman.

Then she closed her eyes, but she felt about with her hand until it clasped the little warm hand of the child.

"Go back to your room now, Cecile, " said Aunt Lydia.

But the dying hand pressed the little hand, and Cecile answered gravely and firmly:

"Stepmother 'ud like me to stay, Aunt Lydia. "

Aunt Lydia did not speak again, and for half an hour there was silence. Suddenly Cecile's stepmother opened her eyes bright and wide.

"Lovedy, " she said, "Lovedy; find Lovedy, " and then she died.

CHAPTER V.

THE TIN BOX AND ITS TREASURE.

Cecile and Maurice D'Albert were the orphan children of a French father and a Spanish mother. Somewhere in the famous valleys of the Pyrenees these two had loved each other, and married. Maurice D'Albert, the father, was a man of a respectable class and for that class of rather remarkable culture. He owned a small vineyard, and had a picturesque chateau, which he inherited from his ancestors, among the hills. Pretty Rosalie was without money. She had neither fortune nor education. She sprang from a lower class than her husband; but her young and childish face possessed so rare an order of beauty that it would be impossible for any man to ask her where she came from, or what she did. Maurice D'Albert loved her at once. He married her when she was little more than a child; and for four years the young couple lived happily among their native mountains; for Rosalie's home had been only as far away as the Spanish side of the Pyrenees.

But at the end of four years clouds came. The vine did not bear; a blight seemed to rest on all vegetation of the prosperous little farm. D'Albert, for the first time in his life, was short of money for his simple needs. This was an anxiety; but worse troubles were to follow. Pretty Rosalie bore him a son; and then, when no one even apprehended danger, suddenly died. This death completely broke down the poor man. He had loved Rosalie so well that when she left him the sun seemed absolutely withdrawn from his life. He lived for many more years, but he never really held up his head again. Rosalie was gone! Even his children now could scarcely make him care for life. He began to hate the place where he had been so happy with his young wife. And when a distant cousin, who had long desired the little property, came and offered to buy it, D'Albert sold the home of his ancestors. The cousin gave him a small sum of money down for the pretty chateau and vineyard, and agreed to pay the rest in yearly instalments, extending over twelve years.

With money in his purse, and secure in a small yearly property for at least some years to come, D'Albert came to England. He had been in London once for a fortnight, when quite a little lad; and it came into his head that the English children looked healthy and happy, and he thought it might give him pleasure to bring up his little son and daughter as English children. He took the baby of three months, and the girl of a little over two years, to England; and, in a poor and obscure corner of the great world of London, established himself with his babies. Poor man! the cold and damp English climate proved anything but the climate of his dreams. He caught one cold, then another, and after two or three years entered a period of confirmed ill-health, which was really to end in rapid consumption. His children, however, throve and grew strong. They both inherited their young mother's vigorous life. The English climate mattered nothing to them, for they remembered no other. They learned to speak the English tongue, and were English in all but their birth. When they were babies their father stayed at home, and nursed them as tenderly as any woman, allowing no hired nurse to interfere. But when they were old enough to be left, and that came before long, Cecile growing *so* wise and sensible, so dependable, as her father said, D'Albert went out to look for employment.

He was, as I have said, a man of some culture for his class. As he knew Spanish fluently, he obtained work at a school, as teacher, of Spanish, and afterward he further added to his little income by giving lessons on the guitar. The money too came in regularly from the French chateau, and D'Albert was able to put by, and keep his children in tolerable comfort.

He never forgot his young wife. All the love he had to bestow upon woman lay in her Pyrenean grave. But nevertheless, when Cecile was six years old, and Maurice four, he asked another woman to be his wife. His home was neglected; his children, now that he was out so much all day, pined for more care. He married, but not loving his wife, he did not add to his happiness. The woman who came into the house came with a sore and broken heart. She brought no love for either father or children. All the love in her nature was centered on her own lost child. She came and gave no love, and received none, except from Cecile. Cecile loved everybody. There was that in the little half-French, half-Spanish girl's nature—a certain look in her long almond-shaped blue eyes, a melting look, which could only be caused by the warmth of a heart brimful of loving kindness. Woe be to anyone who could hurt the tender heart of this little one! Cecile's stepmother had often pained her, but Cecile still loved on.

Two years after his second marriage D'Albert died. He died after a brief fresh cold, rather suddenly at the end, although he had been ill for years.

The Children's Pilgrimage

To his wife he explained all his worldly affairs, He received fifty pounds a year from his farm in France. This would continue for the next few years. There was also a small sum in hand, enough for his funeral and present expenses. To Cecile he spoke of other things than money—of his early home in the sunny southern country, of her mother, of little Maurice. He said that perhaps some day Cecile could go back and take Maurice with her to see with her own eyes the sunny vineyards of the south, and he told her what the child had never learned before, that she had a grandmother living in the Pyrenees, a very old woman now, old and deaf, and knowing not a single word of the English tongue. "But with a loving heart, Cecile", added her father, "with a loving mother's heart. If ever you could find your grandmother, you would get a kiss from her that would be like a mother's kiss."

Shortly after Maurice D'Albert died, and the children lived on with their stepmother. Without loving them, the second Mrs. D'Albert was good to her little stepchildren. She religiously spent all their father's small income on them, and when she died, she had so arranged money matters that her sister Lydia would be well paid with the fifty pounds a year for supporting them at her farm in the country.

This fifty pounds still came regularly every half-year from the French farm. It would continue to be paid for the next four years, and the next half-year's allowance was about due when the children left London and went to the farm in Kent.

The few days that immediately followed Mrs. D'Albert's death were dull and calm. No one loved the poor woman well enough to fret really for her. The child she had lost was far away and knew nothing, and Lydia Purcell shed few tears for her sister. True, Cecile cried a little, and went into the room where the dead woman lay, and kissed the cold lips, registering again, as she did so, a vow to find Lovedy, but even Cecile's loving heart was only stirred on the surface by this death. The little girl, too, was so oppressed, so overpowered by the care of the precious purse of money, she lived even already in such hourly dread of Aunt Lydia finding it, that she had no room in her mind for other sensations; there was no place in the lodgings in which they lived to hide the purse of bank notes and gold. Aunt Lydia seemed to be a woman who had eyes in the back of her head, she saw everything that anyone could see; she was here, there, and everywhere at once. Cecile dared not take the bag from inside the bosom of her frock, and its weight, physical as well as mental, brought added pallor to her thin cheeks. The kind young doctor, who had been good to Mrs. D'Albert, and had written to her sister to come to her, paid the children a hasty visit. He noticed at once Cecile's pale face and languid eyes.

"This child is not well, " he said to Lydia Purcell. "What is wrong, my little one? " he added, drawing the child forward tenderly to sit on his knee.

"Please, I'm quite well, " answered Cecile, "'tis only as father did say as I was a very dependable little girl. I think being dependable makes you feel a bit old—don't it, doctor? "

"I have no doubt it does, " answered the doctor, laughing. And he went away relieved about the funny, old-fashioned little foreign girl, and from that moment Cecile passed out of his busy and useful life.

The next day the children, Toby, and Aunt Lydia went down to the farm in Kent. Neither Cecile, Maurice, nor their town-bred dog had ever seen the country, to remember it before, and it is not too much to say that all three went nearly wild with delight. Not even Aunt Lydia's sternness could quench the children's mirth when they got away into the fields, or scrambled over stiles into the woods. Beautiful Kent was then rich in its autumn tints. The children and dog lived out from morning to night. Provided they did not trouble her, Lydia Purcell was quite indifferent as to how the little creatures committed to her care passed their time. At Cecile's request she would give her some broken provisions in a basket, and then never see or think of the little trio again until, footsore and weary after their day of wandering, they crept into their attic bedroom at night.

It was there and then, during those two delicious months, before the winter came with its cold and dreariness, that Cecile lost the look of care which had made her pretty face old before its time. She was a child again—rather she was a child at last. Oh! the joy of gathering real, real flowers with her own little brown hands. Oh! the delight of sitting under the hedges and listening to the birds singing. Maurice took it as a matter of course; Toby sniffed the country air solemnly, but with due and reasonable appreciation; but to Cecile these two months in the country came as the embodiment of the babyhood and childhood she had never known.

The Children's Pilgrimage

In the country Cecile was only ten years old.

When first they had arrived at the old farm she had discovered a hiding place for her purse. Back of the attic, were she had and Maurice and Toby slept, was a little chamber, so narrow—running so completely away into the roof—that even Cecile could only explore it on her hands and knees.

This little room she did examine carefully, holding a candle in her hand, in the dead of night, when every soul on the busy farm was asleep.

Woe for Cecile had Aunt Lydia heard a sound; but Aunt Lydia Purcell slept heavily, and the child's movements were so gentle and careful that they would scarcely have aroused a wakeful mouse. Cecile found in the extreme corner of this tiny attic in the roof an old broken wash-hand-stand lying on its back. In the wash-hand-stand was a drawer, and inside the drawer again a tidy little tin box. Cecile seized the box, sat down on the floor, and taking the purse from the bosom of her frock, found that it fitted it well. She gave a sigh of relief; the tin box shut with a click; who would guess that there was a purse of gold and notes inside!

Now, where should she put it? Back again into the old drawer of the old wash-stand? No; that hiding place was not safe enough. She explored a little further, almost lying down now, the roof was so near her head. Here she found what she had little expected to see—a cupboard cunningly contrived in the wall. She pushed it open. It was full, but not quite full, of moldy and forgotten books. Back of the books the tin box might lie hidden, lie secure; no human being would ever guess that a treasure lay here.

With trembling hands she pushed it far back into the cupboard, covered it with some books, and shut the door securely.

Then she crept back to bed a light-hearted child. For the present her secret was safe and she might be happy.

CHAPTER VI.

MERCY BELL.

The farm in Kent, called Warren's Grove, belonged to an old lady. This lady was very old; she was also deaf and nearly blind. She left the management of everything to Lydia Purcell, who, clever and capable, was well equal to the emergency. There was no steward or overseer of the little property, but the farm was thoroughly and efficiently worked. Lydia had been with Mrs. Bell for over twenty years. She was now trusted absolutely, and was to all intents and purposes the mistress of Warren's Grove. This had not been so when first she arrived; she had come at first as a sort of upper servant or nurse. The old lady was bright and active then. She had a son in Australia, and a bonnie grandchild to wake echoes in the old place and keep it alive. This grandchild was a girl of six, and Lydia was its nurse. For a year all went well; then the child, partly through Lydia's carelessness, caught a malignant fever, sickened, and died. Lydia had taken her into an infected house. This knowledge the woman kept to herself. She never told either doctor or grandmother—she dared not tell—and the grief, remorse, and pain changed her whole nature.

Before the death of little Mercy Bell, Lydia had been an ordinary young woman. She had no special predisposition to evil. She was a handsome, bold-looking creature, and where she chose to give love, that love was returned. She had loved her pretty little charge, and the child had loved her and died in her arms. Mrs. Bell, too, had loved Lydia, and Lydia was bright and happy, and looked forward to a home of her own some day.

But from the moment the grave had closed over Mercy, and she felt herself in a measure responsible for her death, all was changed in the woman. She did not leave her situation; she stayed on, she served faithfully, she worked hard, and her clever and well-timed services became more valuable day by day. But no one now loved Lydia, not even old Mrs. Bell, and certainly she loved nobody. Of course the natural consequences followed—the woman, loving neither God nor man, grew harder and harder. At forty-five, the age she was when the children came to Warren's Grove, she was a very hard woman indeed.

It would be wrong, however, to say that she had *no* love; she loved one thing—a base thing—she loved money. Lydia Purcell was saving money; in her heart she was a close miser.

She was not, however, dishonest; she had never stolen a penny in her life, never yet. Every farthing of the gains which came in from the well-stocked and prosperous little farm she sent to the county bank, there to accumulate for that son in Australia, who, childless as he was, would one day return to find himself tolerably rich. But still Lydia, without being dishonest, saved money. When old Mrs. Bell, a couple of years after her grandchild's death, had a paralytic stroke, and begged of her faithful Lydia, her dear Lydia, not to leave her, but to stay and manage the farm which she must give up attending to, Lydia had made a good compact for herself.

"I will stay with you, Mistress Bell, " she had replied, addressing the old dame in the fashion she loved. "I will stay with you, and tend you, and work your farm, and you shall pay me my wages. "

"And good wages, Lydia—good wages they must be, " replied the old lady.

"They shall be fair wages, " answered Lydia. "You shall give me a salary of fifty pounds a year, and I will have in the spring every tenth lamb, and every tenth calf, to sell for myself, and I will supply fowl and eggs for our own use at table, and all that are over I will sell on my own account. "

"That is fair—that is very fair, " said Mrs. Bell.

On these terms Lydia stayed and worked. She studied farming, and the little homestead throve and prospered. And Lydia too, without ever exceeding by the tenth of an inch her contract, managed to put by a tidy sum of money year by year. She spent next to nothing on dress; all her wants were supplied. Nearly her whole income, therefore, of fifty pounds a year could go by untouched; and the tenth of the flock, and the money made by the overplus of eggs and poultry, were by no means to be despised.

Lydia was not dishonest, but she so far looked after her own interests as to see that the hen-houses were warm and snug, that the best breeds of poultry were kept up, and that those same birds should lay their golden eggs to the tune of a warm supper. Lydia, however, though very careful, was not always very wise. Once a quarter she regularly took her savings to the bank in the little town of F—t, and on one of these occasions she was tempted to invest one hundred pounds of her savings in a very risky speculation. Just about the time that the children were given into her charge this speculation was pronounced in danger, and Lydia, when she brought Cecile and Maurice home, was very anxious about her money.

Now, if Mrs. D'Albert did not care for children, still less did Lydia Purcell. It was a strange fact that in both these sisters their affection for all such little ones should lie buried in a lost child's grave. It was true that, as far as she could tell, Mrs. D'Albert's love might be still alive. But little Mercy Bell's small grave in the churchyard contained the only child that Lydia Purcell could abide. That little grave was always green, and remained, summer and winter, not quite without flowers. But though she clung passionately to Mercy's memory, yet, because she had been unjust to this little one, she disliked all other children for her sake.

It had been great pain and annoyance to Lydia to bring the orphan D'Alberts home, and she had only done so because of their money; for she reflected that they could live on the farm for next to nothing, and without in the least imagining herself dishonest, she considered that any penny she could save from their fifty pounds a year might be lawfully her own.

Still the children were unpleasant to her, and she wished that her sister had not died so inopportunely.

As the two children sat opposite to her in the fly, during their short drive from the country station to the farm, Lydia regarded them attentively.

Maurice was an absolutely fearless child. No one in all his little life had ever said a cross word to Maurice, consequently he considered all the people in the world his slaves, and treated them with lofty indifference. He chattered as unreservedly to Lydia Purcell as he did to Cecile or Toby, and for Maurice in consequence Lydia felt no special dislike; his fearlessness made his charm. But Cecile was different. Cecile was unfortunate enough to win at once this disagreeable woman's antipathy. Cecile had timid and pleading eyes. Her eyes said plainly, "Let me love you."

The Children's Pilgrimage

Now, Mercy's eyes too were pleading; Mercy's eyes too had said, "let me love you, " Lydia saw the likeness between Mercy and Cecile at a glance, and she almost hated the little foreign girl for resembling her lost darling.

Old Mrs. Bell further aggravated her dislike; she was so old and invalidish now that her memory sometimes failed.

The morning after the children's arrival, she spoke to Lydia.

"Lydia, that was Mercy's voice I heard just now in the passage. "

"Mercy is dead, " answered Lydia, contracting her brows in pain.

"But, Lydia, I *did* hear her voice. "

"She is dead, Mistress Bell. That was another child. "

"Another child! Let me see the other child. "

Lydia was obliged to call in Cecile, who came forward with a sweet grave face, and stood gently by the little tremulous old woman, and took her hand, and then stooped down to kiss her.

Cecile was interested in such great age, and kept saying to herself, "Perhaps my grandmother away in the Pyrenees is like this very old woman, " and when Mrs. Bell warmly returned her soft little caress, Cecile wondered to herself if this was like the mother's kiss her father and told her of when he was dying.

But when Cecile had gone away, Mrs. Bell turned to Lydia and said in a tone of satisfaction:

"How much our dear Mercy has grown. "

After this nothing would ever get the idea out of the old lady's head that Cecile was Mercy.

CHAPTER VII.

A GUIDE TO THE PYRENEES.

I have said, for the first two months of Cecile's life in the country she was a happy and light-hearted child. Her purse of money was safe for the present. Her promise lay in abeyance. Even her dead stepmother, anxious as she was to have Lovedy found, had counseled Cecile to delay her search until she was older. Cecile, therefore, might be happy. She might be indeed what she was—a child of ten. This happiness was not to last. Clouds were to darken the life of this little one; but before the clouds and darkness came, she was to possess a more solid happiness—a happiness that, once it found entrance into such a heart as hers, could never go away again.

The first beginning of this happiness was to come to Cecile through an unexpected source—even through the ministrations of an old, partly blind, and half-simple woman.

Mrs. Bell from the first took a fancy to Cecile, and liked to have her about her. She called her Mercy, and Cecile grew accustomed to the name and answered to it. This delusion on the part of poor old Mrs. Bell was great torture to Lydia Purcell, and when the child and the old woman were together she always left them alone.

One afternoon Mrs. Bell said abruptly:

"Mercy, I thought—or was it a dream? —I thought you were safe away with Jesus for the last few years. "

"No, Mistress Bell, " answered Cecile in her slow and grave tones, "I've only been in London these last few years. "

"Now you're puzzling me, " said Mrs. Bell in a querulous voice, "and you know I hate being puzzled. Lydia Purcell, too, often puzzles me lately, but you, Mercy, never used to. Sit down, child, and stitch at your sampler, and I'll get accustomed to the sight of you, and not believe that you've been away with my blessed Master, as I used to dream. "

The Children's Pilgrimage

"Is your blessed Master the same as Jesus that you thought I had gone to live with? " asked Cecile, as she pulled out the faded sampler and tried to work the stitches.

"Yes, my darling, He's my light and my stay, the sure guide of a poor old woman to a better country, blessed be His holy Name! "

"A guide! " said Cecile. This name attracted her—a guide would be so useful by and by when she went into a foreign land to look for Lovedy. "Do you think as He'd guide me too, Mistress Bell? "

"For sure, deary, for sure. Don't He call a little thing like you one of His lambs? 'Tis said of Him that He carries the lambs in His arms. That's a very safe way of being guided, ain't it, Mercy? "

"Yes, ma'am. Only I hope as He'll take you in His arms too, Mistress Bell, for you don't look as though you could walk far. And will He come soon, Mistress? "

"I don't say as 'twill be long, Mercy. I'm very old and very feeble, and He don't ever leave the very old and feeble long down here. "

"And is the better country that the blessed Master has to guide you to, away in France, away in the south of France, in the Pyrenees? " asked Cecile with great excitement and eagerness.

But Mrs. Bell had never even heard of the Pyrenees. She shook her old head and frowned.

"Tis called the Celestial City by some, " she said, "and by some again the New Jerusalem, but I never yet heard anyone speak of it by that other outlandish name. Now you're beginning your old game of puzzling, Mercy Bell. "

Cecile bent over her work, and old Mrs. Bell dozed off to sleep.

But the words the old woman had spoken were with Cecile when later in the day she went out to play with Maurice and Toby; were with her when she lay down to sleep that night. What a pity Jesus only guided people to the Celestial City and to the New Jerusalem! What a pity that, as He was so very good, He did not do more! What a pity that He could not be induced to take a little girl who was very young, and very ignorant, but who had a great care and anxiety on her mind, into France, even as far as, if necessary, to the south of France! Cecile wondered if He could be induced to do it. Perhaps old Mrs. Bell, who knew Him so well, would ask Him. Cecile guessed that Jesus must have a very kind heart. For what did that girl say who once sat upon a doorstep, and sang about him?

"I am so glad Jesus loves even me. "

That girl was as poor as Cecile herself. Nay, indeed, she was much poorer. How white was her thin face, how ragged her shabby gown! But then, again, how triumphant was her voice as she sang! What a happy light filled her sunken eyes!

There was no doubt at all that Jesus loved this poor girl; and if He loved her, why might He not love Cecile too? Yes, He surely had a great and loving heart, capable of taking in everybody; for Cecile's stepmother, though she was not *very* nice, had smiled when that little story of the poor girl on the doorstep had been told to her; had smiled and seemed comforted, and had repeated the words, "Jesus loves even me, " softly over to herself when she was dying.

Cecile, too, now looking back over many things, remembered her own father. Cecile's father, Maurice D'Albert, was a Roman Catholic by birth. He was a man, however, out of whose life religion had slipped.

During his wife's lifetime, and while he lived on his little farm in the Pyrenees, he had done as his neighbors did, gone to confession, and professed himself a good Catholic; but when trouble came to him, and he found his home in the bleaker land of England, there was found to be no heart in his worship. He was an amiable, kind-hearted man, but he forgot the religious part of life. He went neither to church nor chapel, and he brought up his children like himself, practically little heathens. Cecile, therefore, at ten years old was more ignorant than it would be possible to find a respectable English child. God, and heaven, and the blessed hope of a future life were things practically unknown to her.

What fragmentary ideas she had gleaned in her wanderings about the great city with her little brother were vague and unformed. But even Cecile, thinking now of her father's deathbed, remembered words which she had little thought of at the time.

Just before he breathed his last, he had raised two feeble hands, and placed one on her head, and one on Maurice's, and said in a faltering, failing voice:

"If the blessed and adorable Jesus be God, may He guide you, my children. "

These were his last words, and Cecile, lying on her little bed to-night, remembered them vividly.

Who was this Jesus who was so loving, and who was so willing to guide people? She must learn more about Him, for if *He* only promised to go with her into France, then her heart might be light, her fears as to the success of her great mission might be laid to rest.

Cecile resolved to find out all she could about Jesus from old Mrs. Bell.

The next morning, immediately after breakfast, Aunt Lydia called the little girl aside, and gave her as usual a basket of broken provisions.

"There is a good piece of apple-tart in the basket this morning, Cecile, and a bottle of fresh milk. Don't any of you three come worriting me again before nightfall; there, run away quickly, child, for I'm dreadful busy and put out to-day. "

For a brief moment Cecile looked eagerly and pityingly into the hard face. There was love in her gentle eyes, and, as they filled with love, they grew so like Mercy's eyes that Lydia Purcell almost loathed her. She gave her a little push away, and said sharply:

"Get away, get away, do, " and turned her back, pretending to busy herself over some cold meat.

Cecile went slowly and sought Maurice. She knew there would be no dinner in store for her that day. But what was dinner compared to the knowledge she hoped to gain!

"Maurice, dear, " she said, as she put the basket into his hand, "this is a real lovely day, and you and Toby are to spend it in the woods, and I'll come presently if I can. And you might leave a little bit of dinner if you're not very hungry, Maurice. There's lovely apple-pie in the basket, and there's milk, but a bit of bread will do for me. Try and leave a little bit of bread for me when I come. " Maurice nodded, his face beaming at the thought of the apple-pie and the milk. But Toby's brown eyes said intelligently:

"We'll keep a little bit of *every*thing for you, Cecile, and I'll take care of Maurice. " And Cecile, comforted that Toby would take excellent care of Maurice, ran away into old Mrs. Bell's room.

"May I sit with you, and may I do a little bit more of Mercy's sampler, please, Mistress Bell? " she asked.

The old lady, who was propped up in the armchair in the sunshine, received her in her usual half-puzzled half-pleased way.

"There, Mercy, child, you've grown so queer in your talk that I sometimes fancy you're half a changeling. May you sit with your grandam? What next? There, there, bring yer bit of a stool, and get the sampler out, and do a portion of the feather-stitch. Mind ye're careful, Mercy, and see as you count as you work. "

Cecile sat down willingly, drew out the faded sampler, and made valiant efforts to follow in the dead Mercy's finger marks. After a moment or two of careful industry, she laid down her work and spoke:

"Mistress Bell, when 'ull you be likely to see Jesus next, do you think? "

"Lawk a mercy, child! ain't you near enough to take one's breath away. Do you want to kill your old grandam, Mercy? Why, in course I can't see my blessed Saviour, the Lord Jesus, till I'm dead. "

"Oh! " said Cecile, with a heavy sigh, "I did think as He lived down yere, and that He came in and out to see you sometimes, seeing as you love Him so. You said as He was a guide. How can He be a guide when He's dead? "

"A guide to the New Jerusalem and the Celestial City, " murmured old Mrs. Bell, beginning to wander a little. "Yes, yes, my blessed Lord and faithful and sure guide. "

"But how can He be a guide when He's dead? " questioned Cecile.

The Children's Pilgrimage

"Mercy, child, put in another feather in yer sampler, and don't worry an old woman. The Lord Jesus ain't dead—no, no; He died once, but He rose—He's alive for evermore. Don't you ask no strange questions, Mercy, child. "

"Oh! but I must—I must, " answered Cecile, now grown desperate. She threw her sampler on the floor, rose to her feet, and confronted the old woman with her eyes full of tears. "Whether I'm Mercy or not don't matter, but I'm a very, very careworn little girl—I'm a little girl with a deal, a great deal of care on my mind—and I want Jesus most terrible bad to help me. Mistress Bell, dear Mistress Bell, when you die and see Jesus, won't you ask Him, won't you be certain sure to ask Him to guide me too? "

"Why, my darling, He's sure to guide you. There ain't no fear, my dear life. He's sure, sure to take my Mercy, too, to the Celestial City when the right time comes. "

"But I don't want Him to take me to the Celestial City. I haven't got to look for nobody in the Celestial City. 'Tis away to France, down into the south of France I've got to go. Will you ask Jesus to come and guide me down into the Pyrenees in the south of France, please, Mistress Bell? "

"I don't know nothing of no such outlandish place, " said old Mrs. Bell, once more irritated and thrown off her bearings, and just at this moment, to Cecile's serious detriment, Lydia Purcell entered.

Lydia was in one of her worst tempers, and old Mrs. Bell, rendered cross for the moment, spoke unadvisedly:

"Lydia, I do think you're bringing up the child Mercy like a regular heathen. She asks me questions as 'ud break her poor father, my son Robert's heart ef he was to hear. She's a good child, but she's *that* puzzling. You bid her mind her sampler, and not worry an old woman, Lydia Purcell. "

Lydia's eyes gazed stormily at Cecile.

"I'll bid her see and do what she's told, " she said, going up to the little girl and giving her a shake. "You go out of the house this minute, miss, and don't let me never see you slinking into this yere room again without my leave. " She took the child to the door and shut it on her.

Mrs. Bell began to remonstrate feebly. "Lydia, don't be harsh on my little Mercy, " she began. "I like to have her along o' me. I'm mostly alone, and the child makes company. "

"Yes, but you have no time for her this morning, for, as I've told you a score of times already to-day, Mr. Preston is coming, " replied Lydia.

Now Mr. Preston was Mrs. Bell's attorney, and next to her religion, which was most truly real and abiding in her poor old heart, she loved her attorney.

CHAPTER VIII.

"THE UNION."

Lydia had just then plenty of cause for anxiety; for that kind of anxiety which such a woman would feel. She was anxious about the gold she had been so carefully saving, putting by here a pound and there a pound, until the bank held a goodly sum sufficient to support her in comfort in the not very distant day when her residence in Warren's Grove would come to an end.

Whenever Mrs. Bell died, Lydia knew she must look out for a fresh home, and that day could surely now not be very distant.

The old woman had seen her eighty-fifth birthday. Death must be near one so feeble, who was also eighty-five years of age. Lydia would be comfortably off when Mrs. Bell died, and she often reflected with satisfaction that this money, as she enjoyed it, need trouble her with no qualms of conscience—it was all the result of hard work, of patient industry. In her position she could have been dishonest, and it would be untrue to deny that the temptation to be dishonest when no one would be the wiser, when not a soul could possibly ever know, had come to her more than once. But she had never yet yielded to the temptation. "No, no, " she had said to her own heart, "I will enjoy my money by and by with clean hands. It shall be good money. I'm a hard woman, but nothing mean nor unclean shall touch me. " Lydia made these resolves most often sitting by Mercy's grave. For week after week did she visit this little grave, and kept it bright with flowers and green with all the love her heart could ever know.

But all the same it was about this money which surely she had a right to enjoy, and feel secure and happy in possessing, that Lydia was so anxious now.

She had ground for her fears. As I said before Lydia Purcell had once done a foolish thing. Now her folly was coming home to her. She had been tempted to invest two hundred pounds in an unlimited company. Twenty per cent. she was to receive for this money. This twenty per cent. tempted her. She did the deed, thinking that for a year or two she was safe enough.

But this very morning she had been made uneasy by a letter from Mr. Preston, her own and Mrs. Bell's man of business.

He knew she had invested this money. She had done so against his will.

He told her that ugly rumors were afloat about this very company. And if it went, all Lydia's money, all the savings of her life would be swept away in its downfall.

When he called, which he did that same morning, he could but confirm her fears.

Yes, he would try and sell out for her. He would go to London for the purpose that very day.

Lydia, anxious about her golden calf, the one idol of her life, was not a pleasant mistress of the farm. She was never particularly kind to the children; but now, for the next few days, she was rough and hard to everyone who came within her reach.

The dairymaid and the cook received sharp words, which, fortunately for themselves, they were powerful enough to return with interest. Poor old Mrs. Bell cowered lonely and sad by her fireside. Now and then she asked querulously for Mercy, but no Mercy, real or imaginary, ever came near her; and then her old mind would wander off from the land of Beulah, where she really lived, right across to the Celestial City at the other side of the river. Mrs. Bell was too old and too serene to be rendered really unhappy by Lydia's harsh ways! Her feet were already on the margin of the river, and earth's discords had scarcely power to touch her.

But those who did suffer, and suffer most from Lydia's bad temper, were the children.

They were afraid to stay in her presence. The weather had suddenly turned cold, wet, and wintry. Cecile dared not take Maurice out into the sleet showers which were falling about every ten minutes. All the bright and genial weather had departed. Their happy days in the woods and fields were over, and there was nothing for them but to spend the whole day in their attic bedroom. Here the wind howled fiercely. The badly-fitting window in the roof not only shook, but let in plenty of rain. And Maurice cried from cold and fright. In his

The Children's Pilgrimage

London home he had never undergone any real roughing. He wanted a fire, and begged of Cecile to light one; and when she refused, the little spoiled unhappy boy nearly wept himself sick. Cecile looked at Toby, and shook her head despondingly, and Toby answered her with more than one blink from his wise and solemn eyes.

Neither Cecile nor Toby would have fretted about the cold and discomfort for themselves, but both their hearts ached for Maurice.

One day the little boy seemed really ill. He had caught a severe cold, and he shivered, and crouched up now in Cecile's arms with flushed cheeks. His little hands and feet, however, were icy cold. How Cecile longed to take him down to Mrs. Bell's warm room. But she was strictly forbidden to go near the old lady.

At last, rendered desperate, she ventured to do for Maurice what nothing would have induced her to do for herself. She went downstairs, poked about until she found Lydia Purcell, and then in a trembling voice begged from her a few sticks and a little coal to build a fire in the attic bedroom.

Lydia stared at the request, then she refused it.

"That grate would not burn a fire even if you were to light it, " she said partly in excuse.

"But Maurice is so cold. I think he is ill from cold, and you don't like us to stay in the kitchen, " pleaded the anxious little sister.

"No, I certainly can't have children pottering about in my way here, " replied Lydia Purcell. "And do you know, Cecile—for if you don't 'tis right you should—all that money I was promised for the care of you and your brother, and the odious dog, has never come. You have been living on me for near three months now, and not a blessed sixpence have I had for my trouble. That uncle, or cousin, or whoever he is, in France, has not taken the slightest notice of my letter. There's a nice state of things—and you having the impudence to ask for a fire up in yer very bedroom. What next, I wonder? "

"I can't think why the money hasn't come, " answered Cecile, puckering her brows; "that money from France always did come to the day—always exactly to the day, it never failed. Father used to say our cousin who had bought his vineyard and farm was reliable. I can't think, indeed, why the money is not here long ago, Mrs. Purcell. "

"Well, it han't come, child, and I have got Mr. Preston to write about it, and if he don't have an answer soon and a check into the bargain, out you and Maurice will have to go. I'm a poor woman myself, and I can't afford to keep no beggar brats. That'll be worse nor a fire in your bedroom, I guess, Cecile. "

"If the money don't come, where'll you send us, Mrs. Purcell, please? " asked Cecile, her face very pale.

"Oh! 'tis easy to know where, child—to the Union, of course. "

Cecile had never heard of the Union.

"Is it far away? and is it a nice place? " she asked innocently.

Lydia laughed and held up her hands.

"Of all the babies, Cecile D'Albert, you beat them hallow, " she said. "No, no, I'll tell you nothing about the Union. You wait till you see it. You're so queer, maybe you'll like it. There's no saying —and Maurice'll get his share of the fire. Oh, yes, he'll get his share. "

"And Toby! Will Toby come too? " asked Cecile.

"Toby! bless you, no. There's a yard of rope for Toby. He'll be managed cheaper than any of you. Now go, child, go! "

The Children's Pilgrimage

CHAPTER IX.

"THE ADVENT OF THE GUIDE."

Cecile crept upstairs again very, very slowly, and sat down by Maurice's side.

"Maurice, dear, " she said to her little brother, "I ha' no good news for you. Aunt Lydia won't allow no fire, and you must just get right into bed, and I'll lie down and put my arms round you, and Toby shall lie at your feet. You'll soon be warm then, and maybe if you're a very good boy, and don't cry, I'll make up a little fairy tale for you, Maurice. "

But Maurice was sick and very miserable, and he was in no humor even to be comforted by what at most times he considered the nicest treat in the world—a story made up by Cecile.

"I hate Aunt Lydia Purcell, " he said; "I hate her, Cecile. "

"Oh, don't! Maurice, darling. Father often said it was wrong to hate anyone, and maybe Aunt Lydia does find us very expensive. Do you know, Maurice, she told me just now that our cousin in France has never sent her any money all this time? And you know how reliable our cousin always was; and Aunt Lydia says if the money does not come soon, she will send us away, quite away to another home. We are to go to a place called 'The Union. ' She says it is not very far away, and that it won't be a bad home. At least, you will have a fire to warm yourself by there, Maurice. "

"Oh! " said Maurice excitedly, "don't you *hope* our cousin in France won't send the money, Cecile? Couldn't you write, or get someone to write to him, telling him not to send the money? "

"I don't know writing well enough to put it in a letter, Maurice, and, besides, it would not be fair to Aunt Lydia, after her having such expense with us all these months. Don't you remember that delicious apple pie, Maurice, and the red, red apples to eat with bread in the fields? 'Tis only the last few days Aunt Lydia has got really unkind, and perhaps we are very expensive little children. Besides, Maurice, darling, I did not like to tell you at first, but there is one dreadful, dreadful thing about the Union. However nice a home it might be for you and me, we could not take Toby with us, Maurice. Aunt Lydia said Toby would not be taken in. "

"Then what would become of our dog? " asked Maurice, opening his velvety brown eyes very wide.

"Ah! that I don't understand. Aunt Lydia just laughed, and said Toby should have a yard of rope, and 'twould be cheaper than the Union. I can't in the least find out what she meant. "

But here Maurice got very red, so red, down below his chin, and into his neck, and even up to the roots of his hair, that Cecile gazed at him in alarm, and feared he had been taken seriously ill.

"Oh, Cecile! " he gasped. "Oh! oh! oh! " and here he buried his head on his sister's breast.

"What is it, Maurice? Maurice, speak to me, " implored his sister. "Maurice, are very ill? Do speak to me, darling? "

"No, Cecile, I'm not ill, " said the little boy, when he could find voice after his agitation. "But, oh! Cecile, you must never be angry with me for hating Aunt Lydia again. Cecile, Aunt Lydia is the dreadfullest woman in all the world. *Do* you know what she meant by a yard of rope? "

"No, Maurice; tell me, " asked Cecile, her face growing white.

"It means, Cecile, that our dog—our darling, darling Toby—is to be hung, hung till he dies. Our Toby is to be murdered, Cecile, and Aunt Lydia is to be his murderer. That's what it means. "

"But, Maurice, how do you know? Maurice, how can you tell? "

"It was last week, " continued the little boy, "last week, the day you would not come out, Toby and me were in the wood, and we came on a dog hanging to one of the trees by a bit of rope, and the poor dog was dead, and a big boy stood by. Toby howled when he saw the dog, and the big boy laughed; and I said to him, 'What is the matter with the poor dog? ' And the dreadful boy laughed again, Cecile, and he said, 'I've been giving him a yard of rope. '

"And I said, 'But he's dead. '

"And the boy said, 'Yes, that was what I gave it him for.' That boy was a murderer, and I would not stay in the wood all day, and that is what Aunt Lydia will be; and I hate Aunt Lydia, so I do."

Here Maurice went into almost hysterical crying, and Cecile and Toby had both as much as they could do for the next half hour to comfort him.

When he was better, and had been persuaded to get into bed, Cecile said:

"Me and you need not fret about Toby, Maurice, for our Toby shan't suffer. We won't go into no Union wherever it is, and if the money don't come from France, why, we'll run away, me and you and Toby."

"We'll run away," responded Maurice with a smile, and sleepy after his crying fit, and comforted by the warmth of his little bed, he closed his eyes and dropped asleep. His baby mind was quite happy now, for what could be simpler than running away?

Cecile sat on by her little brother's side, and Toby jumped into her lap. Toby had gone through a half hour of much pain. He had witnessed Maurice's tears, Cecile's pale face, and had several times heard his own name mentioned. He was too wise a dog not to know that the children were talking about some possible fate for him, and, by their tones and great distress, he guessed that the fate was not a pleasant one. He had his anxious moments during that half hour. But when Maurice dropped asleep and Cecile sat droopingly by his side, instantly this noble-natured mongrel dog forgot himself. His mission was to comfort the child he loved. He jumped on Cecile's lap, thereby warming her. He licked her face and hands, he looked into her eyes, his own bright and moist with a great wealth of canine love.

"Oh, Toby," said the little girl, holding him very tight, "Toby! I'd rather have a yard of rope myself than that you should suffer."

Toby looked as much as to say:

"Pooh, that's a trivial matter, don't let's think of it," and then he licked her hands again.

The Children's Pilgrimage

Cecile began to wonder if it would not be better for them not to wait for that letter from France. There was no saying, now that Aunt Lydia was really proved to be a wicked woman, what she might do, if they gave her time after the letter arrived. Would it not be best for Cecile, Maurice, and Toby to set off at once on that mission into France? Would it not be wisest, young as Cecile was, to begin the great search for Lovedy without delay? The little girl thought she had better secure her purse of money, and set off at once. But oh! she was so ignorant, so ignorant, and so young. Should she, Maurice, and Toby go east, west, north, or south? She had a journey before her, and she did not know a step of the way.

"Oh, Toby, " she said again to the watchful dog, "if only I had a guide. I do want a guide so dreadfully. And there is a guide called Jesus, and He loves everybody, and He guides people and little children, and perhaps dogs like you, Toby, right across to the New Jerusalem and the Celestial City. But I want Him to guide us into the south of France. He's so kind He would take us into his arms when we were tired and rest us. You and me, Toby, are strong, but Maurice is only a baby. If Jesus would guide us, He would take Maurice into His arms now and then. But Mistress Bell says she never heard of Jesus guiding anybody into the south of France, into the Pyrenees. Oh, how I wish He would! "

"Yes, " answered Toby, by means of his expressive eyes, and wagging his stumpy tail, "I wish He would. "

That night when Cecile and Maurice were asleep, and all the house was still, a messenger of kingly aspect came to the old farm.

Had Cecile opened her eyes then, and had she been endowed with power to tear away the slight film which hides immortal things from our view, she would have seen the Guide she longed for. For Jesus came down, and in her sleep took Mrs. Bell across the river. Without a pang the old pilgrim entered into rest, and no one knew in that slumbering household the moment she went home.

But I think—it may be but a fancy of mine—still I think Jesus did more. I think He went up still higher in that old farmhouse. I think He entered an attic bedroom and bent over two sleeping children, and smiled on them, and blessed them, and said to the anxious heart of one, "Certainly I will be with thee. I will guide My little lamb every step of the way. "

For Cecile looked so happy in her childish slumbers. Every trace of care had left her brow. The burden of responsibility was gone from her heart.

I think, before He left the room, Jesus stooped down and gave her a kiss of peace.

CHAPTER X.

"TOPSY-TURVY."

It may have seemed a strange thing, but, nevertheless, it was a fact, that one who appeared to make no difference to anybody while she was alive should yet be capable of causing quite a commotion the moment she was dead.

This was the case with old Mrs. Bell. For years she had lived in her pleasant south room, basking in the sun in summer, and half sleeping by the fire in winter. She never read; she spoke very little; she did not even knit, and never, by any chance, did she stir outside those four walls. She was in a living tomb, and was forgotten there. The four walls of her room were her grave. Lydia Purcell, to all intents and purposes, was mistress of all she surveyed.

But from the moment it was discovered that Mrs. Bell was dead—from the moment it was known that the time had come to shut her up in four much smaller walls—the aspect of everything was changed. She was no longer a person of no importance.

No importance! Her name was in everybody's mouth. The servants talked of her. The villagers whispered, and came and asked to look at her; and then they commented on the peaceful old face, and one or two shed tears and inwardly breathed a prayer that their last end might be like hers.

The house was full of subdued bustle and decorous excitement; and all the bustle and all the excitement were caused by Mrs. Bell.

Mrs. Bell, who spent her days from morning to night alone while she was living, who had even died alone! It was only after death she seemed worth consideration.

Between the day of death and the funeral, Mr. Preston, the lawyer, came over to Warren's Grove many times. He was always shut up with Lydia Purcell when he came, though, had anyone listened to their conversation, they would have found that Mrs. Bell was the subject of their discourse.

But the strange thing, the strangest thing about it all, was that Lydia Purcell and Mrs. Bell, from the moment Mrs. Bell was dead, appeared to have changed places. Lydia, from ruling all, and being feared by all, was now the person of no account. The cook defied her; the dairymaid openly disobeyed her in some important matter relating to the cream; and the boy whose business it was to attend to Lydia's own precious poultry, not only forgot to give them their accustomed hot supper, but openly recorded his forgetfulness over high tea in the kitchen that same evening; and the strange thing was that Lydia looked on, and did not say a word. She did not say a word or blame anybody, though her face was very pale, and she looked anxious.

The children noticed the changed aspect of things, and commented upon them in the way children will. To Maurice it was all specially surprising, as he had scarcely been aware of Mrs. Bell's existence during her lifetime.

"It must be a good thing to be dead, Cecile, " he said to his little sister, "people are very kind to you after you are dead, Cecile. Do you think Aunt Lydia Purcell would give me a fire in our room after I'm dead? "

"Oh, Maurice! don't, " entreated Cecile, "you are only a little baby boy, and you don't understand. "

"But I understood about the yard of rope, " retorted Maurice slyly.

Yes, Cecile owned that Maurice had been very clever in that respect, and she kissed him, and told him so, and then, taking his hand, they ran out.

The weather was again fine, the short spell of cold had departed, and the children could partly at least resume their old life in the woods. They had plenty to eat, and a certain feeling of liberty which everyone in the place shared. The cook, who liked them and pitied them, supplied them with plenty of cakes and apples, and the dairymaid treated Maurice to more than one delicious drink of cream.

Maurice became a thoroughly happy and contented little boy again, and he often remarked to himself, but for the benefit of Cecile and Toby, what a truly good thing it was that Mrs. Bell had died. Nay, he

The Children's Pilgrimage

was even heard to say that he wished someone could be always found ready to die, and so make things pleasant in a house.

Cecile, however, looked at matters differently. To her Mrs. Bell's death was a source of pain, for now there was no one at all left to tell her how to find the guide she needed. Perhaps, however, Mrs. Bell would talk to Jesus about it, for she was to see Jesus after she was dead.

Cecile used to wonder where the old woman had gone, and if she had found the real Mercy at last.

One day, as Jane, the cook, was filling the children's little basket, Cecile said to her:

"Has old Mrs. Bell gone into the Celestial City? "

"No, no, my dear, into heaven, " replied the cook; "the blessed old lady has gone into heaven, dear. "

Cecile sighed. "She always *spoke* about going to the Celestial City and the New Jerusalem, " she said.

Now the dairymaid, who happened to be a Methodist, stood near. She now came forward.

"Ain't heaven and the New Jerusalem jest one and the same, Jane Parsons? What's the use of puzzling a child like that? Yes, Miss Cecile, honey, the old lady is in heaven, or the New Jerusalem, or the Celestial City, which you like to call it. They all means the same. "

Cecile thanked the dairymaid and walked away. She was a little comforted by this explanation, and a tiny gleam of light was entering her mind. Still she was very far from the truth.

The halcyon days between Mrs. Bell's death and her funeral passed all too quickly. Then came the day of the funeral, and the next morning the iron rule of Lydia Purcell began again. Whatever few words she said to cook, dairymaid, and message-boy, they once more obeyed her and showed her respect. And there was no more cream for Maurice, nor special dainties for the little picnic basket. That same day, too, Lydia and Mr. Preston had a long conversation.

"It is settled then, " said the lawyer, "and you stay on here and manage everything on the old footing until we hear from Mr. Bell. I have telegraphed, but he is not likely to reply except by letter. You may reckon yourself safe not to be disturbed out of your present snug quarters for the winter. "

"And hard I must save, " said Lydia; "I have but beggary to face when I'm turned out. "

"Some of your money will be secured, " replied the lawyer. "I can promise you at least three hundred. "

"What is three hundred to live on? "

"You can save again. You are still a young woman. "

"I am forty-five, " replied Lydia Purcell. "At forty-five you don't feel as you do at twenty-five. Yes, I can save; but somehow there's no spirit in it. "

"I am sorry for you, " replied the lawyer. Then he added, "And the children — the children can remain here as long as you stay. "

But at the mention of the children, the momentary expression of softness, which had made Lydia's face almost pleasing, vanished.

"Mr. Preston, " she said, rising, "I will keep those children, who are no relations to me, until I get a letter from France. If a check comes with the letter, well and good; if not, out they go — out they go that minute, sure as my name is Lydia Purcell. What call has a Frenchman's children on me? "

"Where are they to go? " asked Mr. Preston.

"To the workhouse, of course. What is the workhouse for but to receive such beggar brats? "

"Well, I am sorry for them, " said the lawyer, now also rising and buttoning on his coat. "They don't look fit for such a life; they look above so dismal a fate. Poor little ones! That boy is very handsome, and the girl, her eyes makes you think of a startled fawn. Well, good-day, Mrs. Purcell. I trust there will be good news from France. "

The Children's Pilgrimage

Just on the boundary of the farm Mr. Preston met Maurice. Some impulse, for he was not a softhearted man himself, made him stop, call the pretty boy to his side, and give him half a sovereign.

"Ask your sister to take care of it for you, and keep it, both of you, my poor babes, for a rainy day."

CHAPTER XI.

A MONTH TO PREPARE.

Mr. Preston's visits were now supposed to have ceased. But the next afternoon, when Lydia was busy in the dairy, he came again to the farm.

He came now with both important and unpleasant tidings.

The heir in Australia had telegraphed: "He was not coming back to England. Everything was to be sold; farm and all belongings to it were to be got rid of as quickly as possible. "

Lydia clasped her hands in dismay at these tidings. No time for any more saving, no time for any more soft living, for the new owners of Warren's Grove would be very unlikely to need her services.

"And there is another thing, Mrs. Purcell, " continued the lawyer, "which I confess grieves me even more than this. I have heard from France. I had a letter this morning. "

"There was no check in it, I warrant, " said Lydia.

"No, I am sorry to tell you there was no check in it. The children's cousin in France refuses to pay any more money to them. He says their father is dead, and the children have no claim; besides, the vineyard has been doing badly the last two years, and he considers that he has given quite enough for it already; in short, he refuses to allow another penny to these poor little orphans. "

"But my sister Grace, the children's stepmother, said there was a regular deed for this money, " said Lydia. "She had it, and I believe it is in an old box of hers upstairs. If there is a deed, could not the man be forced to pay, Mr. Preston? "

"We could go to law with him, certainly; but the difficulty of a lawsuit between a Frenchman and an English court would be immense; the issue would be doubtful, and the sum not worth the risk. The man owes four fifties, that is two hundred pounds; the whole of that sum would be expended on the lawsuit. No; I fear we shall gain nothing by that plan. "

The Children's Pilgrimage

"Well, of course I am sorry for the children, " said Lydia Purcell, "but it is nothing to me. I must take steps to get them into the workhouse at once; as it is, I have been at considerable loss by them. "

"Mrs. Purcell, believe me, that loss you will never feel; it will be something to your credit at the right side of the balance some day. And now tell me how much the support of the little ones costs you here. "

Lydia considered, resting her chin thoughtfully on her hand.

"They have the run of the place, " she said. "In a big place like this 'tis impossible, however careful you may be, not to have odds and ends and a little waste; the children eat up the odds and ends. Yes; I suppose they could be kept here for five shillings a week each. "

"That is half a sovereign between them. Mrs. Purcell, you are sure to remain at Warren's Grove for another month; while you are here I will be answerable for the children; I will allow them five shillings a week each—you understand? "

"Yes, I understand, " said Lydia, "and I'm sure they ought to be obliged to you, Mr. Preston. But should I not take steps about the workhouse? "

"I will take the necessary steps when the time comes. Leave the matter to me. "

That evening Lydia called Cecile to her side.

"Look here, child, you have got a kind friend in Mr. Preston. He is going to support you both here for a month longer. It is very good of him, for you are nothing, either of you, but little beggar brats, as your cousin in France won't send any more money. "

"Our cousin in France won't send any more money! " repeated Cecile. Her face grew very pale, her eyes fell to the ground; in a moment she raised them.

"Where are we to go at the end of the month, Aunt Lydia Purcell? "

"To the workhouse. "

The Children's Pilgrimage

"You said before it was to the Union. "

"Yes, child, yes; 'tis all the same. "

But here Maurice, who had been busy playing with Toby and apparently not listening to a single word, scrambled up hastily to his feet and came to Cecile's side.

"But Cecile and me aren't going into no Union, wicked Aunt Lydia Purcell! " he said.

"Heity-teity! " said Lydia, laughing at his little red face and excited manner.

The laugh enraged Maurice, who had a very hot temper.

"I hate you, Aunt Lydia Purcell! " he repeated, "I hate you! and I'm not going to be afraid of you. You said you'd give our Toby a yard of rope; if you do you'll be a murderer. I think you're so wicked, you're one already. "

Those words, striking at some hidden, deep-seated pain in Lydia's heart, caused her to wince and turn pale. She rose from her seat, shaking her apron as she did so. But before she left the room she cast a look of unutterable aversion on both the children.

Cecile now knew what she had before her. She, Maurice, and Toby had just a month to prepare—just a month to get ready for the great task of Cecile's life. At the end of a month they must set forth—three pilgrims without a guide. Cecile felt that it was a pity this long journey which they must take in secret should begin in the winter. Had she the power of choice, she would have put off so weary a pilgrimage until the days were long and the weather mild. But there was no choice in the matter now; just when the days were shortest and worst, just at Christmas time, they must set out. Cecile was a very wise child for her years. Her father had called her dependable. She was dependable. She had thought, and prudence, and foresight. She made many schemes now. At night, as she lay awake in her attic bedroom, in the daytime, as she walked by Maurice's side, she pondered them. She had two great anxieties, —first, how to find the way; second, how to make the money last. Fifteen pounds her stepmother had given her to find Lovedy with. Fifteen pounds seemed to such an inexperienced head as Cecile's a very large sum of money — indeed, quite an inexhaustible sum. But Mrs. D'Albert had assured her that it was not a large sum at all. It was not even a large sum for one, she said, even for Cecile herself. To make it sufficient she must walk a great deal, and sleep at the smallest village inns, and eat the plainest food. And how much shorter, then, would the money go, if it had to supply two with food and the other necessities of the journey? Cecile resolved that, if possible, they would not touch the money laid in the Russia-leather purse until they really got into France. Her present plan was to walk to London. London was not so very far out of Kent, and once in London, the place where she had lived all, or almost all her life, she would feel at home. Cecile even hoped she might be able to earn a little money in London, money enough to take Maurice and Toby and herself into France. She had not an idea how the money was to be earned, but even if she had to sweep a crossing, she thought she could do it. And, for their walk into London, there was that precious half sovereign, which kind Mr. Preston had given Maurice, and which Cecile had put by in the same box which held the leather purse. They might have to spend a shilling or two of that half sovereign, and for the rest, Cecile began to consider what they could do to save now. It was useless to expect such foresight on Maurice's part. But for herself, whenever she got an apple or a nut, she put it carefully aside. It was not that her little teeth did not long to close in the juicy fruit, or to crack the hard shell and secure the kernel. But far greater than these physical longings was her earnest desire to keep true to her solemn promise to the dead — to find, and give her mother's message and her mother's gift to the beautiful, wayward English girl who yet had broken that mother's heart.

CHAPTER XII.

THE CUPBOARD IN THE WALL.

But poor Cecile had greater anxieties than the fear of her journey before her.

Mrs. D'Albert—when she gave her that Russia-leather purse—had said to her solemnly, and with considerable fear:

"Keep it from Lydia Purcell. Let Lydia know nothing about it, for Lydia loves money so well that no earthly consideration would make her spare you. Lydia would take the money, and all my life-work, and all your hope of finding Lovedy, would be at an end. "

This, in substance, was Mrs. D'Albert's speech; and Cecile had not been many hours in Lydia Purcell's company without finding out how true those words were.

Lydia loved money beyond all other things. For money she would sell right, nobleness, virtue. All those moral qualities which are so precious in God's sight Lydia would part with for that possession which Satan prizes—money.

Cecile, when she first came to Warren's Grove, had put her treasure into so secure and out-of-the-way a hiding place that she felt quite easy about it. Lydia would never, never think of troubling her head about that attic sloping down to the roof, still less would she poke her fingers into the little secret cupboard where the precious purse lay.

Cecile's mind therefore was quite light. But one morning, about a week after Mrs. Bell's funeral, as she and Maurice were preparing to start out for their usual ramble, these words smote on her ears with a strange and terrible sense of dread.

"Jane, " said Lydia, addressing the cook, "we must all do with a cold dinner to-day, and not too much of that, for, as you write a very neat hand, I want you to help me with the inventory, and it has got to be begun at once. I told Mr. Preston I would have no agent pottering about the place. 'Tis a long job, but I will do it myself. "

The Children's Pilgrimage

"What's an inkin-dory? " asked Maurice, raising a curious little face to Jane.

"Bless yer heart, honey, " said Jane, stooping down and kissing him, "an inventory you means. Why, 'tis just this—Mrs. Purcell and me—we has got to write down the names of every single thing in the house —every stick, and stone, and old box, and even, I believe, the names of the doors and cupboards. That's an inventory, and mighty sick we'll be of it. "

"Come, Jane, stop chattering, " said Lydia. "Maurice, run out at once. You'll find me in the attics, Jane, when you've done. We'll get well through the attics to-day. "

Aunt Lydia turned on her heel, and Maurice and Cecile went slowly out. Very slow, indeed, were Cecile's footsteps.

"How dull you are, Cecile! " said the little boy.

"I'm not very well, " said Cecile. "Maurice, " she continued suddenly, "you go and play with Toby, darling. Go into the fields, and not too far away; and don't stay out too late. Here's our lunch. No, I don't want any. I'm going to lie down. Yes, maybe I'll come out again. "

She ran away before Maurice had even time to expostulate. She was conscious that a crisis had come, that a great dread was over her, that there might yet be time to take the purse from its hiding place.

An inventory meant that every box was looked into, every cupboard opened. What chance then had her purse in its tin box in a forgotten cupboard? That cupboard would be opened at last, and her treasure stolen away. Aunt Lydia was even now in the attics, or was she? Was there any hope that Cecile might be in time to rescue the precious purse?

She flew up the attic stairs, her heart beating, her head giddy. Oh! if she might be in time!

Alas! she was not. Aunt Lydia was already in full possession of Cecile's and Maurice's attic. She was standing on tiptoe, and taking down some musty books from a shelf.

The Children's Pilgrimage

"Go away, Cecile, " she said to the little girl, "I'm very busy, and I can't have you here; run out at once. "

"Please, Aunt Lydia, I've such a bad headache, " answered poor Cecile. This was true, for her agitation was so great she felt almost sick. "May I lie down on my bed? " she pleaded.

"Oh, yes, child! if your head is bad. But you won't get much quiet here, for Jane and I have our work cut out for us, and there'll be plenty of noise. "

"I don't mind a noise, if I may lie down, " answered Cecile thankfully.

She crept into her bed, and lay as if she was asleep. In reality, with every nerve strung to the highest tension, sleep was as impossible for her as though such a boon had never been granted to the world. Whenever Aunt Lydia's back was turned, her eyes were opened wide. Whenever Aunt Lydia looked in her direction, the poor little creature had to feign the sleep which was so far away. As long as it was only Maurice's and Cecile's attic, there was some rest. There was just a shadowy hope that Aunt Lydia might go downstairs for something, that five minutes might be given her to snatch her treasure away.

Lydia Purcell, however, a thoroughly clever woman, was going through her work with method and expedition. She had no idea of leaving the attics until she had taken a complete and exhaustive list of what they contained.

Cecile began to count the articles of furniture in her little bedroom. Alas! they were not many. By the time Jane appeared, a complete list of them was nearly taken.

"Jane, go into that little inner attic, and poke out the rubbish, " said Aunt Lydia, "poke out every stick and stone, and box. Don't overlook a thing. I'll be with you in a minute. "

"Nasty, dirty little hole, " remarked Jane. "I'll soon find what it contains; not sixpence worth, I'll warrant. "

But here the rack of suspense on which poor Cecile was lying became past endurance, the child's fortitude gave way.

Sitting up in bed, she cried aloud in a high-pitched, almost strained voice, her eyes glowing, her cheeks like peonies:

"Oh! not the little cupboard in the wall. Oh! please—oh! please, not the little cupboard in the wall. "

"What cupboard? I know of no cupboard, " exclaimed Aunt Lydia.

Jane held up her hands.

"Preserve us, ma'am, the poor lamb must be wandering, and look at her eyes and hands. "

"What is it, Cecile? Speak! what is it, you queer little creature? " said Aunt Lydia, in both perplexity and alarm, for the child was sobbing hard, dry, tearless sobs.

"Oh, Aunt Lydia! be merciful, " she gasped. "Oh! oh! if you find it don't keep it. 'Tisn't mine, 'tis Lovedy's; 'tis to find Lovedy. Oh! don't, don't, don't keep the purse if you find it, Aunt Lydia Purcell. "

At the word "purse" Aunt Lydia's face changed. She had been feeling almost kind to poor Cecile; now, at the mention of what might contain gold, came back, sweeping over her heart like a fell and evil wind, the love of gold.

"Jane, " she said, turning to her amazed handmaiden; "this wicked, silly child has been hiding something, and she's afraid of my finding it. Believe me, I will look well into the inner attic. She spoke of a cupboard. Search for a cupboard in the wall, Jane. "

Jane, full of curiosity, searched now with a will. There was but a short moment of suspense, then the sliding panel fell back, the little tin box was pulled out, and Cecile's Russia-leather purse was held up in triumph between Jane's finger and thumb.

There was a cry of pleasure from Aunt Lydia. Cecile felt the attic growing suddenly dark, and herself as suddenly cold. She murmured something about "Lovedy, Lovedy, lost now, " and then she sank down, a poor unconscious little heap, at Aunt Lydia's feet.

CHAPTER XIII.

ON THE ROAD TO THE CELESTIAL CITY.

When Cecile awoke from the long swoon into which she had sunk, it was not to gaze into the hard face of Lydia Purcell. Lydia was nowhere to be seen, but bending over her, with eyes full of compassion, was Jane. Jane, curious as she was, felt now more sorrow than curiosity for the little creature struck down by some mysterious grief.

At first the child could remember nothing.

"Where am I? " she gasped, catching hold of Jane's hand and trying to raise herself.

"In yer own little bed, honey. You have had a faint and are just coming round; you'll be all right in a minute or two. There, just one tiny sup more wine and I'll get you a nice hot cup of tea. "

Cecile was too weak and bewildered not to obey. She sipped the wine which Jane held to her lips, then lay back with a little sigh of relief and returning consciousness.

"I'm better now; I'm quite well now, Jane, " she murmured in a thankful voice.

"Yes, honey, you are a deal better now, " answered Jane, stooping down and kissing her. "And now never don't you stir a bit, and don't worry about nothing, for Jane will fetch you a nice cup of tea, and then see how pleasant you'll feel. "

The kind-hearted girl hurried away, and Cecile was left alone in the now quiet attic.

What thing had happened to her? What weight was at her heart? She had a desire, not a keen desire, but still a feeling that it would give her pleasure to be lying in the grave by her father's side. She felt that she did not much care for anyone, that anything now might happen without exciting her. Why was not her heart beating with love for Maurice and Toby? Why had all hope, all longing, died within her? Ah! she knew the reason. It came back to her slowly, slowly, but surely. All that dreadful scene, all those moments of suspense too terrible even to be borne, they returned to her memory.

Her Russia-leather purse of gold and notes were gone, the fifteen pounds she was to spend in looking for Lovedy, the forty pounds she was to give as her dead mother's dying gift to the wandering girl, had vanished. Cecile felt that as surely as if she had flung it into the sea, was that purse now lost. She had broken her promise, her solemn, solemn promise to the dead; everything, therefore, was now over for her in life.

When Jane came back with the nice hot tea, Cecile received it with a wan smile. But there was such a look of utter, unchildlike despair in her lovely eyes that, as the handmaiden expressed it, telling the tale afterward, her heart went up into her mouth with pity.

"Cecile, " said the young woman, when the tea-drinking had come to an end, "I sees by yer face, poor lamb, as you remembers all about what made you drop down in that faint. And look you here, my lamb, you've got to tell me, Jane Parsons, all about it; and what is more, if I can help you I will. You tell Jane all the whole story, honey, for it 'ud go to a pagan's heart to see you, and so it would; and you needn't be feared, for she ain't anywheres about. She said as she wanted no dinner, and she's safe in her room a-reckoning the money in the purse, I guess. "

"Oh, Jane! " said little Cecile, "the purse! the Russia-leather purse! I think I'll die, since Aunt Lydia Purcell has found the Russia-leather purse. "

"Well, tell us the whole story, child. It do seem a wonderful thing for a bit of a child like you to have a purse of gold, and then to keep it a-hiding. I don't b'lieve as you loves gold like Miss Purcell do; it don't seem as if you could have come by so much money wrong, Cecile. "

"No, Jane, I didn't come by it wrong. Mrs. D'Albert, my stepmother, gave me that Russia-leather purse, with all the gold and notes in it, when she was dying. I know exactly how much was in it, fifteen pounds in gold, and forty pounds in ten-pound Bank of England notes. I can't ever forget what was in that dreadful purse, as my stepmother told me I was never to lose until I found Lovedy. "

The Children's Pilgrimage

"And who in the name of fortune is Lovedy, Cecile? You do tell the queerest stories I ever listened to."

"Yes, Jane, it is a very queer tale, and though I understand it perfectly myself, I don't suppose I can get you to understand."

"Oh, yes! my deary, I'm very smart indeed at picking up a tale. You tell me all about Lovedy, Cecile."

Thus admonished, Cecile did tell her tale. All that long sad story which the dying woman had poured into the child's listening ears was now told again to the wondering and excited cook. Jane listened with her mouth open and her eyes staring. If there was anything under the sun she dearly, dearly loved, it was a romance, and here was one quite unknown in her experience. Cecile told her little story in childish and broken words—words which were now and then interrupted by sobs of great pain—but she told it with the power which earnestness always gives.

"I'll never find Lovedy now; I've broken my promise—I've broken my promise," she said in conclusion.

"Well," answered Jane, drawing a long breath when the story was over, "that is interesting, and the queerest bit of a tale I ever set my two ears to listen to. Oh, yes! I believes you, child. You ain't one as'll tell lies—and that I'm gospel sure on. And so yer poor stepmother wanted you not to let Lydia Purcell clap her eyes on that purse. Ah, poor soul! she knew her own sister well."

"Yes, Jane, she said I'd never see it again if Aunt Lydia found it out. Oh, Jane! I did think I had hid the purse so very, very secure."

"And so you had, deary—real beautiful, and if it hadn't been for that horrid inventory, it might ha' lain there till doomsday. But now do tell me, Cecile—for I am curious, and that I won't go for to deny — suppose as you hadn't lost that purse, however 'ud a little mite like you go for to look for Lovedy?"

"Oh, Jane! the purse is lost, and I can never do it now—never until I can earn it all back again my own self. But I'd have gone to France — me and Maurice and Toby had it all arranged quite beautiful—we were going to France this very winter. Lovedy is quite safe to be in France; and you know, Jane, me and Maurice ain't little English

The Children's Pilgrimage

children. We are just a little French boy and girl; so we'd be sure to get on well in our own country, Jane."

"Yes, yes, for sure," said Jane, knowing nothing whatever of France, but much impressed with Cecile's manner; "there ain't no doubt as you're a very clever little girl, Cecile, and not the least bit English. I dare say, young as you are, that you would find Lovedy, and it seems a real pity as it couldn't be."

"I wanted the guide Jesus very much to go with us," said Cecile, raising her earnest eyes and fixing them on Jane's face. "If *He* had come, we'd have been sure to find Lovedy. For me and Maurice, we are very young to go so far by ourselves. Do you know anything about that guide, Jane? Mistress Bell said when she was alive, that He took people into the New Jerusalem and into the Celestial City. But she never heard of His being a guide to anybody into France. I think 'tis a great, great pity, don't you?"

Now Jane was a Methodist. But she was more, she was also a Christian.

"My dear lamb," she said, "the blessed Lord Jesus'll guide you into France, or to any other place. Why, 'tis all on the road to the Celestial City, darling."

"Oh! is it? Oh! would He really, really be so kind and beautiful?" said Cecile, sitting up and speaking with sudden eagerness and hope. "Oh, dear Jane! how I love you for telling me this! Oh! if only I had my purse of gold, how surely, how surely I should find Lovedy now."

"Well, darling, there's no saying what may happen. You have Jane Parsons for your friend anyhow, and what is more, you have the Lord Jesus Christ. Eh! but He does love a little faithful thing like you. But see here, Cecile, 'tis getting dark, and I must run downstairs; but I'll send you up a real good supper by Maurice, and see that he and Toby have full and plenty. You lie here quite easy, Cecile, and don't stir till I come back to you. I'll bring you tidings of that purse as sure as my name's Jane, and ef I were you, Cecile, I'd just say a bit of a prayer to Jesus. Tell Him your trouble, it'll give you a power of comfort."

"Is that praying? I did not know it was that."

"That is praying, my poor little lamb; you tell it all straight away to the loving Jesus."

"But He isn't here."

"Oh, yes, darling! He'll be very nigh to you, I guess, don't you be frightened."

"Does Jesus the guide come in the dark?"

"He'll be with you in the dark, Cecile. You tell Him everything, and then have a good sleep."

CHAPTER XIV.

WHAT JANE PARSONS KNEW.

When, a couple of hours later, Maurice, very tired and fagged after his long day's ramble, came upstairs, followed by Toby, and thrust into Cecile's hand a great hunch of seed-cake, she pushed it away, and said in an earnest, impressive whisper:

"Hush! "

"Oh, why? " asked Maurice; "you have been away all the whole day, Cecile; and Toby and me had no one to talk to, and now when I had such a lot to tell you, you say 'Hush' Why do you say 'Hush' Cecile? "

"Oh, Maurice! don't talk, darling, 'tis because Lord Jesus the guide is in the room, and I think He must be asleep, for I have prayed a lot to Him, and He has not answered. Don't let's disturb Him, Maurice; a guide must be so tired when he drops asleep. "

"Where is He? " asked Maurice; "may I light a candle and look for Him? "

"No, no, you mustn't; He only comes to people in the dark, so Jane says. You lie down and shut your eyes. "

"If you don't want your cake, may I eat it then? "

"Yes, you may eat it. And, Toby, come into my arms, dear dog. "

Maurice was soon in that pleasant land of a little child's dreams, and Toby, full of most earnest sympathy, was petting and soothing Cecile in dog fashion.

Meanwhile, Jane Parsons downstairs was not idle.

Cecile's story, told after Cecile's fashion, had fired her honest heart with such sympathy and indignation that she was ready both to dare and suffer in her cause.

The Children's Pilgrimage

Jane Parsons had been brought up at Warren's Grove from the time she was a little child. Her mother had been cook before her, and when her mother got too old, Jane, as a matter of course, stepped into her shoes. Active, honest, quiet, and sober, she was a valuable servant. She was essentially a good girl, guided by principle and religion in all she did.

Jane had never known any other home but Warren's Grove, and long as Lydia Purcell had been there, Jane was there as long.

Now she was prepared—prepared, if necessary—to give up her home. She meant, as I said, to run a risk, for it never even occurred to her not to help Cecile in her need. Let Lydia Purcell quietly pocket that money—that money that had been saved and hoarded for a purpose, and for such a purpose! Let Lydia spend the money that had, as Jane expressed it, a vow over it! Not if her sharp wits could prevent it.

She thought over her plan as she bustled about and prepared the supper. Very glum she looked as she stepped quickly here and there, so much so that the dairymaid and the errand-boy chaffed her for her dull demeanor.

Jane, however, hasty enough on most occasions, was too busy now with her own thoughts either to heed or answer them.

Well she knew Lydia Purcell, equally well she knew that to tell Cecile's tale would be useless. Lydia cared for neither kith nor kin, and she loved money beyond even her own soul.

But Jane, a clever child once, a clever woman now, had not been unobservant of some things in Lydia's past, some things that Lydia supposed to be buried in the grave of her own heart. A kind-hearted girl, Jane had never used this knowledge. But now knowledge was power. She would use it in Cecile's behalf.

Ever since the finding of the purse, Lydia had been alone.

In real or pretended indignation, she had left Cecile to get out of her faint as best she could. For six or seven hours she had now been literally without a soul to speak to. She was not, therefore, indisposed to chat with Jane—who was a favorite with her—when

The Children's Pilgrimage

that handmaid brought in a carefully prepared little supper, and laid it by her side.

"That's a very shocking occurrence, Jane, " she began.

"Eh? " said Jane.

"Why, that about the purse. Who would have thought of a young child being so depraved? Of course the story is quite clear. Cecile poking about, as children will, found the purse; but, unlike a child, hid it, and meant to keep it. Well, to think that all this time I have been harboring, and sheltering, and feeding, and all without a sixpence to repay myself, a young thief! But wait till I tell Mr. Preston. See how long he'll keep those children out of the workhouse after this! Oh! no wonder the hardened little thing was in a state of mind when I went to search the attics! "

"Heaven give me patience! " muttered Jane to herself. Aloud she said, "And who, do you think, the money belongs to, ma'am? "

"I make no doubt whose it is, Jane, " said Lydia Purcell quietly and steadily. "It is my own. This is my purse. It is the one poor old Mrs. Bell lost so many years ago. You were a child at the time, but there was some fuss made about it. I am short of money now, sadly short! and I count it a providence that this, small as it is, should have turned up. "

"You mean to keep it then? " said Jane.

"Why, yes, I certainly do. You don't suppose I will hand it over to that little thief of a French girl? Besides, it is my own. Is it likely I should not know my own purse? "

"Is there much money in it? " asked Jane as quietly as before.

"No, nothing to make a fuss about. Only a few sovereigns and some silver. Nothing much, but still of value to a hard-working woman. "

"After that lie, I'll not spare her, " muttered Jane to herself. Aloud she said, "I was only a child of ten years or so, but I remember the last time poor Mistress Bell was in that attic. "

"Indeed. And when was that? " asked Lydia.

The Children's Pilgrimage

"I suppose it was then as she dropped the purse, and it got swept away in all the confusion that followed, " continued Jane, now placing herself in front of Lydia, and gazing at her.

Lydia was helping herself to another mutton-chop, and began to feel a little uncomfortable.

"When was Mrs. Bell last in the attics? " she said.

"I was with her, " continued Jane. "I used to play a good bit with Missie Mercy in those days, you remember, ma'am? Mrs. Bell was poking about, but I was anxious for Mercy to come home to go on with our play, and I went to the window. I looked out. There was a fine view from that 'ere attic window. I looked out, and I saw—"

"What? " asked Lydia Purcell. She had laid down her knife and fork now, and her face had grown a trifle pale.

"Oh! nothing much. I saw you, ma'am, and Missie Mercy going into that poor mason's cottage, him as died of the malignant fever. You was there a good half hour or so. It was a day or two later as poor Missie sickened. "

"I did not think it was fever, " said Lydia. "Believe me, believe me, Jane, I did not know it certainly until we were leaving the cottage. Oh! my poor lamb, my poor innocent, innocent murdered lamb! "

Lydia covered her face with her hands; she was trembling. Even her strong, hard-worked hands were white from the storm of feeling within.

"You knew of this, you knew this of me all these years, and you never told. You never told even *me* until to-night, " said Lydia presently, raising a haggard face.

"I knew it, and I never told even you until to-night, " repeated Jane.

"Why do you tell me to-night? "

"May I take away the supper, ma'am, or shall you want any more? "

"No, no! take it away, take it away! You *don't* know what I have suffered, girl; to be the cause, through my own carelessness, of the

The Children's Pilgrimage

death of the one creature I loved. And—and—yes, I will tell the truth—I had heard rumors; yes, I had heard rumors, but I would not heed them. I was fearless of illness myself, and I wanted a new gown fitted. Oh! my lamb, my pretty, pretty lamb! "

"Well, ma'am, nobody ever suspected it was you, and 'tis many years ago now. You don't fret. Good-night, ma'am! "

Lydia gave a groan, and Jane, outside the door, shook her own hand at herself.

"Ain't I a hard-hearted wretch to see her like that and not try to comfort? Well, I wonder if Jesus was there would He try a bit of comforting? But I'm out of all patience. Such feeling for a child as is dead and don't need it, and never a bit for a poor little living child, who is, by the same token, as like that poor Mercy as two peas is like each other. "

Jane felt low-spirited for a minute or two, but by the time she returned to the empty kitchen she began to cheer up.

"I did it well. I think I'll get the purse back, " she said to herself.

She sat down, put out the light, and prepared to wait patiently.

For an hour there was absolute stillness, then there was a slight stir in the little parlor. A moment later Lydia Purcell, candle in hand, came out, on her way to her bedroom. Jane slipped off her shoes, glided after her just far enough to see that she held a candle in one hand and a brandy bottle in the other.

"God forgive me for driving her to it, but I had to get the purse, " muttered Jane to herself. "I'm safe to get the purse now. "

CHAPTER XV.

GOING ON PILGRIMAGE.

It was still quite the middle of the night when a strong light was flashed into Cecile D'Albert's eyes, and she was aroused from a rather disturbed sleep by Jane, who held up the Russia-leather purse in triumph.

"Here it is, Cecile, " she said, "here it is. I guess Jesus Christ heard your bit of a prayer real wonderful quick, my lamb. "

"Oh, Jane! He did not answer me once, " said Cecile, starting up and too surprised and bewildered to understand yet that her lost purse was really hers again. "He never heard me, Jane; I suppose He was asleep, for I did ask Him so often to let me have my purse back. "

"There wasn't much sleep about Him, " said Jane; "the Lord don't never slumber nor sleep; and as to not answering, what answer could be plainer than yer purse, Cecile? Here, you don't seem to believe it, take it in yer hand and count. "

"My own purse; Lovedy's own purse, " said Cecile, in rather a slow, glad voice. The sense of touch had brought to her belief. She opened her eyes wide and looked hard at Jane. Then a great light of beauty, hope, and rapture filled the lovely eyes, and the little arms were flung tight round the servant's honest neck.

"Dear, dear Jane, I do love you. Oh! *did* Aunt Lydia really give the purse back? "

"You have got the purse, Cecile, and you don't ask no questions. Well, there, I don't mind telling you. She had it in her hand when she dropped asleep; she wor sleeping very sound, it was easy to take the purse away. "

"My own and Lovedy's purse, " repeated Cecile. "Oh, Jane! it seems too good of Jesus to give it back to me again. "

"Aye, darling, He'll give you more than that if you ask Him, for you're one o' those as He loves. But now, Cecile, we ha' a deal to do

The Children's Pilgrimage

before morning. You open the purse, and see that all the money is safe. "

Cecile did as she was bid, and out fell the fifteen sovereigns and the four Bank of England notes.

"'Tis all there, Jane, " she said, "even to the little bit of paper under the lining. "

"What's that, child? "

"I don't know, there's some writing on it, but I can't read writing. "

"Well, but I can, let me read it, darling. "

Cecile handed the paper to her, and Jane read aloud the following words:

"'This purse contains fifty-five pounds. Forty pounds in Bank of England ten-pound notes, for my dear and only child, Lovedy Joy; fifteen pounds in gold for my stepdaughter, Cecile D'Albert. To be spent by her in looking for my daughter, and for no other use whatever.

"'Signed by me, Grace D'Albert, on this ninth day of September, 18 — '

"Cecile, " said Jane suddenly, "you must let me keep this paper. I will send it back to you if I can, but you must let me keep it for the present. What I did to-night might have got me into trouble. But this will save me, if you let me keep it for a bit. "

"Yes, Jane, you must keep it; it only gives directions; I know all about them down deep in my heart. "

"And now, little one, I'm sorry to say there's no more sleep for you this night. You've got to get up; you and Maurice and Toby have all three of you to get up and be many, many miles away from here before the morning, for if Lydia found you in the house in the morning, you would not have that purse five minutes, child, and I don't promise as I could ever get it back again. "

The Children's Pilgrimage

"I always meant to go away, " said Cecile quietly. "I did not know it would come so soon as to-night, but I'm quite ready. Me and Maurice and Toby, we'll walk to London. I have got half a sovereign that Mr. Preston gave to Maurice. We'll go to London first, and then to France. Yes, Jane, I'm quite ready. Shall I wake Maurice, and will you open the door to let us out? "

"I'll do more than that, my little lamb; and ain't it enough to break one's heart to hear the poor innocent, and she taking it so calm and collected-like? Now, Cecile, tell me have you any friends in London? "

"I once met a girl who sat on a doorstep and sang, " answered Cecile. "I think she would be my friend, but I don't know where she lives. "

"Then she ain't no manner of good, deary. Jane Parsons can do better for you than that. Now listen to what I has got to say. You get up and dress, and wake Maurice and get him dressed, and then you, Maurice, and Toby slip downstairs as soft as little mice; make no noise, for ef *she* woke it 'ud be all up with us. You three come down to the kitchen, and I'll have something hot for you to drink, and then I'll have the pony harnessed to the light cart, and drive you over to F—- in time to catch the three o'clock mail train. The guard'll be good to you for he's a friend of mine, and I'll have a bit of a note writ, and when you get to London the guard'll put you in a cab, and you'll drive to the address written on the note. The note is to my cousin, Annie West, what was Jones. She's married in London and have one baby, and her heart is as good and sweet and soft as honey. She'll keep you for a week or two, till 'tis time for you to start into France. Now be quick up, deary, and hide that purse in yer dress, werry safe. "

"Oh, Jane, what a beautiful, beautiful plan! And will Maurice's half-sovereign help us all that much? "

"The half-sovereign won't have nothing to say to it; 'tis Jane Parsons' own work, and her own money shall pay it. You keep that half-sovereign for a rainy day, Cecile. "

"That's what Mr. Preston said when he gave it, " echoed Cecile. And then the kind-hearted servant hurried downstairs to complete her arrangements.

The Children's Pilgrimage

"Maurice," said Cecile, stooping down and waking her little brother. "Get up, Maurice, darling; 'tis time for us to commence our journey."

"Oh, Cecile!" said the little fellow, "in the very middle of the night, and I'm so sleepy."

"For Toby's sake, Maurice, dear."

"Toby shall have no yard of rope, wicked Aunt Lydia," said Maurice at these words, starting up and rubbing his brown eyes to try and open them. Ten minutes later the three little pilgrims were in the kitchen being regaled with cake and hot coffee, which even Toby partook of with considerable relish.

Then Jane, taking a hand of each little child, led them quietly out, and without any noise they all—even Toby—got into the light cart, and were off, numberless twinkling stars looking down on them. Lydia Purcell, believing she had the purse in her hand, was sleeping the sleep of the sin-laden and unhappy. She thought that broken and miserable rest worth the money treasure she believed she had secured. She little guessed that already it had taken to itself wings, and was lying against the calm and trustful heart of a little child; but the stars knew, and they smiled on the children as they drove away.

Jane, when they got to the railway station, saw the guard, with whom, indeed, she was great friends, and he very gladly undertook to see to the children, and even to wink at the rule about dogs, and allow Toby to travel up to London with them. What is more, he put them into a first-class carriage which was empty, and bade them lie down and never give anything a thought till they found themselves in London.

"Do you think Jesus the Guide is doing all this for us?" asked Cecile in a whisper, with her arms very tight around Jane's neck.

"Yes, darling, 'tis all along His doing."

"Oh! how easy He is making the first bit of our pilgrimage!" said Cecile.

The whistle sounded. The train was off, and Jane found herself standing on the platform with tears in her eyes. She turned, once more got into the light cart, and drove quickly back to Warren's Grove.

CHAPTER XVI.

"LYDIA'S RESOLVE."

Lydia Purcell had hitherto been an honest woman. Now, in resolving to keep the purse, she but yielded to a further stage of that insidious malady which for so long had been finding ample growth in her moral and spiritual nature. She did not, however, know that the purse was Cecile's. The child's agony, and even terror, she put down with considerable alacrity to an evil conscience. How would it be possible for all that money to belong to a little creature like Cecile?

Lydia's real thought with regard to the Russia-leather purse was that it belonged to old Mrs. Bell—that it had been put into the little tin box, and, unknown to anyone, had got swept away as so much lumber in the attic. Cecile, poking about, had found it, and had made up her mind to keep it: hence her distress.

Lydia had really many years ago lost a purse, about which the servants on the farm had heard her talk. It darted into her head to claim this purse, full of all its sweet treasure, as her own lost property. There was foundation to her tale. The servants would have no reason not to believe her.

Mrs. Bell's heir was turning her out. She would avenge herself in this way on him. She would keep the money which he might lawfully claim. Thus she would once more lay by a nest-egg for a rainy day.

Sitting in her own room, the door locked behind her, and counting the precious money, Lydia had made up her mind to do this. It was so easy to become a thief—detection would be impossible. Yes; she knew in her heart of hearts she was stealing, but looking at the delightful color of the gold—feeling the crisp banknotes—she did not think it very wrong to steal.

She was in an exultant frame of mind when she went down to supper. When Jane appeared she was glad to talk to her.

She little knew that Jane was about to open the sore, sore place in her heart, to probe roughly that wound that seemed as if it would never heal.

The Children's Pilgrimage

When Jane left her, she was really trembling with agitation and terror. Another, then, knew her secret. If that was so, it might any day be made plain to the world that she had caused the death of the only creature she loved.

Lydia was so upset that the purse, with its gold and notes, became for the time of no interest to her.

There was but one remedy for her woes. She must sleep. She knew, alas! that brandy would make her sleep.

Just before she laid her head on her pillow, she so far remembered the purse as to take it out of her pocket, and hold it in her hand. She thought the feel of the precious gold would comfort her.

Jane found it no difficult task to remove the purse from her nerveless fingers. When she awoke in the morning, it was gone.

Lydia had, however, scarcely time to realize her loss, scarcely time to try if it had slipped under the bedclothes, before Jane Parsons, with her bonnet and cloak still on, walked into the room. She came straight up to the bed, stood close to Lydia, and spoke:

"You will wonder where I have been, and what I have been doing? I have been seeing the children, Cecile and Maurice D'Albert, and their dog Toby, off to London. Before they went, I gave the leather purse back to Cecile. It was not your purse, nor a bit like it. I took it out of your hand when you were asleep. There were forty pounds in banknotes, ten-pound banknotes, in the purse, and there were fifteen pounds in gold. Your sister Mrs. D'Albert had given this money to Cecile. You know your own sister's writing. Here it is. That paper was folded under the lining of the purse; you can read it. The purse is gone, and the children are in London before now. You can send a detective after them if you like. "

With these last words, Jane walked out of the room.

For nearly an hour Lydia stayed perfectly still, the folded paper in her hand. At the end of that time she opened the paper, and read what it contained. She read it three times very carefully, then she got up and dressed, and came downstairs.

When Jane brought her breakfast into the little parlor, she said a few words:

"I shall send no detective after those children; they and their purse may slip out of my life, they were never anything to me. "

"May I have the bit of paper with the writing on it back? " asked Jane in reply.

Lydia handed it to her. Then she poured herself out a cup of coffee, and drank it off.

SECOND PART.

"FINDING THE GUIDE."

"As often the helpless wanderer,
  Alone in a desert land,
Asks the guide his destined place of rest,
  And leaves all else in his hand."

CHAPTER I.

"LOOKING FOR THE OLD COURT."

When Jane Parsons left the children, and they found themselves in that comfortable first-class railway carriage on their way to London, Maurice and Toby, with contented sighs, settled themselves to resume their much-disturbed sleep. But Cecile, on whom the responsibility devolved, sat upright without even thinking of slumbering. She was a little pilgrim beginning a very long pilgrimage. What right had she to think of repose? It was perfectly natural for Maurice and Toby to shut their eyes and go off into the land of dreams; they were only following in her footsteps, doing trustfully just what she told them. But for the head of the pilgrim band, the "Great Heart" of the little party, such a pleasant and, under other circumstances, desirable course was impossible.

When the train had first moved off she had taken the precious purse, which hitherto she had held in her hand, and restored it to its old hiding place in the bosom of her frock. Had she but known it, her treasure was safe enough there, for no one could suspect so poor-looking a child of possessing so large a sum of money. After doing this Cecile sat very upright, gravely watching, with her sweet wide-open blue eyes, the darkness they rushed through, and the occasional lights of the sleepy little stations which they passed. Now and then they stopped at one of these out-of-the-way stations, and then a very weary-looking porter would come yawning up, and there would be a languid attempt at bustle and movement, and then the night mail would rush on again into the winter's night. Yes, it was mid-winter now, and bitterly cold. The days, too, were at their very shortest, for it was just the beginning of December, and by the time they reached Victoria, not a blink of real light from the sky had yet come.

Maurice felt really cross when he was awakened a second time in what seemed like the middle of the night, and even long-suffering Toby acknowledged to himself that it was very unpleasant.

But Cecile's clear eyes looked up with all kinds of thanks into the face of the big guard as he put them into a cab, and gave the cabby directions where to drive them to.

"A sweet child, bless her, " he said to himself, as he turned away. The cabby had been desired to drive the children to Mrs. West's home, and the address Jane had written out was in his hand. The guard, too, had paid the fare; and Cecile was told that in about half an hour they would all find themselves in snug quarters.

"Will they give us breakfast in 'snug quarters'? " asked Maurice, who always took things literally. "I wonder, Cecile, if 'snug quarters' will be nice? "

Alas! poor little children. When the cab at last drew up at the door in C—— Street, and the cabby got down and rang the bell, and then inquired for Mrs. West, he was met by the discouraging information that Mrs. West had left that address quite a year ago. No, they could not tell where she had gone, but they fancied it was to America.

"What am I to do now with you two little tots, and that 'ere dawg? " said the cabby, coming up to the cab door. "There ain't no Mrs. West yere. And that 'ere young party"—with a jerk of his thumb at the slatternly little individual who stood watching and grinning on the steps—"her says as Mrs. West have gone to 'Mericy. Ain't there no one else as I can take you to, little uns? "

"No, thank you, " answered Cecile. "We'll get out, please, Cabby. This is a nice dry street. Me, and Maurice, and Toby can walk a good bit. You couldn't tell us though, please, what's the nearest way from here to France? "

"To France! Bless yer little heart, I knows no jography. But look yere, little un. Ha'n't you no other friends as I could take you to? I will, and charge no fare. There! I'll be generous for the sake of that pretty little face. "

But Cecile only shook her head.

The Children's Pilgrimage

"We don't know nobody, thank you, Cabby" she said, "except one girl, and I never learned where her home was. We may meet her if we walk about, and I want very badly, very badly, indeed, to see her again. "

"Well, my dear, I'm feared as I must leave you, though I don't like to. "

"Oh, yes! and thank you for the drive. " Here Cecile held out her little hand to the big rough cabby, and Maurice instantly followed her example; but Toby, who in his heart of hearts saw no reason for this excessive friendliness, stood by without allowing his tail to move a quarter of an inch. Then the little party turned the corner and were lost to view.

"They aren't at all snug quarters, Cecile, " said Maurice, in a complaining tone.

"Oh, darling! " answered Cecile, "they aren't so bad. See, the sun is coming out, and it will be quite pleasant to walk, and we're back in London again. We know London, you must not forget, Maurice. And, Maurice, me and you have got to be very brave now. We have a great, great deal before us. We have got something very difficult but very splendid to do. We have got to be very brave, Maurice, and we must not forget that we are a little French boy and girl, and not disgrace ourselves before the English children. "

"And has Toby got to be brave too? " asked Maurice.

"Yes, Toby is always brave, I think. Now, Maurice, listen to me. The first thing we'll do is to get some breakfast. I have got all your half-sovereign. You don't forget your half-sovereign. We will spend a little, a very little, of that on some breakfast, and then afterward we will look for a little room where we can live until I find out from someone the right way to go to France. "

The thought of breakfast cheered Maurice up very much, and when a few moments later the two children and the dog found themselves standing before a coffee-stall, and Maurice had taken two or three sips of his sweet and hot coffee and had attacked with much vigor a great hunch of bread and butter, life began once more to assume pleasant hues to his baby mind. Cecile paid for the coffee and bread and butter with her half sovereign; and though the man at the coffee

The Children's Pilgrimage

stall looked at it very hard, and also looked at her, and tested the good money by flinging it up and down on the stall several times and even taking it between his teeth and giving it a little bite, he returned the right change, saying, as he did so, "Put that away careful, young un, or you're safe to be robbed. " But again the poor look of the little group proved their safeguard. For Cecile and Maurice in their hurry had come away in their shabbiest clothes, and Cecile's hat was even a little torn at the brim, and Maurice's toes were peeping out of his worn little boots, and his trousers were patched. This was all the better for Cecile's hidden treasure, and as she was a wise little girl, she took the hint given her by the coffee-man, and not only hid her money, but next time she wanted anything offered very small change. This was rendered easy, for the man at the coffee-stall had given her mostly sixpences and pence.

The sun was now shining brilliantly. The day was frosty and bright; there would be a bitter night further on, but just now the air was fresh and invigorating. The children and dog, cheered and warmed by their breakfast, stepped along gayly, and Cecile began to think that going on pilgrimage was not such a bad thing.

Having no one to consult, Cecile was yet making up her plans with rare wisdom for so young a child. They would walk back to the part of London that they knew. From there they would make their inquiries, those inquiries which were to land them in France. In their old quarters, perhaps in their old home, they might get lodgings.

Walking straight on, Cecile asked every policeman she met to direct them to Bloomsbury, but whether the police were careless and told them wrong, whether the distance was too great, or whether Cecile's little head was too young to remember, noon came, and noon passed, and they were still far, far away from the court where their father and stepmother had died.

The Children's Pilgrimage

CHAPTER II.

"A NIGHT'S LODGINGS."

Soon after noon, Cecile, Maurice, and Toby sat down to shelter and rest themselves on a step under the deep porch of an old church. The wind had got up, and was very cold, and already the bright morning sky had clouded over.

There was a promise of snow in the air and in the dull sky, and the children shivered and drew close to each other.

"We won't mind looking any longer for our old court to-day, Maurice, " said Cecile. "As soon as you are rested, darling, we'll go straight and get a night's lodging. I am afraid we must do it as cheap as possible, but you shan't walk any more to-day. "

To all this Maurice, instead of replying in his usual grumbling fashion, laid his head on his sister's lap, and dropped off into a heavy sleep. His pretty baby face looked very white as he slept, and when Cecile laid her hand on his cheek it was cold.

She felt a fresh dread coming over her. Was Maurice too completely a baby boy to go on such a long and weary pilgrimage? And oh! if this was the case, what should she do? For they had nothing to live on. There seemed no future at all before the little girl but the future of finding Lovedy.

Cecile buried her head in her hands, and again the longing rose up strong, passionate, fervent, that Jesus, the good Guide, would come to her. He had come once. He was in the dark room last night. He answered her though He made no sound, though, listen as she would, she could not hear the faintest whisper from His lips. Still He was surely there. Jane had said so, and Jane knew Him well; she said it was He who had sent back her purse. Suppose she met Him in the street to-day, and He knew her? Suppose He came out of the church behind them? Or suppose, suppose He came to her again in the dark in that "lodging for the night, " where they must go? Cecile wished much that Jesus would come in the daylight; she wanted to see His face, to look into His kind eyes. But even to feel that He would be with her in the dark was a great comfort in her present desolation.

The Children's Pilgrimage

Cecile was aroused from her meditations by something very soft and warm rubbing against her hand. She raised her eyes to encounter the honest and affectionate gaze of Toby.

Toby's eyes were bright, and he was wagging his tail, and altogether seeming as if he found life agreeable. He gamboled a little when Cecile looked at him, and put his forepaws on her lap. Toby meant nothing by this but to please and cheer his little mistress. He saw she was down and tired, and he was determined to put a bold face on things, and to get a bit of sunshine, even on this December afternoon, into his own honest eyes, if it would come nowhere else. Generally Cecile was the brightest of the party; now Toby was determined to show her that he was a dog worth having in adversity.

She did think so. Tears sprang to her own blue eyes. She threw her arms round Toby's neck and gave him a great hug. In the midst of this caress the dog's whole demeanor changed; he gave a quick spring out of Cecile's embrace, and uttered an angry growl. A girl was approaching by stealthy steps at the back of the little party.

The moment she heard Toby's bark she changed her walk to a quick run and threw herself down beside Cecile with an easy hail-fellow-well-met manner.

"Well, you're a queer un, you ere, " she said, looking up pertly in Cecile's face, "a-hugging of that big dawg, and a-sitting on the church steps of St. Stephen's on the werry bitterest evening that has come this year yet. Ha'n't you no home, now, as you sits yere? "

"No; but I am going to look out for a night's lodging at once, " answered Cecile.

"For you and that ere little un, and the dawg? "

"Yes, we must all three be together whatever happens. Do you know of a lodging, little girl? "

"My name's Jessie—Jessie White. Yes, I knows where I goes myself. 'Tis werry warm there. 'Tis a'most *too* warm sometimes. "

"And is it cheap? " asked Cecile. "For me, and Maurice, and Toby, we have got to do things *very* cheap. We shall only be a day or two in London, and we must do things *very*, very cheap while we stay. "

The Children's Pilgrimage

"Oh! my eyes! hasn't we all to do things cheap? What does you say to a penny? A penny is wot I pays for a share of a bed, and I s'pose as you and that ere little chap could have one all to yerselves for tuppence, and the dawg, he ud lie in for nothink. I calls tuppence uncommon cheap to be warm for so many hours. "

"Tuppence? " said Cecile. "Two pennies for Maurice and me and Toby. Yes, I suppose that is cheap, Jessie White. I don't know anything about prices, but it does not sound dear. We will go to your lodgings if you will tell us the right street, and I hope it is not far away, for Maurice is very tired. "

"No, it ain't far, but you can't go without me; you would not get in nohow. Now, I works in the factory close by, and I'm just out for an hour for my dinner. I'll call for you yere, ef you like, at five o'clock, and take you straight off, and you can get into bed at once. And now s'pose as we goes and has a bit of dinner? I has tuppence for my dinner. I did mean to buy a beautiful hartificial flower for my hat instead, but somehow the sight of you three makes me so starved as I can't stand it. Will you come to my shop and have dinner too? "

To this proposition Cecile, Maurice (who had awakened), and Toby all eagerly agreed; and in a moment or two the little party found themselves being regaled at the ragged girl's directions with great basins of hot soup and hunches of bread. She took two basins of soup, and two hunches of bread herself. But though Maurice and Cecile wished very much for more, Cecile—even though it was to be paid for with their own money—felt too timid to ask again, and the strange girl appeared to think it impossible they could want more than one supply.

"I'm off now, " she said to Cecile, coming up to her and wiping her mouth.

"Yes; but where are we to meet you for the lodging? " asked the little girl anxiously—"Maurice is *so* tired—and you promised to show us. Where shall we get the lodging for the night? "

The girl gave a loud rude laugh.

"'Tis in Dean Street, " she said. "Dean Street's just round the corner—'tis number twenty. I'll turn up if I ha' money. "

The Children's Pilgrimage

"But you said we could not get in without you, " said Cecile.

"Well, what a bother you ere! I'll turn up if I can. You be there at the door, and if I can I'll be there too. " Then she nodded violently, and darted out of the shop.

Cecile wondered why she was in such a hurry to go, and at the change in her manner, but she understood it a little better when she saw that the ragged girl had so arranged matters that Cecile had to pay for all the dinners!

"I won't never trust ragged girls like that again, " was her wise mental comment; and then she, Maurice, and Toby recommenced their weary walking up and down. Their dinner had once more rested and refreshed them, and Cecile hoped they might yet find the old court in Bloomsbury. But the great fatigue of the morning came back a little sooner in the short and dull winter's afternoon, and the child discovered now to her great distress that she was lagging first. The shock and trouble she had gone through the day before began to tell on her, and by the time Maurice suddenly burst into tears her own footsteps were reeling.

"I think you're unkind, Cecile, " said the little boy, "and I don't believe we are ever, ever going to find our old court, or the lodgings for the night. "

"There's a card up at this house that we're passing" said Cecile. "I'll ask for a lodging at this very house, Maurice. "

She rang the bell timidly, and in a moment or so a pert girl with a dirty cap on her head came and answered it.

"Please, " said Cecile, raising her pretty anxious little face, "have you got a lodging for the night for two little children and a dog? I see a card up. We don't mind its being a very small lodging, only it must be cheap. "

The girl burst out laughing, and rude as the ragged girl's laugh had been, this struck more painfully, with a keener sense of ridicule, on Cecile's ear.

"Well, I never, " said the servant-maid at last; "*you* three want a lodging in this yere house? A night's lodging she says, for her and the little un and the dog she says, and she wants it cheap, she says. Go further afield, missy, this house ain't for the likes of you, " and then the door was slammed in Cecile's face.

"Look, look, " said Maurice excitedly, "there's a crowd going in there; a great lot of people, and they're all just as ragged as me and you and Toby. Let's go in and get a bed with the ragged people, Cecile. "

Cecile raised her eyes, then she exclaimed joyfully:

"Why, this is Dean Street, Maurice. Yes, and that's, that's number twenty. We can get our night's lodging without that unkind ragged girl after all. "

Then the children, holding each other's hands, and Toby keeping close behind, found themselves in the file of people, and making their way into the house, over the door of which was written:

"CHEAP LODGINGS FOR THE NIGHT FOR WOMEN AND CHILDREN. "

Early as the hour was, the house seemed already full from attic to cellar. Cecile and Maurice were pushed into a good-sized room about halfway up the first flight of stairs.

At the door of this room a woman stood, who demanded pennies of everyone before they were allowed to enter the room.

Cecile had some slight difficulty in getting hers out of the bosom of her frock; she did so with anxiety, and some effort at concealment, which was observed by two people:

One was a red-faced, wicked-looking girl of about sixteen; the other was a pale woman, who turned her worn faded brown eyes, with a certain look of pathos in them, on the little pair.

The moment the people got into the room, there was a scramble for the beds, which were nothing better than wooden boards, with canvas bags laid on them, and a second piece of canvas placed for covering. But bad and comfortless as these beds looked, without either pillow or bolster, they were all eagerly coveted, and all soon full. Two and even three got into each, and those who could not get accommodation in that way were glad to throw themselves on the floor, as near to a great stove, which burned hot and red, as possible.

It would have fared very badly with Cecile and Maurice were it not for the woman who noticed them at the door. But as they were looking round bewildered, and Toby was softly licking Cecile's hand, the little girl felt a touch from this woman.

"I ha' my own bed laid ready in this corner, and you are both welcome to share it, my little dears. "

"Oh! they may come with me. I has my corner put by too, " said the red-faced girl, who also came up.

"Please, ma'am, we'll choose your bed, if Toby may sleep with us, " said Cecile, raising her eyes, and instinctively selecting the right company.

The woman gave a faint, sad smile, the girl turned scowling away, and the next moment Maurice found himself curled up in the most comfortable corner of the room. He was no longer cold, and hard as his bed was, he was too tired to be particular, and in a moment he and Toby were both sound asleep.

But Cecile did not sleep. Weary as she was, the foul air, the fouler language, smote painfully on her ears. The heat, too, soon became almost unbearable, and very soon the poor child found herself wishing for the cold streets in preference to such a night's lodging.

There was no chance whatever of Jesus coming to a place like this, and Cecile's last hope of His helping her vanished.

The strong desire that He would come again and do something wonderful, as He had done the day before, had been with her for many dreary hours; and when this hope disappeared, the last drop in her cup of trouble was full, and poor, brave, tired little pilgrim that she was, she cried long and bitterly. The pale woman by her side was long ago fast asleep. Indeed silence, broken only by loud snores, was already brooding over the noisy room. Cecile was just beginning to feel her own eyes drooping, when she was conscious of a little movement. There was a gas jet turned down low in the room, and by its light she could see that unpleasant red-faced girl sitting up in bed. She was not only sitting up, but presently she was standing up, and

The Children's Pilgrimage

then the little girl felt a cold chill of fear coming over her. She came up to the bedside.

Cecile almost thought she must scream, when suddenly the pale woman, who had appeared so sound asleep, said quietly:

"Go back to yer bed at once, Peggie Jones. I know what you're up to."

The girl, discomfited, slunk away; and for ten minutes there was absolute silence. Then the woman, laying her hand on Cecile's shoulder, said very softly:

"My dear, you have a little money about you?"

"Yes," answered the child.

"I feared so. You must come away from here at once. I can protect you from Peggie. But she has accomplices who'll come presently. You'd not have a penny in the morning. Get up, child, you and the little boy. Why, 'twas the blessed Jesus guided you to me to save. Come, poor innocent lambs!"

There was one thing the woman had said which caused Cecile to think it no hardship to turn out once more into the cold street. She rose quite quietly, her heart still and calm, and took Maurice's hand, and followed the woman down the stairs, and out once again.

"Now, as you ha' a bit of money, I'll get you a better lodging than that," said the kind woman; and she was as good as her word, and took the children to a cousin of her own, who gave them not only a tiny little room, and a bed which seemed most luxurious by contrast, but also a good supper, and all for the sum of sevenpence.

So Cecile slept very sweetly, for she was feeling quite sure again that Jesus, who had even come into that dreadful lodging to prevent her being robbed, and to take care of her, was going to be her Guide after all.

CHAPTER III.

IN THE CORNER BEHIND THE ORGAN.

The next morning the children got up early. The woman of the house, who had taken a fancy to them, gave them a good breakfast for fourpence apiece, and Toby, who had always hitherto had share and share alike, was now treated to such a pan of bones, and all for nothing, that he could not touch the coffee the children offered him.

"Now, " said Mrs. Hodge, "that ere dawg has got food enough and plenty for the whole day. When a dawg as isn't accustomed to it gets his fill o' bones 'tis wonderful how sustaining they is. "

"And may we come back again here to-night, ma'am? " asked Cecile eagerly.

But here a disappointment awaited them. Mrs. Hodge, against her will, was obliged to shake her head. Her house was a popular one. The little room the children had occupied was engaged for a month from to-night. No—she was sorry—but she had not a corner of her house to put them in. It was the merest chance her being able to take them in for that one night.

"It is a pity you can't have us, for I don't think you're a wicked woman, " said Maurice, raising his brown eyes to scan her face solemnly.

Mrs. Hodge laughed.

"Oh! what a queer, queer little baby boy! " she said, stooping down to kiss him. "No, my pet; it 'ud be a hard heart as 'ud be wicked to you. "

But though Mrs. Hodge was sorry, she could not help the children, and soon after ten o'clock they once more stepped out into the streets. The sun was shining, and Maurice's spirits were high. But Cecile, who had the responsibility, felt sad and anxious. She was footsore and very tired, and she knew no more than yesterday where or how to get a night's lodging. She saw plainly that it would not do, with all that money about her, to venture into a penny lodging; and she feared that, even careful as they were, the ten shillings would

The Children's Pilgrimage

soon be spent; and as to her other gold, she assured herself that she would rather starve than touch it until they got to France. The aim and object then of her present quest must be to get to France.

Where was France? Her father said it lay south. Where was south? The cabby, when she asked him, said he could not tell her, for he did not know jography. What was jography? Was it a thing, or a person? Whoever or whatever it was, it knew the way to France, to that haven of her desire. Cecile must then endeavor to find jography. But where, and how? A church door stood open. Some straggling worshipers came out. The children stood to watch them. The door still remained open. Taking Maurice's hand, Cecile crept into the silent church; it felt warm and sheltered. Toby slipped under one of the pews; Cecile and Maurice sat side by side on a hassock. Maurice was still bright and not at all sleepy, and Cecile began to think it a good opportunity to tell him a little of the life he had before him.

"Maurice, " she said, "do you mind having to walk a long way, having to walk hundreds and hundreds of miles, and do you mind having to keep on walking for days and weeks? "

"Yes, " said Maurice. "I don't like walking; I'd rather go back to our old court. "

"But you'd like to pick flowers—pretty, pretty flowers growing by the waysides; and there'd be lots of sunshine all day long. It would not be like England, it would be down South. "

"Is it warm down South? " asked Maurice.

"Why, Maurice, of course, that was where our father lived and where our own, own mother died; 'tis lovely, lovely down South. "

"Then I don't mind walking, Cecile; let's set of South at once. "

"Oh! I wish—I wish we could, darling. We have very little money, Maurice; 'tis most important for me and you and Toby to go to France as soon as possible. But I don't know the way. The cabby said something about Jography. If Jography is a person, *he* knows the way to France. I should like to find Jography, and when we get to France, I have a hope, a great hope, that Jesus the Guide will come with us. Yes, I do think He will come. "

The Children's Pilgrimage

"That's Him as you said was in the dark in our attic? "

"Yes, that's the same; and do you know He came into the dark of that other dreadful attic again last night, and 'twas He told the woman to take us out and give us those much nicer lodgings. Oh, Maurice! I *do* think, yes, I do think, after His doing that, that He has quite made up His mind to take us to France. "

Maurice was silent. His baby face looked puzzled and thoughtful. Suddenly he sprang to his feet. His eyes were bright. He was possessed with an idea.

"Cecile, " he said, "let's get back to our old court. Do you know that back of our old court there's a square, and in that square a lovely, lovely garden? I have often stood at the rails and wanted to pick the flowers. There are heaps of them, and they are of all colors. Cecile, p'raps that garden is South. I should not mind walking in there all day. Let's go back at once and try to find it. "

"One moment, one moment first, Maurice, " said Cecile. She, too, had a thought in her head. "You and Toby stay here. I'll be back in a moment, " she exclaimed.

Behind the organ was a dark place. In this short winter's day it looked like night.

The idea had darted into Cecile's head that Jesus might be there. She went to the dark corner; yes, it was very gloomy. Peer hard as she would, she could not see into all its recesses. Jesus might be there. No one had ever taught her to kneel, but instinctively she fell on her knees and clasped her hands.

"Jesus, " she said, "I think you're here. I am most grateful to you, Jesus the Guide, for what you did for me and Maurice and Toby the last two nights. Jesus the Guide, will you tell me how to find Jography and how to get to France? and when we go there will you guide us? Please do, though it isn't the New Jerusalem nor the Celestial City. But I have very important business there, Jesus, very important. And Maurice is so young, he's only a baby boy, and he'll want you to carry him part of the way. Will you, who are so very good, come with us little children, and with Toby, who is the dearest dog in the world? And will you tell some kind, kind woman to give us a lodging for the night in a safe place where I won't be robbed of my money? "

Here, while Cecile was on her knees still praying, a wonderful thing happened. It might have been called a coincidence, but I, who write the story of these little pilgrims, think it was more; for into Cecile's dark corner, unperceived by her, a man had come, and this man began to fill the great organ with wind, and then in a moment the whole church began to echo with sweet sounds, and in the midst of the music came a lull, and then one voice rose triumphant, joyful, and reassuring on the air.

"Certainly, I will be with thee, " sang the voice, "I will be with thee, I will be with thee. "

CHAPTER IV.

THE WOMAN WITH THE KINDEST FACE.

Cecile went back to where she had left Maurice sitting on the church hassock, and, taking his hand, said to him, "Come. "

Her little, worn face was bright and some of the sweetness of the music she had been listening to had got into her blue eyes.

"Come, Maurice, " said Cecile. "I know now what to do. Everything will be quite right now. I have told Jesus all about it, and Jesus the Guide has answered me, and said He would come with us. Did you hear that wonderful, lovely music? That was Jesus answering me. And, Maurice, I asked Him to let us find a kind woman who will help us to a night's lodging, and I know He will do that too. "

"A kind woman? " said Maurice. "The kindest woman I ever saw is coming up the church steps this minute. "

Cecile looked in the direction in which Maurice pointed.

A woman, with a pail in one hand and a large sweeping brush in the other, was not only coming up the steps, but had now entered the church door. Cecile and Maurice stood back a little in the shadow. The woman could not see them, but they could gaze earnestly at her. She was a stout woman with a round face, rosy cheeks, and bright, though small and sunken, brown eyes. Her eyes had, however, a light in them, and her wide lips were framed in smiles. She must have been a women of about fifty, but her broad forehead was without a wrinkle. Undoubtedly she was very plain. She had not a good feature, not even a good point about her ungainly figure. Never in her youngest days could this woman have been fair to see, but the two children, who gazed at her with beating hearts, thought her beautiful. Goodness and loving-kindness reigned in that homely face; so triumphantly did they reign, these rare and precious things, that the little children, with the peculiar penetration of childhood, found them out at once.

"She's a *lovely* woman, " pronounced Maurice. "I'm quite sure she has got a night's lodging. I'll run and ask her. "

The Children's Pilgrimage

"No, no, she might not like it," whispered the more timid Cecile.

But just then Toby, who had been standing very quiet and motionless behind Maurice, perceived a late, late autumn fly, sailing lazily by, within reach of his nose. That fly was too much for Toby; he made a snap at it, and the noise which ensued roused the woman's attention.

"Oh! my little Honies," she said, coming forward, "we don't allow dogs in the church. Even a nice dog like that is against the rules. I'm very sorry, my loves, but the dog must go out of church."

"Don't Jesus like dogs then?" asked Maurice.

"And please, ma'am," suddenly demanded Cecile, before the woman had time to answer Maurice, "*is* that Jesus the Guide playing the beautiful music up there?"

"That, my dears! You shock me! That is only Mr. Ward the organist. He's practicing for tomorrow. To-morrow's Sunday, you know. Why, you *are* a queer little pair."

"We're going on a pilgrimage," said Maurice. "We're going South; and Cecile has been talking a great deal lately to Jesus the Guide; and she asked Him just now to find us a woman with a kind face to give us a night's lodging, and we both think you are quite lovely. Will you give us a night's lodging, ma'am?"

"Will I? Hark to the baby! Well, I never! And are you two little orphans, dears?"

"Yes," said Cecile, "our father is dead, and our mother, and our stepmother, and we have no one to care for us, except Jane Parsons, and we can't stay with Jane any longer, for if we did, we should only be sent to the Union."

"And we couldn't go to the Union, though there *are* good fires there," interrupted Maurice, "because of Toby. If we went to the Union, our dog Toby would get a yard of rope, that would be murder. We can never, never, never go to the Union on account of murdering Toby."

The Children's Pilgrimage

"So we came away. " continued Cecile. "Jane Parsons sent us to London with the guard yesterday. We are not English, we are foreign; me and Maurice are just a little French boy and girl, and we are going back to France, if we can find Jography to tell us how. But we want a night's lodging first. Will you give us a night's lodging, ma'am? We can pay you, please, ma'am. "

"Oh, yes, I've no doubt you can pay me well, and I'm like to want yer bit of money, and I suppose you want to bring Toby too. "

"Yes and Toby too, " said Maurice.

"Well, I never did hear the like, never. John, I say, John, come here. "

The man addressed as John came forward with great strides.

He was a tall man about double the height of his stout wife.

"John, honey, " said the little stout woman, "yere's the queerest story. Two mites, all alone, with only a dog belonging to them; father dead, mother dead, and they asks ef that's Jesus playing the organ, and they wants a night's lodging, and I have the kindest face. Hark to the rogues! and will I give it to 'em? What say you, John? "

"What say *you*, Molly? Have you room for 'em, old girl? "

"The house is small, " said the woman, "but there *is* the little closet back of our bedroom, and Susie's mattress lying vacant. I could make 'em up tidy in that little closet. "

The man laughed, and chucked his wife under the chin.

"Where's the use o' asking me, " he said, "when you knows as you *can't* say no to no waif nor stray as hever walked? "

He went away, for he was employed just then in blowing the organ, and the organist was beckoning to him, so the woman turned to the children.

"My name is Mrs. Moseley, darlings, and ef you're content with a werry small closet for you and yer dog, why, yer welcome, and I'll promise as it shall be clean. Why, ef that'll do for the night's lodging, you three jest get back into the church pew, and hide Toby well under the seat, and I'll have done my work in about an hour, and then we'll go back home to dinner. "

CHAPTER V.

A HOUSE WITHOUT A DOOR.

The children in their wanderings the day before, and again this morning, had quite unknown to themselves traveled quite away from Bloomsbury, and when they entered the church, and sat down in that pew, and hid Toby underneath, they were in the far-famed East-End quarter of the great town. They knew nothing of this themselves, though Cecile did think the houses very poor and the people very dirty. They were, therefore, doubly fortunate in coming across Mrs. Moseley.

Mrs. Moseley was sextoness to the very new and beautiful church in Mile End. Her husband was a policeman at present on night duty, which accounted for his being at leisure to blow the organ in the church. This worthy couple had a little grave to love and tend, a little grave which kept their two hearts very green, but they had no living child. Mrs. Moseley had, however, the largest of mother's hearts—a heart so big that were it not for its capacity of acting mother to every desolate child in Mr. Danvers' parish, it must have starved. Now, she put Cecile and Maurice along with twenty more into that big heart of hers, and they were a truly fortunate little pair when she took them home.

Such a funny home was hers, but so clean when you got into it.

It was up a great many pairs of stairs, and the stairs at the top were a good deal broken, and were black with use, and altogether considerably out of repair. But the strangest part, though also the most delightful to Maurice and Cecile in their funny new home, was the fact that it had no door at all.

When you got to the top and looked for the door, you were confronted with nothing but a low ceiling over your head, and a piece of rope within reach of your hand. If you pulled the rope hard enough, up would suddenly jump two or three boards, and then there was an opening big enough for you to creep into the little kitchen.

Yes, it was the queerest entrance into the oddest little home. But when once you got there how cozy it all was!

The Children's Pilgrimage

The proverbial saying, "eating off the floor, " might have been practiced on those white boards. The little range shone like a looking glass, and cups and saucers were ranged on shelves above it. In the middle of the floor stood a bright and thick crimson drugget. The window, dormer though it was, was arranged quite prettily with crimson curtains, while some pots of sweet-smelling herbs and flowers stood on its ledge. There were two or three really good colored prints on the white-washed walls and several illuminated texts of Scripture. The little deal table, too, was covered with a crimson cloth.

A canary bird hung in a cage in the window, and it is not too much to say that this poor bird, born and bred in the East End, was thoroughly happy in his snug home. A soft-furred gray cat purred before the little range. The bedroom beyond was as clean and neat as the kitchen, and the tiny room where Cecile, Maurice and Toby were to sleep, though nearly empty at present, would, Mrs. Moseley assured them, make a sleeping chamber by no means to be despised by and by.

When they got into the house, Maurice ran all over it in fearless ecstasies. Cecile sat on the edge of a chair, and Toby, after sniffing at the cat, decided to make friends with her by lying down in the delicious warmth by her side.

"What's yer name, dear heart? " asked Mrs. Moseley to the rather forlorn-looking little figure seated on the edge of a chair.

"Cecile, please, ma'am. "

"Cecil! That sounds like a boy's name. It ain't English to give boy names to little girls. But then you're foreign, you say—French, ain't it? I once knew a girl as had lived a long time in France and loved it dearly. Well, well, but here's dinner ready; the potatoes done to a turn, and boiled bacon and greens. Now, where's my good man? We won't wait for him, honey. Come, Maurice, my man, I don't doubt but you're rare and hungry. "

"Yes, " answered Maurice; "me and Cecile and Toby are very hungry. We had bad food yesterday; but I like this dinner, it smells good. "

"It will eat good too, I hope. Now, Cecile, why don't you come? "

The Children's Pilgrimage

Cecile's face had grown first red and then pale.

"Please, " she said earnestly, "that good dinner that smells so delicious may be very dear. We little children and our dog we have got to be most desperate careful, please, Mrs. Moseley, ma'am. We can't eat that nice dinner if 'tis dear. "

"But s'pose 'tis cheap, " said Mrs. Moseley; "s'pose 'tis as cheap as dirt? Come, my love, this dinner shan't cost you nothink; come and eat. Don't you see that the poor little man there is fit to cry? "

"And nothink could be cheaper than dirt, " said Maurice, cheering up. "I'm so glad as this beautiful, delicious dinner is as cheap as dirt. "

"Now we'll say grace, " said Mrs. Moseley.

She folded her hands and looked up.

"Lord Jesus, bless this food to me and to Thy little ones, and use us all to Thy glory. "

Her eyes were shut while she was speaking; when she opened them she felt almost startled by the look Cecile had given her. A look of wonder, of question, of appeal.

"You want to ask me some'ut, dear? " she said gently to the child.

"Oh, yes! oh, yes! "

"Well, I'm very busy now, and I'll be busy all the afternoon. But we has tea at six, and arter tea my man 'ull play wid Maurice, and you shall sit at my knee and ask me what you like. "

CHAPTER VI.

CECILE GIVES HER HEART.

It was thus, sitting at Mrs. Moseley's knee in that snug kitchen, that Cecile got her great question answered. It was Mrs. Moseley who explained to the longing, wondering child, what Jesus the Guide would do, who Jesus the Guide really was. It was Mrs. Moseley who told Cecile what a glorious future she had before her, and how safe her life down in this world really was.

And Cecile listened, half glad, half sorry, but, if the truth must be known, dimly understanding. For Cecile, sweet as her nature was had slow perceptions.

She was eight years old, and in her peculiar, half English, half foreign life, she had never before heard anything of true religion. All the time Mrs. Moseley was speaking, she listened with bright eyes and flushed cheeks. But when the sweet old story came to an end, Cecile burst into tears.

"Oh! I'm glad and I'm sorry, " she sobbed; "I wanted a real, real guide. I'm glad as the story's quite true, but I wanted someone to hold my hand, and to carry Maurice when he's ever so tired. I'm glad and sorry. "

"But I'm not sorry, " said Maurice, who was lying full length on the hearth-rug, and listening attentively. "I'm glad, I am—and I'd like to die; I'd much rather die than go south. "

"Oh, Maurice! " said Cecile.

"Yes, Cecile. I'd much rather die. I like what that kind woman says about heaven, and I never did want to walk all that great way. Do Jesus have little boys as small as me in heaven, Mrs. Moseley, ma'am? "

"Lord bless the child. Yes, my sweet lamb. Why, there's new-born babes up there; and I had a little un, he wor a year younger nor you. But Jesus took him there; it near broke my heart, but he went there. "

"Then I'll go too, " said Maurice. "I'll not go south; I'll go to heaven. "

"Bless the bonnie children both, " said Mrs. Moseley softly under her breath. She laid her hand on Cecile's head, who was gazing at her little brother in a sort of wonder and consternation. Then the good woman rose to get supper.

The next day ushered in the most wonderful Sunday Cecile had ever spent. In the first place, this little girl, who had been so many years of her little life in our Christian England, went to church. In her father's time, no one had ever thought of so employing part of their Sunday. The sweet bells sounded all around, but they fell on unheeding ears. Cecile's stepmother, too, was far too busy working for Lovedy to have time for God's house, and when the children went down to Warren's Grove, though Lydia Purcell regularly Sunday after Sunday put on her best bonnet, and neat black silk gown, and went book in hand into the simple village church, it had never occurred to her to take the orphan children with her. Therefore, when Mrs. Moseley said to Cecile and Maurice:

"Now come and let me brush your hair, and make you tidy for church, " they were both surprised and excited. Maurice fretted a little at the thought of leaving Toby behind, but, on the whole, he was satisfied with the novelty of the proceeding.

The two children sat very gravely hand in hand. The music delighted them, but the rest of the service was rather above their comprehension.

Cecile, however, listened hard, taking in, in her slow, grave way, here a thought and there an idea.

Mrs. Moseley watched the children as much as she listened to the sermon, and as she said afterward to her husband, she felt her heart growing full of them.

The rest of the Sunday passed even more delightfully in Maurice's estimation. Mrs. Moseley's pudding was pronounced quite beyond praise by the little hungry boy, and after dinner Moseley showed him pictures, while Mrs. Moseley amused Cecile with some Bible stories.

But a strange experience was to come to the impressionable Cecile later in the day.

The Children's Pilgrimage

Quite late, when all the light had faded, and only the lamps were lit, and Maurice was sound asleep in his little bed in Mrs. Moseley's small closet, that good woman, taking the little girl's hand, said to her:

"When we go to church we go to learn about Jesus. I took you to one kind of church this morning. I saw by yer looks, my little maid, as you were trying hard to understand. Now I will take you to another kind of church. A church wot ain't to call orthodox, and wot many speaks against, and I don't say as it ha'n't its abuses. But for all that, when Molly Moseley wants to be lifted clean off her feet into heaven, she goes there; so you shall come to-night with me, Cecile."

All religious teaching was new to Cecile, and she gave her hand quite willingly to her kind friend.

They went down into the cold and wet winter street, and presently, after a few moments' quick walking, found themselves in an immense, square-built hall. Galleries ran round it, and these galleries were furnished with chairs and benches. The whole body of the hall was also full of seats, and from the roof hung banners, with texts of Scripture printed on them, and the motto of the Salvation Army:

"Fire and Blood."

Cecile, living though she had done in its very midst had never heard of this great religious revival. To such as her, poor little ignorant lost lamb, it preached, but hitherto no message had reached her. She followed Mrs. Moseley, who seated herself on a bench in the front row of a gallery which was close to the platform. The space into which she and Cecile had to squeeze was very small, for the immense place was already full to overflowing.

"We'll have three thousand to-night, see if we don't, " said a thin-faced girl, bending over to Mrs. Moseley.

"Oh, ma'am! " said another, who had a very worn, thin, but sweet face, "I've found such peace since I saw you last. I never could guess how good Jesus would be to me. Why, now as I'm converted, He never seems to leave my side for a minute. Oh! I do ache awful with this cough and pain in my chest, but I don't seem to mind it now, as Jesus is with me all day and all night. "

The Children's Pilgrimage

Another, nudging her, here said:

"Do you know as Black Bess ha' bin converted too? "

"Oh, praise the Lord! " said this girl, sinking back on her seat, being here interrupted by a most violent fit of coughing.

The building filled and filled, until there was scarcely room to stand. A man passing Mrs. Moseley said:

"'Tis a glorious gathering, all brought together by prayer and faith, all by prayer and faith. "

Mrs. Moseley took Cecile on her lap.

"They'll sing in a moment, darling, and 'twill be all about your Guide, the blessed, blessed Jesus. " And scarcely were the words out of her mouth, when the whole vast building rang again to the words:

> "Come, let us join our cheerful songs:
> Hallelujah to the Lamb who died on Mount Calvary.
> Hallelujah, hallelujah, hallelujah! Amen. "

Line after line was sung exultantly, accompanied by a brass band.

Immediately afterward a man fell on his knees and prayed most earnestly for a blessing on the meeting.

Then came another hymn:

> "I love thee in life, I love thee in death;
> If ever I love thee, my Jesus, 'tis now. "

This hymn was also sung right through, and then, while a young sergeant went to fetch the colors, the whole great body of people burst into perfectly rapturous singing of the inspiriting words:

> "The angels stand on the Hallelujah strand,
> And sing their welcome home. "

"Oh! Maurice would like that, " whispered Cecile as she leant up against Mrs. Moseley. She never forgot the chorus of that hymn, it was to come back to her with a thrill of great comfort in a dark day

The Children's Pilgrimage

by and by. Mrs. Moseley held her hand firmly; she and her little charge were looking at a strange sight.

There were three thousand faces, all intensely in earnest, all bearing marks of great poverty, many of great and cruel hardship —many, too, had the stamp of sin on their brows. That man looked like a drunken husband; that woman like a cruel mother. Here was a lad who made his living by stealing; here a girl, who would sink from this to worse. Not a well-dressed person in the whole place, not a soul who did not belong to the vast army of the very poor. But for all that, there was not one in this building who was not getting his heart stirred, not one who was not having the best of him awakened into at least a struggling life, and many, many poor and outcast as they were, had that indescribable look on their worn faces which only comes with "God's peace."

A man got up to speak. He was pale and thin, and had long, sensitive fingers. He shut his eyes, clenched his hand, and began:

"Bless thy word, Lord." This he repeated three times.

The people caught it up, they shouted it through the galleries, all over the building. He waved his hand to stop them, then opening his eyes, he began:

"I want to tell you about *Jesus*. Jesus is here tonight, He's down in this hall, He's walking about, He's going from one to another of you, He's knocking at your hearts. Brothers and sisters, the Lord Jesus is knocking at your hearts. Oh! I see His face, and 'tis very pale, 'tis very sad, 'tis all burdened with sadness. What makes it so sad? *Your sins*, your great, awful *black* sins. Sometimes He smiles, and is pleased. When is that? That is when a young girl, or a boy, or even a little child, opens the door of the heart, and He can take that heart and make it His own, then the Lord Jesus is happy. Now, just listen! He is talking to an old woman, she is very old, her face is all wrinkled, her hands shake, she *must* die soon, she can't live more than a year or so, the Lord Jesus is standing by her, and talking to her. He is saying, 'Give me thy heart, give me thy heart.'

"She says she is so old and so wicked, she has been a bad wife, a bad mother, and bad friend; she is an awful drunkard.

The Children's Pilgrimage

"'Never mind,' says Jesus, 'Give me thy heart, I'll forgive thee, poor sinner; I'll make that black heart white.'

"Then she gives it to Him, and she is happy, and her whole face is changed, and she is not at all afraid to die.

"Now, do you see that man? He is just out of prison. What was he in prison for? For beating his wife. Oh! what a villain, what a coward! How cruel he looks! Respectable people, and kind people, don't like to go near him, they are afraid of him. What a strong, brutal face he has! But the blessed Jesus isn't afraid. See, He is standing by this bad man, and He says, 'Give me thy heart.'

"'Oh! go away,' says the man; 'do go away, my heart is too bad.'

"'I'll not go away without thy heart,' says Jesus; ''tis not too bad for me.'

"And then the man, just because he can't help it, gives this heart, and hard as stone it is, to Jesus, and Jesus gives it back to him quite soft and tender, and there's no fear that *he* will beat his wife again.

"Now, look where Jesus is; standing by the side of a little child—of a little, young, tender child. That little heart has not had time to grow hard, and Jesus says, 'Give it to Me. I'll keep it soft always. It shall always be fit for the kingdom of heaven;' and the little child smiles, for she can't help it, and she gives her baby heart away at once. Oh! how glad Jesus is! What a beautiful sight! look at her face; is not it all sunshine? I think I see just such a little child there in front of me."

Here the preacher paused, and pointed to Cecile, whose eyes, brilliant with excitement, were fixed on his face. She had been listening, drinking in, comprehending. Now when the preacher pointed to her, it was too much for the excitable child, she burst into tears and sobbed out:

"Oh! I give my heart, I give my heart."

"Blessings on thee, sweet lamb," came from several rough but kindly voices.

Mrs. Moseley took her in her arms and carried her out. She saw wisely that she could bear no more.

As they were leaving the hall, again there came a great burst of singing:

"I love Jesus, Hallelujah!
I love Jesus; yes, I do.
I love Jesus, He's my Saviour;
Jesus smiles and *loves me too.* "

CHAPTER VII.

"SUSIE."

Cecile had never anything more to say to the Salvation Army. What lay behind the scenes, what must shock a more refined taste, never came to her knowledge. To her that fervent, passionate meeting seemed always like the very gate of heaven. To her the Jesus she had long been seeking had at last come, come close, and entered into her heart of hearts. She no longer regretted not seeing Him in the flesh; nay, a wonderful spiritual sight and faith seemed born in her, and she felt that this spiritual Christ was more suited to her need. She got up gravely the next morning; her journey was before her, and the Guide was there. There was no longer the least reason for delay, and it was much better that she, Maurice, and Toby should start for France, while they had a little money that they could lawfully spend. When she had got up and dressed herself, she resolved to try the new powerful weapon she had got in her hand. This weapon was prayer; the Guide who was so near needed no darkness to enable Him to listen to her. She did not kneel, she sat on the side of her tiny bed, and, while Maurice still slept, began to speak aloud her earnest need:

"Jesus, I think it is hotter that me, and Maurice, and Toby should go to France while we have a little money left. Please, Jesus, if there is a man called Jography, will you help us to find him to-day, please? " Then she paused, and added slowly, being prompted by her new and great love, "But it must be just as you like, Jesus. " After this prayer, Cecile resolved to wait in all day, for if there was a man called Jography, he would be sure to knock at the door during the day, and come in and say to Cecile that Jesus had sent him, and that he was ready to show her the way to France. Maurice, therefore, and Toby, went out together with Mrs. Moseley, and Cecile stayed at home and watched, but though she, watched all day long, and her heart beat quickly many times, there was never any sound coming up the funny stairs; the rope was never pulled, nor the boards lifted, to let in any one of the name of Jography. Cecile, instead of having her faith shaken by this, came to the wise resolution that Jography was not a man at all. She now felt that she must apply to Mrs. Moseley, and wondered how far she dare trust her with her secret.

The Children's Pilgrimage

"You know, perhaps, ma'am, " she began that evening, when Moseley had started on his night duty, and Maurice being sound asleep in bed, she found herself quite alone with the little woman, "You know, perhaps, ma'am, that we two little children and our dog have got to go on a very long journey—a very, very long journey indeed. "

"No, I don't know nothink about it, Cecile, " said Mrs. Moseley in her cheerful voice. "What we knows, my man and me, is, that you two little mites has got to stay yere until we finds some good orphan school to send you to, and you has no call to trouble about payment, deary, for we're only too glad and thankful to put any children into our dead child's place and into Susie's place. "

"But we can't stay, " said Cecile; "we can't stay, though we'd like to ever so. I'm only a little girl. But there's a great deal put on me—a great, great care. I don't mind it now, 'cause of Jesus. But I mustn't neglect it, must I? "

"No, darling: Only tell Mammie Moseley what it is. "

"Oh! May I call you that? "

"Yes; for sure, love. Now tell me what's yer care, Cecile, honey. "

"I can't, Mammie, I can't, though I'd like to. I had to tell Jane Parsons. I had to tell her, and she was faithful. But I think I'd better not tell even you again. Only 'tis a great care, and it means a long journey, and going south. It means all that much for me, and Maurice, and Toby. "

"Going south? You mean to Devonshire, I suppose, child? "

"I don't know. Is there a place called Devonshire there, ma'am? But we has to go to France—away down to the south of France—to the Pyrenees. "

"Law, child! Why, you don't never mean as you're going to cross the seas? "

"Is that the way to France, Mammie Moseley? Oh! Do you *really* know the way? "

The Children's Pilgrimage

"There's no other way that I ever hear tell on, Cecile. Oh, my dear, you must not do that! "

"But it's just there I've got to go, ma'am; and me and Maurice are a little French boy and girl. We'll be sure to feel all right in France; and when we get to the Pyrenees we'll feel at home. 'Tis there our father lived, and our own mother died, and me and Maurice were born there. I don't see how we can help being at home in the Pyrenees. "

"That may be, child; and it may be right to send a letter to yer people, and if they wants you two, and will treat you well, to let you go back to them. But to have little orphans like you wandering about in France all alone, ain't to be thought on, ain't to be thought on, Cecile. "

"But whether my people write for me and Maurice or not, ma'am, I must go, " said Cecile in a low, firm voice. "I must, because I promised—I promised one that is dead. "

"Well, my darling, how can I help you if you won't *conwide* in me? Oh, Cecile! you're for all the world just like what Susie was; only I hopes as you won't treat us as bad. "

"Susie was the girl who slept in our little bedroom, " said Cecile. "Was she older than me, ma'am? and was she yer daughter, ma'am? "

"No, Cecile. Susie was nothink to me in the flesh, though, God knows, I loved her like a child of my own. God never gave me a bonnie girl to love and care for, Cecile. I had one boy. Oh! I did worship him, and when Jesus tuk him away and made an angel of him, I thought I'd go near wild. Well, we won't talk on it. He died at five years old. But I don't mind telling you of Susie. "

"Oh! please, Mammie! "

"It was a year or more after my little Charlie wor tuk away, " said Mrs. Moseley. "My heart wor still sore and strange. I guessed as I'd never have another baby, and I wor so bad I could not bear to look at children. As I wor walking over Blackfriars Bridge late one evening I heard a girl crying. I knew by her cry as she was a very young girl, nearly a child; and, God forgive me! for a moment I thought as I'd hurry on, and not notice her, for I did dread seeing children. However, her cry was very bitter, and what do you think it was?

The Children's Pilgrimage

"'Oh, Mammie, Mammie, Mammie! '

"I couldn't stand that; it went through me as clean as a knife. I ran up to her and said: 'What's yer trouble, honey? '

"She turned at once and threw her arms round me, and clung to me, nearly in convulsions with weeping.

"'Oh! take me to my mother, ' she sobbed. 'I want my mother. '

"'Yes, deary, tell me where she lives, ' I said.

"But the bonnie dear could only shake her head and say she did not know; and she seemed so exhausted and spent that I just brought her home and made her up a bed in your little closet without more ado. She seemed quite comforted that I should take to her, and left off crying for her mother. I asked her the next day a lot of questions, but to everything she said she did not know. She did not know where her mother lived now. She would rather not see her mother, now she was not so lonely. She would rather not tell her real name. I might call her Susie. She had been in France, but she did not like it, and she had got back to England. She had wandered back, and she was very desolate, and she *had* wanted her mother dreadfully, but not now. Her mother had been bad to her, and she did not wish for her now that I was so good. To hear her talk you'd think as she was hard, but at night John and I 'ud hear her sobbing often and often in her little bed, and naming of her mammie. Never did I come across a more willful bit of flesh and blood. But she had that about her as jest took everyone by storm. My husband and I couldn't make enough on her, and we both jest made her welcome to be a child of our own. She was nothing really but a child, a big, fair English child. She said as she wor twelve years old. She was lovely, fair as a lily, and with long, yellow hair. "

"Fair, and with yellow hair? " said Cecile, suddenly springing to her feet. "Yes, and with little teeth like pearls, and eyes as blue as the sky. "

"Why, Cecile, did you know her? " said Mrs. Moseley. "Yes, yes, that's jest her. I never did see bluer eyes. "

"And was her name Lovedy—Lovedy Joy? " asked Cecile.

The Children's Pilgrimage

"I don't know, child; she wouldn't tell her real name; she was only jest Susie to us. "

"Oh, ma'am! Dear Mrs. Moseley, ma'am, where's Susie now? "

"Ah, child! that's wot I can't tell you; I wishes as I could. One day Susie went out and never come back again. She used to talk o' France, same as you talk o' France, so perhaps she went there; anyhow, she never come back to us who loved her. We fretted sore, and we hadvertised in the papers, but we never, never heard another word of Susie, and that's seven years or more gone by. "

CHAPTER VIII.

THE TRIALS OF SECRECY.

The next day Mrs. Moseley went round to see her clergyman, Mr. Danvers, to consult him about Cecile and Maurice. They puzzled her, these queer little French children. Maurice was, it is true, nothing but a rather willful, and yet winsome, baby boy; but Cecile had character. Cecile was the gentlest of the gentle, but she was firm as the finest steel. Mrs. Moseley owned to feeling even a little vexed with Cecile, she was so determined in her intention of going to France, and so equally determined not to tell what her motive in going there was. She said over and over with a solemn shake of her wise little head that she must go there, that a heavy weight was laid upon her, that she was under a promise to the dead. Mrs. Moseley, remembering how Susie had run away, felt a little afraid. Suppose Cecile, too, disappeared? It was so easy for children to disappear in London. They were just as much lost as if they were dead to their friends, and nobody ever heard of them again. Mrs. Moseley could not watch the children all day; at last in her despair she determined to appeal to her clergyman.

"I don't know what to make of the little girl, " she said in conclusion, "she reminds me awful much of Susie. She's rare and winsome; I think she have a deeper nature than my poor lost Susie, but she's lovable like her. And it have come over me, Mr. Danvers, as she knows Susie, for, though she is the werry closest little thing I ever come across, her face went quite white when I telled her about my poor lost girl, and she axed me quite piteous and eager if her name wor Lovedy Joy. "

"Lovedy is a very uncommon name. " said Mr. Danvers. "You had no reason, Mrs. Moseley, to suppose that was Susan's name? "

"She never let it out to me as it wor, sir. Oh, ain't it a trial, as folk *will* be so close and *contrary*. "

Mr. Danvers smiled.

"I will go and see this little Cecile, " he said, "and I must try to win her confidence. "

The Children's Pilgrimage

The good clergyman did go the next afternoon, and finding Cecile all alone, he endeavored to get her to confide in him. To a certain extent he was successful, the little girl told him all she could remember of her French father and her English stepmother. All about her queer old world life with Maurice and their dog in the deserted court back of Bloomsbury. She also told him of Warren's Grove, and of how the French cousin no longer sent that fifty pounds a year which was to pay Lydia Purcell, how in consequence she and Maurice were to go to the Union, and how Toby was to be hung; she said that rather than submit to *that*, she and Maurice had resolved to run away. She even shyly and in conclusion confided some of her religious doubts and difficulties to the kind clergyman. And she said with a frank sweet light in her blue eyes that she was quite happy now, for she had found out all about the Guide she needed. But about her secret, her Russia-leather purse, her motive in going to France, Cecile was absolutely silent.

"I must go to France, " she said, "and I must not tell why; 'tis a great secret, and it would be wrong to tell. I'd much rather tell you, sir, and Mrs. Moseley, but I must not. I did tell Jane Parsons, I could not help that, but I must try to keep my great secret to myself for the future. "

It was impossible not to respect the little creature's silence as much as her confidence.

Mr. Danvers said, in conclusion, "I will not press for your story, my little girl; but it is only right that I as a clergyman, and someone much older than you, should say, that no matter *what* promise you are under, it would be very wrong for you and your baby brother to go alone to France now. Whatever you may feel called on to do when you are grown up, such a step would now be wrong. I will write to your French cousin, and ask him if he is willing to give you and Maurice a home; in which case I must try to find someone who will take you two little creatures back to your old life in the Pyrenees. Until you hear from me again, it is your duty to stay here. "

"Me and Maurice, we asked Mammie Moseley for a night's lodging, " said Cecile. "Will it be many nights before you hear from our cousin in France? Because me and Maurice, we have very little money, please, sir. "

"I will see to the money part, " said Mr. Danvers.

"And please, sir, " asked Cecile, as he rose to leave, "is Jography a thing or a person? "

"Geography! " said the clergyman, laughing. "You shall come to school to-morrow morning, my little maid, and learn something of geography. "

CHAPTER IX.

"A LETTER."

Mr. Danvers was as good as his word and wrote by the next post to the French cousin. He wrote a pathetic and powerful appeal to this man, describing the destitute children in terms that might well move his heart. But whether it so happened that the French relation had no heart to be moved, whether he was weary of an uncongenial subject, or was ill, and so unable to reply—whatever the reason, good Mr. Danvers never got any answer to his letter.

Meanwhile Cecile and Maurice went to school by day, and sometimes also by night. At school both children learned a great many things. Cecile found out what geography was, and her teacher, who was a very good-natured young woman, did not refuse her earnest request to learn all she could about France.

Cecile had long ago been taught by her own dead father to read, and she could write a very little. She was by no means what would be considered a smart child. Her ideas came slowly—she took in gradually. There were latent powers of some strength in the little brain, and what she once learned she never forgot, but no amount of school teaching could come to Cecile quickly. Maurice, on the contrary, drank in his school accomplishments as greedily and easily as a little thirsty flower drinks in light and water. He found no difficulty in his lessons, and was soon quite the pride of the infant school where he was placed.

The change in his life was doing him good. He was a willful little creature, and the regular employment was taming him, and Mrs. Moseley's motherly care, joined to a slight degree of wholesome discipline, was subduing the little faults of selfishness which his previous life as Cecile's sole charge could not but engender.

It is to be regretted that Toby, hitherto, perhaps, the most perfect character of the three, should in these few weeks of prosperity degenerate the most. Having no school to attend, and no care whatever on his mind, this dog decided to give himself up to enjoyment. The weather was most bitterly cold. It was quite unnecessary for him to accompany Cecile and Maurice to school. *His* education had long ago been finished. So he selected to stay in the warm kitchen, and lie as close to the stove as possible. He made dubious and uncertain friends with the cat. He slept a great deal, he ate a great deal. As the weeks flew on, he became fat, lazy-looking, and uninteresting. Were it not for subsequent and previous conduct he would not have been a dog worth writing about. So bad is prosperity for some!

But prosperous days were not the will of their heavenly Father for these little pilgrims just yet, and their brief and happy sojourn with kind Mrs. Moseley was to come to a rather sudden end.

Cecile, believing fully in the good clergyman's words, was waiting patiently for that letter from France, which was to enable Maurice, Toby, and herself to travel there in the very best way. Her little heart was at rest. During the six weeks she remained with Mrs. Moseley, she gained great strength both of body and mind.

She must find Lovedy. But surely Mr. Danvers was right and if she had a grown person to go with her and her little brother, from how many perils would they not be saved? She waited, therefore, quite quietly for the letter that never came; meanwhile employing herself in learning all she could about France. She was more sure than ever now that Lovedy was there, for something seemed to tell her that Lovedy and Susie were one. Of course this beautiful Susie had gone back to France, and once there, Cecile would quickly find her. She had now a double delight and pleasure in the hope of finding Lovedy Joy. She would give her her mother's message, and her mother's precious purse of gold. But she could do more than that. Lovedy's own mother was dead. But there was another woman who cared for Lovedy with a mother's warm and tender heart. Another woman who mourned for the lost Susie she could never see, but for whom she kept a little room all warm and bright. Cecile pictured over and over how tenderly she would tell this poor, wandering girl of the love waiting for her, and longing for her, and of how she herself would bring her back to Mammie Moseley.

Things were in this state, and the children and their adopted parents were all very happy together, when the change that I have spoken of came.

It was a snowy and bleak day in February, and the little party were all at breakfast, when a quick and, it must be owned, very unfamiliar

The Children's Pilgrimage

step was heard running up the attic stairs. The rope was pulled with a vigorous tug, and a postman's hand thrust in a letter.

"'Tis that letter from foreign parts, as sure as sure, never welcome it, " said Moseley, swallowing his coffee with a great gulp, and rising to secure the rare missive.

Cecile felt herself growing pale, and a lump rising in her throat. But Mrs. Moseley, seizing the letter, and turning it over, exclaimed excitedly:

"Why, sakes alive, John, it ain't a foreign letter at all; it have the Norwich post-mark on it. I do hope as there ain't no bad news of mother. "

"Well, open it and see, wife, " answered the practical husband. The wife did so.

Alas! her fears were confirmed. A very old mother down in the country was pronounced dying, and Mrs. Moseley must start without an hour's delay if she would see her alive.

Then ensued bustle and confusion. John Moseley was heard to mutter that it came at a queer ill-conwenient time, Mr. Danvers being away, and a deal more than or'nary put in his wife's hands. However, there was no help for it. The dying won't wait for other people's convenience. Cecile helped Mrs. Moseley to pack her small carpet-bag. Crying bitterly, the loving-hearted woman bade both children a tender good-by. If her mother really died, she would only remain for the funeral. At the farthest she would be back at the end of a week. In the meantime, Cecile was to take care of Moseley for her. By the twelve o'clock train she was off to Norforkshire. She little guessed that those bright and sweet faces which had made her home so homelike for the last two months were not to greet her on her return. Maurice cried bitterly at losing Mammie Moseley. Cecile went to school with a strangely heavy heart. Her only consolation was in the hope that her good friend would quickly return. But that hope was dashed to the ground the very next morning. For Mrs. Moseley, writing to her husband, informed him that her old mother had rallied; that the doctor thought she might live for a week or so longer, but that she had found her in so neglected and sad a condition that she had not the heart to leave her again. Moseley must

The Children's Pilgrimage

get someone to take up her church work for her, for she could not leave her mother while she lived.

It was on the very afternoon of this day that Cecile, walking slowly home with Maurice from school, and regretting very vehemently to her little brother the great loss they both had in the absence of dear, dear Mammie Moseley, was startled by a loud and frightened exclamation from her little brother.

"Oh, Cecile! Oh, look, look! "

Maurice pointed with an eager finger to a woman who, neatly dressed from head to foot in black, was walking in front of them.

"'Tis—'tis Aunt Lydia Purcell—'tis wicked Aunt Lydia Purcell, " said Maurice.

Cecile felt her very heart standing still; her breath seemed to leave her—her face felt cold. Before she could stir a step or utter an exclamation the figure in black turned quickly and faced the children. No doubt who she was. No doubt whose cold gray eyes were fixed on them. Cecile and Maurice, huddling close together, gazed silently. Aunt Lydia came on. She looked at the little pair, but when she came up to them, passed on without a word or sign of apparent recognition.

"Oh! come home, Cecile, come home, " said Maurice.

They were now in the street where the Moseleys lived, and as they turned in at the door, Cecile looked round. Lydia Purcell was standing at the corner and watching them.

The Children's Pilgrimage

CHAPTER X.

STARTING ON THE GREAT JOURNEY.

Cecile and Maurice ran quickly upstairs, pulled the rope with a will, and got into the Moseleys' attic.

"We are safe now, " said the little boy, who had not seen Lydia watching them from the street corner.

Cecile, panting after her rapid run, and with her hand pressed to her heart, stood quiet for a moment, then she darted into their snug little attic bedroom, shut the door, and fell on her knees.

"Lord Jesus, " she said aloud, "wicked Aunt Lydia Purcell has seen us, and we must go away at once. Don't forget to guide me and Maurice and Toby. "

She said this little prayer in a trembling voice. She felt there was not a moment to lose; any instant Aunt Lydia might arrive. She flung the bedclothes off the bed, and thrusting her hand into a hole in the mattress, pulled out the Russia-leather purse. Joined to its former contents was now six shillings and sixpence in silver. This money was the change over from Maurice's half sovereign.

Cecile felt that it was a very little sum to take them to France, but there was no help for it. She and Maurice and Toby must manage on this sum to walk to Dover. She knew enough of geography now to be sure that Dover was the right place to go to.

She slipped the change from the half sovereign into a sixpenny purse which Moseley had given her on Christmas Day. The precious Russia- leather purse was restored to its old hiding place in the bosom of her frock. Then, giving a mournful glance round the little chamber which she was about to quit, she returned to Maurice.

"Don't take off your hat, Maurice, darling; we have got to go. "

"To go! " said Maurice, opening his brown eyes wide. "Are we to leave our nice night's lodging? Is that what you mean? No, Cecile, " said the little boy, seating himself firmly on the floor. "I don't intend

The Children's Pilgrimage

to go. Mammie Moseley said I was to be here when she came back, and I mean to be here."

"But, oh! Maurice, Maurice, I must go south, Will you let me go alone? Can you live without me, Maurice, darling?"

"No, Cecile, you shall not go. You shall stay here too. We need neither of us go south. It's much, much nicer here."

Cecile considered a moment. This opposition from Maurice puzzled her. She had counted on many obstacles, but this came from an unlooked-for quarter.

Moments were precious. Each instant she expected to hear the step she dreaded on the attic stairs. Without Maurice, however, she could not stir. Resolving to fight for her purse of gold, with even life itself if necessary, she sat down by her little brother on the floor.

"Maurice," she said—as she spoke, she felt herself growing quite old and grave—"Maurice, you know that ever since our stepmother died, I have told you that me and you must go on a long, long journey. We must go south. You don't like to go. Nor I don't like it neither, Maurice—but that don't matter. In the book Mrs. Moseley gave me all about Jesus, it says that people, and even little children, have to do lots of things they don't like. But if they are brave, and do the hard things, Jesus the good Guide, is *so* pleased with them. Maurice, if you come with me to-day, you will be a real, brave French boy. You know how proud you are of being a French boy."

"Yes," answered Maurice, pouting his pretty rosy lips a little, "I don't want to be an English boy. I want to be French, same as father. But it won't make me English to stay in our snug night's lodging, where everything is nice and warm, and we have plenty to eat. Why should we go south to-day, Cecile? Does Jesus want us to go just now?"

"I will tell you," said Cecile; "I will trust you, Maurice. Maurice, when our stepmother was dying, she gave me something very precious—something very, very precious. Maurice, if I tell you what it was, will you promise never, never, never to tell anybody else? Will you look me in the face, and promise me that, true and faithful, Maurice?"

The Children's Pilgrimage

"True and faithful, " answered Maurice, "true and faithful, Cecile. Cecile, what did our stepmother give you to hide? "

"Oh, Maurice! I dare not tell you all. It is a purse—a purse full, full of money, and I have to take this money to somebody away in France. Maurice, you saw Aunt Lydia Purcell just now in the street, and she saw me and you. Once she took that money away from me, and Jane Parsons brought it back again. And now she saw us, and she saw where we live. She looked at us as we came in at this door, and any moment she may come here. Oh, Maurice! if she comes here, and if she steals my purse of gold, I *shall die.* "

Here Cecile's fortitude gave way. Still seated on the floor, she covered her face with her hands, and burst into tears.

Her tears, however, did what her words could not do. Maurice's tender baby heart held out no longer. He stood up and said valiantly:

"Cecile, Cecile, we'll leave our night's lodging. We'll go away. Only who's to tell Mammie Moseley and Mr. Moseley? "

"I'll write, " said Cecile; "I can hold my pen pretty well now. I'll write a little note. "

She went to the table where she knew some seldom-used note paper was kept, selected a gay pink sheet, and dipping her pen in the ink, and after a great deal of difficulty, and some blots, which, indeed, were made larger by tear-drops, accomplished a few forlorn little words. This was the little note, ill-spelt and ill-written, which greeted Moseley on his return home that evening:

"Dear Mammie Moseley and Mr. Moseley: The little children you gave so many nights' lodgings to have gone away. We have gone south, but there is no use looking for us, for Cecile must do what she promised. Mammie Moseley, if Cecile can't do what she promised she will die. The little children would not have gone now when mammie was away, but a great, great danger came, and we had not a moment to stay. Some day, Mammie Moseley and Mr. Moseley, me and Maurice will come back and then look for a great surprise. Now, good-by. Your most grateful little children,

"CECILE—MAURICE.

"Toby has to come with us, please, and he is most obliged for all kindness."

This little note made Moseley dash his hand hastily more than once before his eyes, then catching up his hat he rushed off to the nearest police-station, but though all steps were immediately taken, the children were not found. Mrs. Moseley came home and cried nearly as sorely for them as she did for her dead mother.

"John," she said, "I'll never pick up no more strays—never, never. I'll never be good to no more strays. You mark my words, John Moseley."

In answer to this, big John Moseley smiled and patted his wife's cheek. It is needless to add that he knew her better than to believe even her own words on that subject.

THIRD PART.

THE GREAT JOURNEY.

"I know not the way I am going',
But well do I know my Guide. "

CHAPTER I.

ON THE SAND HILL.

There is an old saying which tells us that there is a special Providence over the very young and the very old. This old-world saying was specially proved in the cases of Maurice and Cecile. How two creatures so young, so inexperienced, should ever find themselves in a foreign land, must have remained a mystery to those who did not hold this faith.

Cecile was eight, Maurice six years old; the dog, of no age in particular, but with a vast amount of canine wisdom, was with them. He had walked with them all the way from London to Dover. He had slept curled up close to them in two or three barns, where they had passed nights free of expense. He had jumped up behind them into loaded carts or wagons when they were fortunate enough to get a lift, and when they reached Dover he had wandered with them through the streets, and had found himself by their sides on the quay, and in some way also on board the boat which was to convey them to France. And now they were in France, two miles outside Calais, on a wild, flat, and desolate plain. But neither this fact nor the weather, for it was a raw and bitter winter's day, made any difference, at least at first, to Cecile. All lesser feelings, all minor discomforts, were swallowed up in the joyful knowledge that they were in France, in the land where Lovedy was sure to be, in their beloved father's country. They were in France, their own *belle* France! Little she knew or recked, poor child! how far was this present desolate France from her babyhood's sunny home. Having conquered the grand difficulty of getting there, she saw no other difficulties in her path just now.

"Oh, Maurice! we are safe in our own country, " she said, in a tone of ecstasy, to the little boy.

Maurice, however, —cold, tired, still seasick from his passage across the Channel, —saw nothing delightful in this fact.

"I'm very hungry, Cecile, " he said, "and I'm very cold. How soon shall we find breakfast and a night's lodging? "

"Maurice, dear, it is quite early in the day; we don't want to think of a night's lodging for many hours yet. "

"But we passed through a town, a great big town, " objected Maurice; "why did you not look for a night's lodging there, Cecile? "

"'Twasn't in my 'greement, Maurice, darling. I promised, promised faithful when I went on this search, that we'd stay in little villages and small tiny inns, and every place looked big in that town. But we'll soon find a place, Maurice, and then you shall have breakfast. Toby will take us to a village very soon. "

All Toby's temporary degeneration of character had vanished since his walk to Dover. He was as alert as ever in his care of Maurice, as anxiously solicitous for Cecile's benefit, and had also developed a remarkable and valuable faculty for finding small towns and out-of-the-way villages, where Cecile's slender store of money could be spent to the best advantage.

On board the small boat which had brought the children across the Channel, Cecile's piquant and yet pathetic face had won the captain's good favor. He had not only given all three their passage for nothing, but had got the little girl to confide sufficiently in him to find out that she carried money with her. He asked her if it was French or English money, and on her taking out her precious Russia-leather purse from its hiding-place, and producing with trembling hands an English sovereign, he had changed it into small and useful French money, and had tried to make the child comprehend the difference between the two. When they got to Calais he managed to land the children without the necessity of a passport, of which, of course, Cecile knew nothing. What more he might have done was never revealed, for Cecile, Maurice, and Toby were quickly lost sight of in the bustle on the quay.

The little trio walked off—Cecile, at least, feeling very triumphant—and never paused, until obliged to do so, owing to Maurice's weariness.

The Children's Pilgrimage

"We will find a village at once now, Maurice, " said his little sister. She called Toby, whistled to him, gave him to understand what they wanted, and the dog, with a short bark and glance of intelligence, ran on in front. He sniffed the air, he smelt the ground. Presently he seemed to know all about it, for he set off soberly in a direct line; and after half an hour's walking, brought the children to a little hamlet, of about a dozen poor-looking houses. In front of a tiny inn he drew up and sat down on his haunches, tired, but well pleased.

The door of the little wayside inn stood open. Cecile and Maurice entered at once. A woman in a tall peasant's cap and white apron came forward and demanded in French what she could serve the little dears with. Cecile, looking helpless, asked in English for bread and milk. Of course the woman could not understand a word. She held up her hands and proclaimed the stupendous fact that the children were undoubtedly English to her neighbors, then burst into a fresh volley of French.

And here first broke upon poor little Cecile the stupendous fact that they were in a land where they could not speak a word of the language. She stood helpless, tears filling her sweet blue eyes. A group gathered speedily round the children, but all were powerless to assist. It never occurred to anyone that the helpless little wanderers might be hungry. It was Maurice at last who saw a way out of the difficulty. He felt starving, and he saw rolls of bread within his reach.

"Stupid people! " said the little boy. He got on a stool, and helped himself to the longest of the fresh rolls. This he broke into three parts, keeping one himself, giving one to Cecile, and the other to Toby.

There was a simultaneous and hearty laugh from the rough party. The peasant proprietor's brow cleared. She uttered another exclamation and darted into her kitchen, from which she returned in a moment with two steaming bowls of hot and delicious soup. She also furnished Toby with a bone.

Cecile, when they had finished their meal, paid a small French coin for the food, and then the little pilgrims left the village.

"The sun is shining brightly, " said Cecile. "Maurice, me and you will sit under that sand hill for a little bit, and think what is best to be done. "

The Children's Pilgrimage

In truth the poor little girl's brave heart was sorely puzzled and perplexed. If they could not speak to the people, how ever could they find Lovedy? and if they did not find Lovedy, of what use was it their being in France? Then how could she get cheap food and cheap lodgings? and how would their money hold out? They were small and desolate children. It did not seem at all like their father's country. Why had she come? Could she ever, ever succeed in her mission? For a moment the noble nature was overcome, and the bright faith clouded.

"Oh, Maurice! " said Cecile, "I wish—I wish Jesus our Guide was not up in heaven. I wish He was down on earth, and would come with us. I know *He* could speak French. "

"Oh! that don't matter—that don't, " answered Maurice, who, cheered by his good breakfast, felt like a different boy. "I'll always just take things, and then they'll know what I mean. The French don't matter, Cecile. But what I wish is that we might be in heaven— me and you and Toby at once—for if this is South, I don't like it, Cecile. I wish Jesus the Guide would take us to heaven at once. "

"We must find Lovedy first, " said Cecile, "and then—and then— yes, I'd like, too, to die and go—there. "

"I know nothing about dying, " answered Maurice; "I only know I want to go to heaven. I liked what Mammie Moseley told me about heaven. You are never cold there and never hungry. Now I'm beginning to be quite cold again, and in an hour or so I shall be as hungry as ever. I don't think nothing of your South, Cecile; 'tis a nasty place, I think. "

"We have not got South yet, darling. Oh, Maurice, " with a wan little smile, "if even *jography* was a person, as I used to think before I went to school. "

"What is that about jography and school, young 'un, " said suddenly, at that moment over their very heads, a gay English voice, and the next instant, a tall boy of about fourteen, with a little fiddle slung over his shoulder, came round the sand hill, and sat down by the children's side.

CHAPTER II.

JOGRAPHY.

Cecile and Maurice had not only gone to school by day, but at Mr. Danvers' express wish had for a short part of their stay in London attended a small and excellent night-school, which was entirely taught by deaconesses who worked under the good clergyman.

To this same night-school came, not regularly, but by fits and starts, a handsome lad of fourteen—a lad with brilliant black eyes, and black hair flung off an open brow. He was poorly dressed, and his young smooth cheeks were hollow for want of sufficient food. When he was in his best attire, and in his gayest humor, he came with a little fiddle swung across his arm.

But sometimes he made his appearance, sad-eyed, and without his fiddle. On these occasions, his feet were also very often destitute of either shoes or stockings.

He was a troublesome boy, decidedly unmanageable, and an irregular scholar, sometimes, absenting himself for a whole week at a time.

Still he was a favorite. He had a bright way and a winsome smile. He never teased the little ones, and sometimes on leaving school he would play a bright air or two so skilfully and with such airy grace, on his little cracked fiddle, that the school children capered round in delight. The deconesses often tried to get at his history but he never would tell it; nor would he, even on those days when he had to appear without either fiddle, or shoes, or stockings, complain of want.

On the evening when Cecile first went to this night-school, a pretty young lady of twenty called her to her side, and asked her what she would like best to learn?

"In this night-school, " she added, "for those children at least, who go regularly to day-school, we try as much as possible to consult their taste, so what do you like best for me to teach you, dear?"

The Children's Pilgrimage

Cecile, opening her blue eyes wide, answered: "Jography, please, ma'am. I'd rayther learn jography than anything else in all the world."

"But why?" asked the deaconess, surprised at this answer.

"'Cause I'm a little French girl, please, teacher. Me and Maurice we're both French, and 'tis very important indeed for me to know the way to France, and about France, when we get there; and Jography tells all about it, don't it, teacher?"

"Why, yes, I suppose so," said the young teacher, laughing. So Cecile got her first lesson in geography, and a pair of bold, handsome black eyes often glanced almost wistfully in her direction as she learned. That night, at the door of the night-school, the boy with the fiddle came up to Cecile and Maurice.

"I say, little Jography," he exclaimed, "you ain't really French, be you?"

"I'm Cecile D'Albert, and this is Maurice D'Albert," answered Cecile. "Yes, we're a little French boy and girl, me and Maurice. We come from the south, from the Pyrenees."

The tall lad sighed.

"*La Belle France*!" he exclaimed with sudden fervor. He caught Cecile's little hand and wrung it, then he hurried away.

After this he had once or twice again spoken to the children, but they had never got beyond the outside limits of friendship. And now behold! on this desolate sandy plain outside the far-famed town of Calais, the poor little French wanderers, who knew not a single word of their native language, and the tall boy with the fiddle met. It was surprising how that slight acquaintance in London ripened on the instant into violent friendship.

Maurice, in his ecstasy at seeing a face he knew actually kissed the tall boy, and Cecile's eyes over-flowed with happy tears.

"Oh! do sit down near us. Do help us, we're such a perplexed little boy and girl," she said; "do talk to us for a little bit, kind tall English boy."

The Children's Pilgrimage

"You call me Jography, young un. It wor through jography we found each other out. And I ain't an English boy, no more nor you are an English girl; I'm French, I am. There, you call me Jography, young uns; 'tis uncommon, and 'ull fit fine. "

"Oh! then Jography is a person, " said Cecile. "How glad I am! I was just longing that he might be. And I'm so glad you're French; and is Jography your real, real name? "

"Ain't you fit to kill a body with laughing? " said the tall lad, rolling over and over in an ecstasy of mirth on the short grass. "No, I ain't christened Jography. My heyes! what a rum go that ud be! No, no, little uns, yer humble servant have had heaps of names. In Lunnon I wor mostly called Joe Barnes, and once, once, long ago, I wor little Alphonse Malet. My mother called me that, but Jography 'ull fit fine jest now. You two call me Jography, young uns. "

"And please, Jography, " asked Cecile, "are you going to stay in France now you have come? "

"Well, I rather guess I am. I didn't take all the trouble to run away to go back again, I can tell you. And now might I ax you what you two mites is arter? "

In reply to that question Cecile told as much of her story as she dared. She and Maurice were going down south. They wanted to find a girl who they thought was in the south. It was a solemn promise—a promise made to one who was dead. Cecile must keep her promise, and never grow weary till she had found this girl.

"But I was puzzled, " said Cecile in conclusion. I was puzzled just now; for though me and Maurice are a little French boy and girl, we don't know one word of French. I did not know how we could find Lovedy; and I was wishing—oh! I *was* wishing—that Jesus the Guide was living down on earth, and that He would take our hands and guide us. "

"Poor young uns! " said the boy, "Poor little mites! Suppose as I takes yer hands, and guides you two little morsels? "

"Oh! will you, Jography? —oh! will you, indeed? how I shall love you! how I shall! "

The Children's Pilgrimage

"And me too, and Toby too! " exclaimed Maurice. And the two children, in their excitement, flung their arms round their new friend's neck.

"Well, I can speak French anyhow, " said the boy. "But now listen. Don't you two agree to nothink till you hears my story. "

"But 'tis sure to be a nice story, Jography, " said Maurice. "I shall like going south with you. "

"Well, sit on my knee and listen, young un. No; it ain't nice a bit. I'm French too, and I'm South too. I used to live in the Pyrenees. I lived there till I was seven years old. I had a mother and no father, and I had a big brother. I wor a happy little chap. My mother used to kiss me and cuddle me up; and my brother—there was no one like Jean. One day I wor playing in the mountains, when a big black man come up and axed me if I'd like to see his dancing dogs. I went with him. He wor a bad, bad man. When he got me in a lonely place he put my head in a bag, so as I could not see nor cry out, and he stole me. He brought me to Paris; afterward he sold me to a man in Lunnon as a 'prentice. I had to dance with the dogs, and I was taught to play the fiddle. Both my masters were cruel to me, and they beat me often and often. I ha' been in Lunnon for seven year now; I can speak English well, but I never forgot the French. I always said as I'd run away back to France, and find my mother and my brother Jean. I never had the chance, for I wor watched close till ten days ago. I walked to Dover, and made my way across in an old fishing-smack. And here I am in France once more. Now little uns, I'm going south, and I can talk English to you, and I can talk French too. Shall we club together, little mates? "

"But have you any money at all, Jography? " asked Cecile, puckering her pretty brows anxiously; "and—and—are you a honest boy, Jography? "

"Well, ef you ain't a queer little lass! *I* honest! I ain't likely to rob from *you*; no, tho' I ha'n't no money—but ha' you? "

"Yes, dear Jography, I have money, " said Cecile, laying her hand on the ragged sleeve; "I have some precious, precious money, as I must give to Lovedy when I see her. If that money gets lost or stolen Cecile will die. Oh, Jography! you won't, you won't take that money away from me. Promise, promise! "

The Children's Pilgrimage

"I ain't a brute, " said the boy. "Little un, I'd starve first! "

"I believe you, Jography, " said Cecile; "and, Jography, me and Maurice have a little other money to take us down south, and we are to stay in the smallest villages, and sleep in the werry poorest inns. Can you do that? "

"Why, yes, I think I can sleep anywhere; and ef you'll jest lend me Toby there, I'll teach him to dance to my fiddling, and that'll earn more sous than I shall want. Is it a bargain then? Shall I go with you two mites and help you to find this ere Lovedy? "

"Jography, 'twas Jesus the Guide sent you, " said Cecile, clasping his hand.

"And I don't want to go to heaven just now, " said Maurice, taking hold of the other hand.

The Children's Pilgrimage

CHAPTER III.

BLUE EYES AND GOLDEN HAIR.

"And now, " proceeded Joe, *alias* Alphonse, *alias* Jography, "the first thing—now as it is settled as we three club together—the first thing is to plan the campaign. "

"What's the campaign? " asked Maurice, gazing with great awe and admiration at his new friend.

"Why, young un, we're going south. You has got to find some un south, and I has got to find two people south. They may all be dead, and we may never find them; but for all that we has got to look, and look real hard too, I take it. Now, you see as this ere France is a werry big place; I remember when I wor brought away seven years ago that it took my master and me many days and many nights to travel even as far as Paris, and sometimes we went by train, and sometimes we had lifts in carts and wagons. Now, as we has got to walk all the way, and can't on no account go by no train, though we *may* get a lift sometimes ef we're lucky, we has got to know our road. Look you yere, young uns, 'tis like this, " Here Jography caught up a little stick and made a rapid sketch in the sand.

"See! " he exclaimed, "this yere's France. Now we ere up yere, and we want to get down yere. We won't go round, we'll go straight across, and the first thing is to make for Paris. We'll go first to Paris, say I. "

"And are there night's lodgings in Paris? " asked Maurice, "and food to eat? and is it warm, not bitter, bitter cold like here? "

"And is Paris a little town, Jography? " asked Cecile. "For my stepmother, she said as I was to look for Lovedy in all the little towns and in all the tiny inns. "

Jography laughed.

"You two ere a rum pair, " he said. "Yes, Maurice, you shall have plenty to eat in Paris, and as to being cold, why, that 'ull depend on where we goes, and what money we spends. You needn't be cold unless you likes; and Cecile, little Missie, we shall go through hall

The Children's Pilgrimage

the smallest towns and villages, as you like, and we'll ax for Lovedy heverywhere. But Paris itself is a big, big place. I wor only seven years old, but I remember Paris. I wor werry misribble in Paris. Yes, I don't want to stay there. But we must go there. It seems to me 'tis near as big as Lunnon. Why shouldn't your Lovedy be in Paris, Missie? "

"Only my stepmother did say the small villages, Jography. Oh! I don't know what for to do. "

"Well, you leave it to me. What's the use of a guide ef he can't guide you? You leave it to me, little un. "

"Yes, Cecile, come on, for I'm most bitter cold, " said Maurice.

"Stay one moment, young uns; you two ha' money, but this yere Joe ha'n't any, I want to test that dog there. Ef I can teach the dog to dance a little, why, I'll play my fiddle, and we'll get along fine. "

In the intense excitement of seeing Toby going through his first lesson, Maurice forgot all his cold and discomfort; he jumped to his feet, and capered about with delight; nay, at the poor dog's awkward efforts to steady himself on his hind legs, Maurice rolled on the ground with laughter.

"You mustn't laugh at him, " said Joe; "no dog 'ud do anythink ef he wor laughed at. There now, that's better. I'll soon teach him a trick or two. "

It is to be doubted whether Toby would have put up with the indignity of being forced to balance himself on the extreme point of his body were it not for Cecile. Hitherto he had held rather the position of director of the movements of the little party. He felt jealous of this big boy, who had come suddenly and taken the management of everything. When Joe caught him rather roughly by the front paws, and tried to force him to walk about after a fashion which certainly nature never intended, he was strongly inclined to lay angry teeth on his arm. But Cecile's eyes said no, and poor Toby, like many another before him, submitted tamely because of his love. He loved Cecile, and for his love he would submit to this indignity. The small performance over, Joe Barnes, flinging his fiddle over his shoulder, started to his feet, and the little party of pilgrims, now augmented to four, commenced their march. They walked for two hours; Joe, when Maurice was very tired, carrying him part of the way. At the end of two hours they reached another small village. Here Joe, taking his fiddle, played dexterously, and soon the village boys and girls, with their foreign dresses and foreign faces, came flocking out.

"Ef Toby could only dance I'd make a fortune 'ere, " whispered Joe to Cecile.

But even without this valuable addition he did secure enough sous to pay for his own supper and leave something over for breakfast the next morning. Then, in French, which was certainly a trifle rusty for want of use, he demanded refreshments, of which the tired and hungry wanderers partook eagerly. Afterward they had another and shorter march into a still smaller and poorer village, where Joe secured them a very cheap but not very uncomfortable night's lodging.

After they had eaten their supper, and little Maurice was already fast asleep, Cecile came up to the tall boy who had so opportunely and wonderfully acted their friend.

"Jography, " she said earnestly, "do you know the French of blue eyes and golden hair—the French of a red, red mouth, and little teeth like pearls. Do you know the French of all that much, dear Jography? "

"Why, Missie, " answered Joe, "I s'pose as I could manage it. But what do I want with blue eyes and gold hair? That ain't my mother, nor Jean neither. "

"Yes, Jography. But 'tis Lovedy. My stepmother said as I was to ask for that sort of girl in all the small villages and all the tiny inns, dear Jography, "

"Well, well, and so we will, darlin'; we'll ax yere first thing tomorrow morning; and now lie down and go to sleep, for we must be early on the march, Missie. "

Cecile raised her lips to kiss Joe, and then she lay down by Maurice's side. But she did not at once go to sleep. She was thanking Jesus for sending to such a destitute, lonely little pair of children so good and so kind a guide.

While Joe, for his part, wondered could it be possible that this unknown Lovedy could have bluer eyes than Cecile's own.

The Children's Pilgrimage

CHAPTER IV.

THE WORD THAT SETTLED JOE BARNES.

From London to Paris is no distance at all. The most delicate invalid can scarcely be fatigued by so slight a journey.

So you say, who go comfortably for a pleasure trip. You start at a reasonably early hour in the morning, and arrive at your destination in time for dinner. A few of you, no doubt, may dread that short hour and a half spent on the Channel. But even its horrors are mitigated by large steamers and kind and attentive attendants, and as for the rest of the journey, it is nothing, not worth mentioning in these days of rushing over the world.

Yes, the power of steam has brought the gay French capital thus near. But if you had to trudge the whole weary way on foot, you would still find that there were a vast number of miles between you and Paris. That these miles were apt to stretch themselves interminably, and that your feet were inclined to ache terribly; still more would you feel the length of the way and the vast distance of the road, if the journey had to be made in winter. Then the shortness of the days, the length of the nights, the great cold, the bitter winds, would all add to the horrors of this so-called simple journey.

This four little pilgrims, going bravely onward, experienced.

Toby, whose spirits rather sank from the moment Joe Barnes took the management of affairs, had the further misfortune of running a thorn into his foot; and though the very Joe whom he disliked was able to extract it, still for a day or two the poor dog was lame. Maurice, too, was still such a baby, and his little feet so quickly swelled from all this constant walking, that Joe had to carry him a great deal, and in this manner one lad felt the fatigue nearly as much as the other. On the whole, perhaps it was the little Queen of the party, the real Leader of the expedition, who suffered the least. Never did knight of old go in search of the Holy Grail more devoutly than did Cecile go now to deliver up her purse of gold, to keep her sacred promise.

Not a fresh day broke but she said to herself: "I am a little nearer to Lovedy; I may hear of Lovedy to-day. " But though Joe did not fail to

The Children's Pilgrimage

air his French on her behalf, though he never ceased in every village inn to inquire for a fair and blue-eyed English girl, as yet they had got no clew; as yet not the faintest trace of the lost Lovedy could be heard of.

They were now over a week in France, and were still a long, long way from Paris. Each day's proceedings consisted of two marches — one to some small village, where Joe played the fiddle, made a couple of sous, and where they had dinner; then another generally shorter march to another tiny village, where they slept for the night. In this way their progress could not but be very slow, and although Joe had far more wisdom than his little companions, yet he often got misdirected, and very often, after a particularly weary number of miles had been got over, they found that they had gone wrong, and that they were further from the great French capital than they had been the night before.

Without knowing it, they had wandered a good way into Normandy, and though it was now getting quite into the middle of February, there was not a trace of spring vegetation to be discovered. The weather, too, was bitter and wintry. East winds, alternating with sleet showers, seemed the order of the day.

Cecile had not dared to confide her secret to Mr. Danvers, neither had all Mrs. Moseley's motherly kindness won it from her. But, nevertheless, during the long, long days they spent together, she was not proof against the charms of the tall boy whom she believed Jesus had sent to guide her, and who was also her own fellow-countryman.

All that long and pathetic interview which Cecile and her dying stepmother had held together had been told to Jography. Even the precious leather purse had been put into his hands, and he had been allowed to open it and count its contents.

For a moment his deep-black eyes had glittered greedily as he felt the gold running through his fingers, then they softened. He returned the money to the purse, and gave it back, almost reverently, to Cecile.

"Little Missie, " he said, looking strangely at her and speaking in a sad tone, "you ha' showed me yer gold. Do you know what yer gold 'ud mean to me? "

"No, " answered Cecile, returning his glance in fullest confidence.

"Why, Missie, I'm a poor starved lad. I ha' been treated werry shameful. I ha' got blows, and kicks, and rough food, and little of that same. But there's worse nor that; I han't no one to speak a kind word to me. Not one, not *one* kind word for seven years have I heard, and before that I had a mother and a brother. I wor a little lad, and I used to sleep o' nights with my mother, and she used to take me in her arms and pet me and love me, and my big brother wor as good to me as brother could be. Missie, my heart has *starved* for my mother and my brother, and ef I liked I could take that purse full o' gold and let you little children fare as best you might, and I could jump inter the next train and be wid my mother and brother back in the Pyrenees in a werry short time. "

"No, Joe Barnes, you couldn't do that, " answered Cecile, the finest pucker of surprise on her pretty brow.

"You think as I couldn't, Missie dear, and why not? I'm much stronger than you. "

"No, Joe, *you* couldn't steal my purse of gold, " continued Cecile, still speaking quietly and without a trace of fear. "Aunt Lydia Purcell could have taken it away, and I dreaded her most terribly, and I would not tell dear Mrs. Moseley, nor Mr. Danvers, who was so good and kind; I would not tell them, for I was afraid somebody else might hear, or they might think me too young, and take away the purse for the present. But *you* could not touch it, Jography, for if you did anything so dreadful, dreadful mean as that, your heart would break, and you would not care for your mother to pet you, and if your big brother were an honest man, you would not like to look at him. You would always think how you had robbed a little girl that trusted you, and who had a great, great dreadful care on her mind, and you would remember how Jesus the Guide had sent you to that little girl to help her, and your heart would break. You could not do it, Joe Barnes. "

Here Cecile returned her purse to its hiding place, and then sat quiet, with her hands folded before her.

Nothing could exceed the dignity and calm of the little creature. The homeless and starved French boy, looking at her, felt a sudden lump rising in his throat; —a naturally warm and chivalrous nature made

The Children's Pilgrimage

him almost inclined to worship the pretty child. For a moment the great lump in his throat prevented him speaking, then, falling on his knees, he took Cecile's little hand in his.

"Cecile D'Albert, " he said passionately, "I'd rayther be cut in little bits nor touch that purse o' gold. You're quite, quite right, little Missie, it 'ud break my heart. "

"Of course, " said Cecile. "And now, Joe, shall we walk on, for 'tis most bitter cold under this sand hill; and see! poor Maurice is nearly asleep. "

That same evening, when, rather earlier than usual, the children and dog had taken refuge in a very tiny little wayside house, where a woman was giving them room to rest in almost for nothing, Joe, coming close to Cecile, said:

"Wot wor that as you said that Jesus the Guide sent me to you, Missie. I don't know nothink about Jesus the Guide. "

"Oh, Joe! what an unhappy boy you must be! I was *so* unhappy until I learned about Him, and I was a long, long time learning. Yes, He did send you. He could not come His own self, so He sent you. "

"But, indeed, Missie, no; I just runned away, and I got to France, and I heard you two funny little mites talking o' jography under the sand hill. It worn't likely as a feller 'ud forget the way you did speak o' jography. No one sent me, Missie. "

"But that's a way Jesus has, Jography. He does not always tell people when He is sending them. But He does send them all the same. It's very simple, dear Jography, but I was a long, long time learning about it. For a long time I thought Jesus came His own self, and walked with people when they were little, like me. I thought I should see Him and feel His hand, and when me and Maurice found ourselves alone outside Calais, and we did not know a word of French, I did, I did wish Jesus lived down here and not up in heaven, and I said I wished it, and then I said that I even wished jography was a person, and I had hardly said it before you came. Then you know, Joe, you told me you were for a whole long seven years trying to get back to your mother and brother, and you never could run away from your cruel master before. Oh, dear Jography! of course

The Children's Pilgrimage

'twas Jesus did it all, and now we're going home together to our own home in dear south of France. "

"Well, missie, perhaps as you're right. Certain sure it is, as I could never run away before; and I might ha' gone round to the side o' the sand hill and never heerd that word jography. That word settled the business for me, Miss Cecile. "

"Yes, Joe; and you must love Jesus now, for you see He loves you. "

"No, no, missie; nobody never did love Joe since he left off his mother. "

"But Jesus, the good Guide, does. Why, He died for you. You don't suppose a man would die for you without loving you? "

"Nobody died fur me, Missie Cecile—that ere's nonsense, miss, dear. "

"No, Joe; I have it all in a book. The book is called the New Testament, and Mrs. Moseley gave it to me; and Mrs. Moseley never, never told a lie to anybody; and she said that nothing was so true in the world as this book. It's all about Jesus dying for us. Oh, Jography! I *cry* when I read it, and I will read it to you. Only it is very sad. It's all about the lovely life of Jesus, and then how He was killed—and He let it be done for you and me. You will love Jesus when I read from the New Testament about Him, Joe. "

"I'd like to hear it, Missie, darling—and I love you now. "

"And I love you, poor, poor Joe—and here is a kiss for you, Joe. And now I must go to sleep. "

CHAPTER V.

OUTSIDE CAEN.

The morning after this little conversation between Joe and Cecile broke so dismally, and was so bitterly cold, that the old woman with whom the children had spent the night begged of them in her patois not to leave her. Joe, of course, alone could understand a word she said, and even Joe could not make much out of what very little resembled the *Bearnais* of his native Pyrenees; but the Norman peasant, being both kind and intelligent, managed to convey to him that the weather looked ugly; that every symptom of a violent snowstorm was brewing in the lowering and leaden sky; that people had been lost and never heard of again in Normandy, in less severe snowstorms than the one that was likely to fall that night; that in almost a moment all landmarks would be utterly obliterated, and the four little travelers dismally perish.

Joe, however, only remembering France by what it is in the sunny south, and having from his latter life in London very little idea of what a snowstorm really meant, paid but slight heed to these warnings; and having ascertained that Cecile by no means wished to remain in the little wayside cottage, he declared himself ready to encounter the perils of the way.

The old peasant bade the children good-by with tears in her eyes. She even caught up Maurice in her arms, and said it was a direct flying in the face of Providence to let so sweet an angel go forth to meet "certain destruction. " But as her vehement words were only understood by one, and by that one very imperfectly, they had unfortunately little result.

The cottage was small, close, and very uncomfortable, and the children were glad to get on their way.

Soon after noon they reached the old town of Caen. They had walked on for two or three miles by the side of the river Orne, and found themselves in old Caen before they knew it. Following strictly Cecile's line of action, the children had hitherto avoided all towns — thus, had they but known it, making very little real progress. But now, attracted by some washer-women who, bitter as the day was, were busy washing their clothes in the running waters of the Orne, they got into the picturesque town, and under the shadow of the old Cathedral.

Here, indeed, early as it was in the day, the short time of light seemed almost to have disappeared. The sky—what could be seen of it between the tall houses of the narrow street—looked almost black, and little flakes of snow began to fall noiselessly.

Here Joe, thinking of the Norman peasant, began to be a little alarmed. He proposed, as they had got into Caen, that they should run no further risk, but spend the night there.

But this proposition was met by tears of reproach by Cecile. "Oh, dear Jography! and stepmother did say, never, never to stay in the big towns—always to sleep in the little inns. Caen is much, much too big a town. We must not break my word to stepmother—we must not stay here."

Cecile's firmness, joined to her great childish ignorance, could be dangerous, but Joe only made a feeble protest.

"Do you see that old woman, and the little lass by her side making lace?" he said. "That house don't look big; we might get a night's lodging as cheap as in the villages."

But though the little Norman girl of seven nodded a friendly greeting to pretty brown-eyed Maurice as he passed, and though the making of lace on bobbins must be a delightful employment, Cecile felt there could be no tidings of Lovedy for her there; and after partaking of a little hot soup in the smallest cafe they could come across, the little pilgrims found themselves outside Caen and in the desolate and wintry country, when it was still early in the day.

Early it was, not being yet quite two o'clock; but it might have been three or four hours later to judge by the light. The snow, it is true, had for the present ceased to fall, but the blackness of the sky was so great that the ground appeared light by comparison. A wind, which sounded more like a wailing cry than any wind the children had ever heard, seemed to fill the atmosphere.

It was not a noisy wind, and it came in gusts, dying away, and then repeating itself. But for this wailing wind there was absolutely not a sound, for every bird, every living creature, except the three children

The Children's Pilgrimage

and the dog, appeared to have vanished from the face of the earth. Maurice, not caring about the weather, indifferent to these signal flags of danger, was cross, for he wanted to talk to the little lacemaker, and to learn how to manage her bobbins.

Cecile was wondering how soon they should reach a very small village, and find a night's shelter in a tiny inn. Joe, better appreciating the true danger, was full of anxious forebodings and also self-reproach, for allowing himself to be guided by a child so young and ignorant as Cecile. Still it never occurred to him to turn back.

After all, it was given to Toby to suggest, though, alas! when too late, the only sensible line of action. For some time, indeed ever since they left Caen, the dog had walked on a little ahead of his party, with his tail drooping, his whole attitude one of utter despondency.

Once or twice he had looked back reproachfully at Cecile; once or twice he had relieved his feelings with a short bark of utter discomfort. The state of the atmosphere was hateful to Toby. The leaden sky, charged with he knew not what, almost drove him mad. At last he could bear it no longer. There was death for him and his, in that terrible, sighing wind. He stood still, got on his hind legs, and, looking up at the lowering sky, gave vent to several long and unearthly howls, then darting at Cecile, he caught her dress between his teeth, and turned her sharp round in the direction of Caen.

If ever a dog said plainly, "Go back at once, and save our lives, " Toby did then.

"Toby is right, " said Joe in a tone of relief; "something awful is going to fall from that sky, Cecile; we must go back to Caen at once."

"Yes, we must go back, " said Cecile, for even to her rather slow mind came the knowledge that a moment had arrived when a promise must yield to a circumstance.

They had left Caen about a mile behind them. Turning back, it seemed close and welcome, almost at their feet. Maurice, still thinking of his little lacemaker, laughed with glee when Joe caught him in his arms.

The Children's Pilgrimage

"Take hold of my coat-tails, Cecile, " he said; "we must run, we may get back in time. "

Alas! alas! Toby's warning had come too late. Suddenly the wind ceased—there was a hush—an instant's stillness, so intense that the children, as they alone moved forward, felt their feet weighted with lead. Then from the black sky came a light that was almost dazzling. It was not lightning, it was the letting out from its vast bosom of a mighty torrent of snow. Thickly, thicker, thicker—faster, faster—in great soft flakes it fell; and, behold! in an instant, all Caen was blotted out. Trees vanished, landmarks disappeared, and the children could see nothing before them or behind them but this white wall, which seemed to press them in and hem them round.

The Children's Pilgrimage

CHAPTER VI.

IN THE SNOW.

So sudden was the snowstorm when it came, so complete the blinding sense of the loss of all external objects, that the children stood stunned, not fearing, because they utterly failed to realize. Maurice, it is true, hid his pretty head in Joe's breast, and Cecile clung a little tighter to her young companion. Toby, however, again seemed the only creature who had any wits about him. Now it would be impossible to get back to Caen. There was, as far as the little party of pilgrims were concerned, no Caen to return to, and yet they must not stand there, for either the violence of the storm would throw them on their faces, or the intense cold would freeze them to death. Onward must still be their motto. But where? These, perhaps, were Toby's thoughts, for certainly no one else thought at all. He set his keen wits to work. Suddenly he remembered something. The moment the memory came to him, he was an alert and active dog; in fact, he was once more in the post he loved. He was the leader of the expedition. Again he seized Cecile's thin and ragged frock; again he pulled her violently.

"No, no, Toby, " she said in a muffled and sad tone; "there's no use now, dear Toby. "

"Foller him, foller him; he has more sense than we jest now, " said Joe, rousing himself from his reverie.

Toby threw to the tall boy the first grateful look which had issued from his brown eyes. Again he pulled Cecile, and the children, obeying him, found themselves descending the path a little, and then the next moment they were in comparative peace and comfort. Wise Toby had led them to the sheltered side of an old wall. Here the snow did not beat, and though eventually it would drift in this direction, yet here for the next few hours the children might at least breathe and find standing room.

"Bravo, Toby! " said Joe, in a tone of rapture; "we none of us seen this old wall; why, it may save our lives. Now, if only the snow don't last too long, and if only we can keep awake, we may do even yet. "

"Why mayn't we go to sleep? " asked Cecile; "not that I am sleepy at two o'clock in the day. "

"Why mayn't we go to sleep? " echoed Joe. "Now, Missie, dear, I'm a werry hignorant boy, but I knows this much, I knows this much as true as gospel, and them as sleeps in the snow never, never wakes no more. We must none of us drop asleep, we must do hevery think but sleep—you and me, and Maurice and Toby. We must stay werry wide awake, and 'twill be hard, for they do say, as the cruel thing is, the snow does make you so desperate sleepy. "

"Do you mean, Joe Barnes, " asked Cecile, fixing her earnest little face on the tall boy, "that if we little children went to sleep now, that we'd die? Is that what you mean by never waking again? "

Joe nodded. "Yes, Missie, dear, that's about what I does mean, " he said.

"To die, and never wake again, " repeated Cecile, "then I'd see the Guide. Oh, Joe! I'd *see* Him, the lovely, lovely Jesus who I love so very much. "

"Oh! don't think on it, Miss Cecile; you has got to stay awake—you has no call to think on no such thing, Missie. "

Joe spoke with real and serious alarm. It seemed to him that Cecile in her earnest desire to see this Guide might lie down and court the sleep which would, alas! come so easily.

He was therefore surprised when she said to him in a quiet and reproachful tone, "Do you think I would lie down and go to sleep and die, Jography? I should like to die, but I must not die just yet. I'm a very, very anxious little girl, and I have a great, great deal to do; it would not be right for me even to think of dying yet. Not until I have found Lovedy, and given Lovedy the purse of gold, and told Lovedy all about her mother, then after that I should like to die. "

"That's right, Missie; we won't think on no dying to-night. Now let's do all we can to keep awake; let's walk up and down this little sheltered bit under the wall; let's teach Toby to dance a bit; let's jump about a bit"

The Children's Pilgrimage

If there was one thing in all the world poor Toby hated more than another, it was these same dancing lessons. The fact was the poor dog was too old to learn, and would never be much good as a dancing dog.

Already he so much dreaded this new accomplishment which was being forced upon him, that at the very word dancing he would try and hide, and always at least tuck his tail between his legs.

But now, what had transformed him? He heard what was intended distinctly, but instead of shrinking away, he came forward at once, and going close to Maurice's side, sat up with considerable skill, and then bending forward took the little boy's hat off his head, and held it between his teeth.

Toby had an object. He wanted to draw the attention of the others to Maurice. And, in truth, he had not a moment to lose, for what they dreaded had almost come to little Maurice—already the little child was nearly asleep.

"This will never do, " said Joe with energy. He took Maurice up roughly, and shook him, and then drawing his attention to Toby, succeeded in rousing him a little.

The next two hours were devoted by Cecile and Joe to Maurice, whom they tickled, shouted to, played with, and when everything else failed, Joe would even hold him up by his legs in the air.

Maurice did not quite go to sleep, but the cold was so intense that the poor little fellow cried with pain.

At the end of about two hours the snow ceased. The dark clouds rolled away from the sky, which shone down deep blue, peaceful, and star-bespangled on the children. The wind, also, had gone down, and the night was calm, though most bitterly cold.

It had, however, been a very terrible snowstorm, and the snow, quite dazzling white, lay already more than a foot deep on the ground.

"Why, Cecile, " said Joe, "I can see Caen again. "

"Do you think we could walk back to Caen now, Joe? "

The Children's Pilgrimage

"I don't know. I'll jest try a little bit first. I wish we could. You keep Maurice awake, Cecile, and I'll be back in a minute. "

Cecile took her little brother in her arms, and Joe disappeared round the corner of the old wall.

"Stay with the children, Toby, " he said to the dog, and Toby stayed.

"Cecile, " said Maurice, nestling up close to his sister, "'tisn't half so cold now. "

He spoke in a tone of great content and comfort, but his sweet baby voice sounded thin and weak.

"Oh, yes! Maurice, darling, it's much colder. I'm in dreadful pain from the cold. "

"I was, Cecile, but 'tis gone. I'm not cold at all; I'm ever so comfortable. You'll be like me when the pain goes. "

"Maurice, I think we had better keep walking up and down. "

"No, no, Cecile, I won't walk no more. I'm so tired, and I'm so comfortable. Cecile, do they sing away in the South? "

"I don't know, darling. I suppose they do. "

"Well, I know they sing in heaven. Mammie Moseley said so. Cecile, I'd much rather go to heaven than to the South. Would not you? "

"Yes, I think so. Maurice, you must not go to sleep. "

"I'm not going to sleep. Cecile, will you sing that pretty song about glory? Mrs. Moseley used to sing it. "

"That one about *'thousands of children*? '" said Cecile.

"Yes—singing, 'Glory, glory, glory. '"

Cecile began. She sang a line or two, then she stopped. Maurice had fallen a little away from her. His mouth was partly open, his pretty eyes were closed fast and tight. Cecile called him, she shook him, she even cried over him, but all to no effect, he was fast asleep.

The Children's Pilgrimage

Yes, Maurice was asleep, and Cecile was holding him in her arms.

Joe was away? and Toby? —Cecile was not very sure where Toby was.

She and her little brother were alone, half buried in the snow. What a dreadful position! What a terrible danger!

Cecile kept repeating to herself, "Maurice is asleep, Maurice will never wake again. If I sleep I shall never wake again, "

But the strange thing was that, realizing the danger, Cecile did not care. She was not anxious about Joe. She had no disposition to call to Toby. Even the purse of gold and the sacred promise became affairs of little moment. Everything grew dim to her—everything indifferent. She was only conscious of a sense of intense relief, only sure that the dreadful, dreadful pain from the cold in her legs was leaving her —that she, too, no longer felt the cold of the night. Jesus the Guide seemed very, very near, and she fancied that she heard "thousands of children" singing, "Glory, glory, glory. "

Then she remembered no more.

The Children's Pilgrimage

CHAPTER VII.

TOBY AGAIN TO THE RESCUE.

Meanwhile Joe was struggling in a snowdrift. Not ten paces away he had suddenly sunk down up to his waist. Notwithstanding his rough hard life, his want of food, his many and countless privations, he was a strong lad. Life was fresh and full within him. He would not, he could not let it go cheaply. He struggled and tried hard to gain a firmer footing, but although his struggles certainly kept him alive, they were hitherto unavailing. Suddenly he heard a cry, and was conscious that something heavy was springing in the air. This something was Toby, who, in agony at the condition of Cecile and Maurice, had gone in search of Joe. He now leaped on to the lad's shoulder, thus by no means assisting his efforts to free himself.

"Hi, Toby lad! off! off! " he shouted; "back to the firm ground, good dog. "

Toby obeyed, and in so doing Joe managed to catch him by the tail. It was certainly but slight assistance, but in some wonderful way it proved itself enough. Joe got out of the drift, and was able to return with the dog to the friendly shelter of the old wall. There, indeed, a pang of terror and dismay seized him. Both children, locked tightly in each other's arms, were sound asleep.

Asleep! Did it only mean sleep? That deathly pallor, that breathing which came slower and slower from the pretty parted lips! Already the little hands and feet were cold as death. Joe wondered if even now could succor come, would it be in time? He turned to the one living creature besides himself in this scene of desolation.

"Toby, " he said, "is there any house near? Toby, if we cannot soon get help for Cecile and Maurice, they will die. Think, Toby—think, good dog. "

Toby looked hard at Joe Barnes. Then he instantly sat down on his hind legs. Talk of dogs not having thoughts—Toby was considering hard just then. He felt a swelling sense of gratitude and even love for Joe for consulting him. He would put his dog's brain to good use now. Already he had thought of the friendly shelter of the old broken wall. Now he let his memory carry him back a trifle farther.

The Children's Pilgrimage

What else had those sharp eyes of his taken in besides the old wall? Why, surely, surely, just down in the hollow, not many yards away, a little smoke. Did not smoke mean a fire? Did not a fire mean a house? Did not a house mean warmth and food and comfort? Toby was on his feet in a moment, his tail wagging fast. He looked at Joe and ran on, the boy following carefully. Very soon Joe too saw, not only a thin column of smoke, but a thick volume, caused by a large wood fire, curling up amidst the whiteness of the snow. The moment his eyes rested on the welcome sight, he sent Toby back. "Go and lie on the children, Toby. Keep them as warm as you can, good dog, dear dog. " And Toby obeyed.

The Children's Pilgrimage

CHAPTER VIII.

A FARM IN NORMANDY.

A Norman gentleman farmer and his wife sat together in their snug parlor. Their children had all gone to bed an hour ago. Their one excellent servant was preparing supper in the kitchen close by. The warmly-curtained room had a look of almost English comfort. Children's books and toys lay scattered about. The good housemother, after putting these in order, sat down by her husband's side to enjoy the first quiet half hour of the day.

"What a fall of snow we have had, Marie, " said M. Dupois, "and how bitterly cold it is! Why, already the thermometer is ten degrees below zero. I hate such deep snow. I must go out with the sledge the first thing in the morning and open a road. "

Of course this husband and wife conversed in French, which is here translated.

"Hark! " said Mme. Dupois, suddenly raising her forefinger, "is not that something like a soft knocking? Can anyone have fallen down in this deep snow at our door? "

M. Dupois rose at once and pushed aside the crimson curtain from one of the windows.

"Yes, yes, " he exclaimed quickly, "you are right, my good wife; here is a lad lying on the ground. Run and get Annette to heat blankets and make the kitchen fire big. I will go round to the poor boy. "

When M. Dupois did at last reach Joe Barnes, he had only strength to murmur in his broken French, "Go and save the others under the old wall—two children and dog" —before he fainted away.

But his broken words were enough; he had come to people who had the kindest hearts in the world.

It seemed but a moment before he himself was reviving before the blazing warmth of a great fire, while the good farmer with three of his men was searching for the missing children.

The Children's Pilgrimage

They were not long in discovering them, with the dog himself, now nearly frozen, stretched across Cecile's body.

Poor little starving lambs! they were taken into warmth and shelter, though it was a long time before either Cecile or Maurice showed the faintest signs of life.

Maurice came to first, Cecile last. Indeed so long was she unconscious, so unavailing seemed all the warm brandy that was poured between her lips, that Mme. Dupois thought she must be dead.

The farmer's children, awakened by the noise, had now slipped downstairs in their little nightdresses. And when at last Cecile's blue eyes opened once more on this world, it was to look into the bright black orbs of a little Norman maiden of about her own age.

"Oh, look, mamma! Look! her eyes open, she sees! she lives! she moves! Ah, mother! how pleased I am. "

The little French girl cried in her joy, and Cecile watched her wonderingly, After a time she asked in a feeble, fluttering voice:

"Please is this heaven? Have we two little children really got to heaven? "

Her English words were only understood by Mme. Dupois, and not very perfectly by her. She told the child that she was not in heaven, but in a kind earthly home, where she need not think, but just eat something and then go to sleep.

"And oh, mamma! How worn her little shoes are! and may I give her my new hat, mamma? " asked the pretty and pitying little Pauline.

"In the morning, my darling. In the morning we will see to all that. Now the poor little wanderers must have some nice hot broth, and then they shall sleep here by the kitchen fire, "

Strange to say, notwithstanding the terrible hardships they had undergone, neither Cecile nor Maurice was laid up with rheumatic fever. They slept soundly in the warmth and comfort of the delicious kitchen, and awoke the next morning scarcely the worse for their grave danger and peril.

The Children's Pilgrimage

And now followed what might have been called a week in the Palace Beautiful for these little pilgrims. For while the snow lasted, and the weather continued so bitterly cold, neither M. nor Mme. Dupois would hear of their leaving them. With their whole warm hearts these good Christian people took in the children brought to them by the snow. Little Pauline and her brother Charles devoted themselves to Cecile and Maurice, and though their mutual ignorance of the only language the others could speak was owned to be a drawback, yet they managed to play happily and to understand a great deal; and here, had Cecile confided as much of her little story to kind Mme. Dupois as she had done to Joe Barnes, all that follows need never have been written. But alas! again that dread, that absolute terror that her purse of gold, if discovered, might be taken from her, overcame the poor little girl; so much so that, when Madame questioned her in her English tone as to her life's history, and as to her present pilgrimage, Cecile only replied that she was going through France on her way to the South, that she had relations in the South. Joe, when questioned, also said that he had a mother and a brother in the South, and that he was taking care of Cecile and Maurice on their way there.

Mme. Dupois did not really know English well, and Cecile's reserve, joined to her few words of explanation, only puzzled her. As both she and her husband were poor, and could not, even if it were desirable, adopt the children, there seemed nothing for it but, when the weather cleared, to let them continue on their way.

"There is one thing, however, we can do to help them," said M. Dupois. "I have decided to sell that corn and hay in Paris, and as the horses are just eating their heads off with idleness just now in their stables, the men shall take the wagons there instead of having the train expenses; the children therefore can ride to Paris in the wagons."

"That will take nearly a week, will it not, Gustave?" asked Mme. Dupois.

"It will take three or four days, but I will provision the men. Yes, I think it the best plan, and the surest way of disposing advantageously of the hay and corn. The children may be ready to start by Monday. The roads will be quite passable then."

So it was decided, and so it came to pass; Charles and Pauline assuring Joe, who in turn informed Cecile and Maurice, that the delights of riding in one of their papa's wagons passed all description. Pauline gave Cecile not only a new hat but new boots and a new frock. Maurice's scanty and shabby little wardrobe was also put in good repair, nor was poor Joe neglected, and with tears and blessing on both sides, these little pilgrims parted from those who had most truly proved to them good Samaritans.

CHAPTER IX.

O MINE ENEMY!

Whatever good Cecile's purse of gold might be to her ultimately, at present it was but a source of peril and danger.

Had anyone suspected the child of carrying about so large a treasure, her life even might have been the forfeit. Joe Barnes knew this well, and he was most careful that no hint as to the existence of the purse should pass his lips.

During the week the children spent at the happy Norman farm all indeed seemed very safe, and yet even there, there was a secret, hidden danger. A danger which would reveal itself by and by.

As I have said, it was arranged that the little party should go to Paris in M. Dupois' wagons; and the night before their departure Joe had come to Cecile, and begged her during their journey, when it would be impossible for them to be alone, and when they must be at all times more or less in the company of the men who drove and managed the wagons, to be most careful not to let anyone even suspect the existence of the purse. He even begged of her to let him take care of it for her until they reached Paris. But when she refused to part with it, he got her to consent that he should keep enough silver out of its contents to pay their slight expenses on the road.

Very slight these expenses would be, for kind M. Dupois had provisioned the wagons with food, and at night they would make a comfortable shelter. Still Cecile so far listened to Joe as to give him some francs out of her purse.

She had an idea that it was safest in the hiding place next her heart, where her stepmother had seen her place it, and she had made a firm resolve that, if need be, her life should be taken before she parted with this precious purse of gold. For the Russia-leather purse represented her honor to the little girl.

But, as I said, an unlooked-for danger was near—a danger, too, which had followed her all the way from Warren's Grove. Lydia Purcell had always been very particular whom she engaged to work on Mrs. Bell's farm, generally confining herself to men from the same

The Children's Pilgrimage

shire. But shortly before the old lady's death, being rather short of hands to finish the late harvest, a tramp from some distant part of the country had offered his services. Lydia, driven to despair to get a certain job finished before the weather finally broke, had engaged him by the week, had found him an able workman, and had not ever learned to regret her choice. The man, however, was disliked by his fellow-laborers. They called him a foreigner, and accused him of being a sneak and a spy. All these charges he denied stoutly; nevertheless they were true. The man was of Norman-French birth. He had drifted over to England when a lad. His parents had been respectable farmers in Normandy. They had educated their son; he was clever, and had the advantage of knowing both French and English thoroughly. Nevertheless he was a bad fellow. He consorted with rogues; he got into scrapes; many times he saw the inside of an English prison. But so plausible was Simon Watts—as he called himself on the Warren's Grove farm—that Aunt Lydia was completely taken in by him. She esteemed him a valuable servant, and rather spoiled him with good living. Simon, keeping his own birth for many reasons a profound secret, would have been more annoyed than gratified had he learned that the children on the farm were also French. He heard this fact through an accident on the night of their departure. It so happened that Simon slept in a room over the stable where the pony was kept; and Jane Parsons, in going for this pony to harness him to the light cart, awoke Simon from his light slumber. He came down to find her harnessing Bess; and on his demanding what she wanted with the pony at so very early an hour, she told him in her excitement rather more of the truth than was good for him to know.

"Those blessed children were being robbed of quite a large sum of money. They wanted the money to carry them back to France. It had been left to the little girl for a certain purpose by one who was dead. They were little French children, bless them! Lydia Purcell had a heart of stone, but she, Jane, had outwitted her. The children had got back their money, and Jane was about to drive them over to catch the night mail for London, where they should be well received and cared for by a friend of her own."

So explained Jane Parsons, and Simon Watts had listened; he wished for a few moments that he had known about this money a little sooner, and then, seeing that there seemed no help for it, as the children were being moved absolutely out of his reach, had dismissed the matter from his mind.

The Children's Pilgrimage

But, see! how strange are the coincidences of life! Soon after, Simon not only learned that all the servants on the farm were to change hands, that many of them would be dismissed, but he also learned some very disagreeable news in connection with the police, which would make it advisable for him to make himself scarce at a moment's notice. He vanished from Warren's Grove, and not being very far from Dover, worked his way across the Channel in a fishing-smack, and once more, after an absence of ten years, trod his native shores.

Instantly he dropped his character as an Englishman, and became as French as anyone about him. He walked to Caen, found out M. Dupois, and was engaged on his farm. Thus he once more, in the most unlooked-for manner, came directly across the paths of Cecile and Maurice.

But a further queer thing was to happen. Watts now calling himself Anton, being better educated than his fellow-laborers, and having always a wonderful power of impressing others with his absolute honesty, was thought a highly desirable person by M. Dupois to accompany his head-steward to Paris, and assist him in the sale of the great loads of hay and corn. Cecile and Maurice did not know him in the least. He was now dressed in the blouse of a French peasant, and besides they had scarcely ever seen him at Warren's Grove.

But Anton, recognizing the children, thought about them day and night. He considered it a wonderful piece of luck that had brought these little pilgrims again across his path. He was an unscrupulous man, he was a thief, he resolved that the children's money should be his. He had, however, some difficulties to encounter. Watching them closely, he saw that Cecile never paid for anything. That, on all occasions, when a few sous were needed, Joe was appealed to, and from Joe's pocket would the necessary sum be forthcoming.

He, therefore, concluded that Cecile had intrusted her money to Joe. Had he not been so very sure of this—had he for a moment believed that a little child so helpless and so young as Cecile carried about with her so much gold—I am afraid he would have simply watched his opportunity, have stifled the cries of the little creature, have torn her treasure from her grasp, and decamped. But Anton believed that Joe was the purse-bearer, and Joe was a more formidable person to deal with. Joe was very tall and strong for his age; whereas Anton

The Children's Pilgrimage

was a remarkably little and slender man. Joe, too, watched the children day and night like a dragon. Anton felt that in a hand-to-hand fight Joe would have the best of it. Also, to declare his knowledge of the existence of the purse, he would have to disclose his English residence, and his acquaintance with the English tongue. That fact once made known might have seriously injured his prospects with M. Dupois' steward, and, in place of anything better, he wished to keep in the good graces of this family for the present.

Still so clever a person as Anton, *alias* Watts, could go warily to work, and after thinking it all over, he decided to make himself agreeable to Joe. In their very first interview he set his own mind completely at rest as to the fact that the children carried money with them; that the large sum spoken of by Jane Parsons was still intact, and still in their possession.

Not that poor Joe had revealed a word; but when Anton led up to the subject of money there was an eager, too eager avoidance of the theme, joined to a troubled and anxious expression in his boyish face, which told the clever and bad man all he wanted.

In their second long talk together, he learned little by little the boy's own history. Far more than he had cared to confide to Cecile did Joe tell to Anton of his early life, of his cruel suffering as a little apprentice to his bad master, of his bitter hardships, of his narrow escapes, finally of his successful running away. And now of the hope which burned within him night and day; the hope of once more seeing his mother, of once more being taken home to his mother's heart.

"I'd rather die than give it up, " said poor Joe in conclusion, and when he said these words with sudden and passionate fervor, wicked Anton felt that the ball, as he expressed it, was at his feet.

Anton resolved so to work on Joe's fears, so to trade on his affections for his mother and his early home, and if necessary, so to threaten to deliver him up to his old master, who could punish him for running away, that Joe himself, to set himself free, would part with Cecile's purse of gold.

The bad man could scarcely sleep with delight as he formed his schemes; he longed to know how much the purse contained—of course in his eagerness he doubled the sum it really did possess.

The Children's Pilgrimage

He now devoted all his leisure time to the little pilgrims, and all the little party made friends with him except Toby. But wise Toby looked angry when he saw him talking to Cecile, and pretending that he was learning some broken English from her pretty lips.

When they got to Paris, Anton promised to provide the children with both cheap and comfortable lodgings. He had quite determined not to lose sight of them until his object was accomplished.

CHAPTER X.

WARNED OF GOD IN A DREAM.

And now a strange thing happened to Cecile, something which shows, I think, very plainly how near the heavenly Guide really was to His little wandering lamb.

After nearly a week spent on the road M. Dupois' wagons reached Paris in perfect safety, and then Anton, according to his promise, took the three children and their dog to lodge with a friend of his.

M. Dupois' steward made no objection to this arrangement, for Anton seemed a most steady and respectable man, and the children had all made great friends with him.

Chuckling inwardly, Anton led his little charges to a part of Paris called the Cite. This was where the very poor lived, and Anton guessed it would best suit his purpose. The houses were very old and shabby, most of them consisting of only two stories, though a few could even boast of four. These wretched and dirty houses were quite as bad as any London slums. Little particular Maurice declared he did not like the nasty smells, but on Anton informing Cecile that lodgings would be very cheap here, she made up her mind to stay for at least a night. Anton took the children up to the top of one of the tallest of the houses. Here were two fair-sized rooms occupied by an old man and woman. The man was ill and nearly blind, the woman was also too aged and infirm to work. She seemed, however, a good-natured old soul, and told Joe—for, of course, she did not understand a word of English—that she had lost five children, but though they were often almost starving, she could never bring herself to sell these little ones' clothes—she now pointed to them hanging on five peg—on the wall. The old couple had a grandson aged seventeen. This boy, thin and ragged as he was, had a face full of fun and mischief. "He picks up odd jobs, and so we manage to live, " said the old woman to Joe.

Both she and her husband were glad to take the children in, and promised to make them comfortable—which they did, after a fashion.

The Children's Pilgrimage

"We can stay here one night. We shall be quite rested and able to go on down south to-morrow, Joe, " said Cecile.

And Joe nodded, inwardly resolving that one night in such quarters should be all they should spend. For he felt that though of course Anton knew nothing about the existence of the purse, yet, that had it been known, it would not be long in Cecile's possession were she to remain there.

Poor Joe! he little guessed that Anton had heard and understood every word of Cecile's English, and was making up his mind just as firmly as Joe. His intention was that not one of that little band should leave the purlieus of the Cite until that purse with its precious contents was his.

The old couple, however, were really both simple and honest. They had no accommodation that night for Anton; consequently, for that first night Cecile's treasure was tolerably free from danger.

And now occurred that event which I must consider the direct intervention of the Guide Jesus on Cecile's behalf. This event was nothing more nor less than a dream. Now anyone may dream. Of all the common and unimportant things under the sun, dreams in our present day rank as the commonest, the most unimportant. No one thinks about dreams. People, if they have got any reputation for wisdom, do not even care to mention them. Quite true, but there are dreams and dreams; and I still hold to my belief that Cecile's dream was really sent to her direct from heaven.

For instance, there never was a more obstinate child than Cecile D'Albert. Once get an idea or a resolve firmly fixed in her ignorant and yet wise little head, and she would cling to it for bare life. Her dead stepmother's directions were as gospel to the little girl, and one of her directions was to keep the purse at all hazards. Not any amount of wise talking, not the most clear exposition of the great danger she ran in retaining it, could have moved her. She really loved Joe. But Joe's words would have been as nothing to her, had he asked her to transfer the precious leather purse to his care. And yet a dream converted Cecile, and induced her to part with her purse without any further difficulty. Lying on a heap of straw by Maurice's side, Cecile dreamt in that vivid manner which makes a vision of the night so real.

The Children's Pilgrimage

Jesus the Guide came into the room. It was no longer a man or a woman, or even a kind boy sent by Him. No, no, He came Himself. He came radiant and yet human, with a face something as Cecile imagined her own mother's face, and He said, "Lovedy's gold is in danger, it is no longer safe with you. Take it to-morrow to the Faubourg St. G— —. There is an English lady there. Her name will be on the door of a house. Ask to see her. She will be at home. Give her Lovedy's money to keep for her. The money will be quite safe then. "

Immediately after this extraordinary dream Cecile awoke, nor could she close her eyes again that night. The Faubourg St. G— — kept dancing before her eyes. She seemed to see a shabby suburb, and then a long and rather narrow street, and when her eyes were quite weary with all the strange French names, there came a plain unmistakable English name, and Cecile felt that the lady who bore this name must be the caretaker of the precious purse for the present. Yes, she must go to the Faubourg St. G— —. She must find it without delay. Cecile believed in her dream most fervently. She was quite sure there was such a part of the great city—there was such a lady. Had not Jesus the Guide come Himself to tell her to go to her?

Cecile, reading her New Testament for the first time, had vivid memories about its wonderful stories. What, alas! is often hackneyed to older and so-called wiser folks, came with power to the little child. Cecile was not surprised that she should be told what to do in a dream. The New Testament was full of accounts of people who were warned of God in a dream. She, too, had been sent this divine warning. Nothing should prevent her acting upon it. In the morning she resolved to tell Joe all about her vision, and then ask him to take her without delay to the English lady who lived in the Faubourg St. G— —. But when she got up no Joe was visible, and the old woman managed to convey to her that he had gone out to make some inquiries about their journey south, and would not be back for some hours. She then poured out a decoction which she called coffee and gave it to the children, and Cecile drank it off, wondering, as she did so, how she, who did not know a word of French, could find her way alone to the Faubourg St. G— —. As she thought, she raised her eyes and encountered the fixed, amused, and impudent gaze of the old woman's grandson. This lad had taken a fancy to Cecile and Maurice from the first. He now sat opposite to them as they ate. His legs were crossed under him, his hands were folded across his breast. He stared hard. He did nothing but stare. But this occupation seemed to afford him the fullest content.

Maurice said, "Nasty rude man, " and shook his hand at him.

But Pericard, not understanding a single word of English, only laughed, and placidly continued his amusement.

Suddenly a thought came to Cecile:

"Pericard, " she said, "Faubourg St. G——. "

Pericard nodded, and looked intelligent.

"Oui, " he answered, "Faubourg St. G——. "

Cecile then got up, took his hand, and pointed first to the window then to the door. Then she touched herself and Maurice, and again said:

"Faubourg St. G——. "

Pericard nodded again. He understood her perfectly.

"Oui, oui, Mam'selle, " he said, and now he took Cecile's hand, and Cecile took Maurice's, and they went down into the street. They had only turned a corner, when Anton came up to the lodging. The old woman could but inform him that the children had gone out with Pericard. That she did not know when they would be back. That Joe also had gone away quite early.

Anton felt inclined to swear. He had made a nice little plan for this morning. He had sent Joe away on purpose. There was nothing now for it but to wait the children's return, as it would be worse than useless to pursue them over Paris. He only hoped, as he resigned himself to his fate, that they would return before Joe did.

CHAPTER XI.

THE FAUBOURG ST. G— —.

Pericard was a genuine French lad. Perhaps few boys had undergone more hardships in his life; he had known starvation, he had known blows, he had felt in their extremity both winter's cold and summer's heat. True, his old grandmother gave him what she could, both of love and kindness. But the outside world had been decidedly rough on Pericard. An English boy would have shown this on his face. He would have appeared careworn, he would scarcely have seemed gay. Very far otherwise, however, was it with this French lad. His merry eyes twinkled continually. He laughed, he whistled, he danced. His misfortunes seemed to have no power to enter into him; they only swept around.

Had he then a shallow heart? Who can tell? He was a genuine specimen of the ordinary Paris gamin.

Pericard now much enjoyed the idea of taking Cecile and Maurice out to the rather distant suburb called the Faubourg St. G— —.

He knew perfectly how to get there. He knew that Cecile, who understood no French wanted to find herself there. He understood nothing, and cared less for what her object was in going there.

He was to be her guide. He would lead her safely to this faubourg, and then back again to his grandmother's house.

Pericard, for all his rags, had something of a gentleman's heart.

He enjoyed guiding this very fair and pretty little lady.

Of course, Maurice and Toby came too. But Cecile was Pericard's princess on this occasion.

As they walked along, it occurred to him how very pleasant it would be to treat his princess—to buy a dainty little breakfast from one or more of the venders who spread their tempting condiments on different stalls, as they passed. He might purchase some fruit, some chocolate, a roll, some butter. Then! how good these things would be, shared between him and the princess, and, of course, the little brother and the good dog, and eaten in that same faubourg, where the air must be a little better, purer than in Paris proper. If only he had the necessary sous?

Alas! he only possessed one centime, and that would buy no dainties worth mentioning.

As the funny little group walked along, Pericard steering straight and clear in the right direction, they saw an old Jew clothesman walking just in front of them. There was nothing particular about this old fellow. He was, doubtless, doing as lucrative a trade in Paris as elsewhere. But, nevertheless, Pericard's bright eyes lighted up at sight of him.

He felt hastily once again in his ragged coat; there rested his one centime. Nodding to Cecile and Maurice, and making signs that he would return instantly, he rushed after the old Jew—tore his coat from his back, and offered it for sale.

It was an old garment, greasy and much worn, but the lining was still good, and, doubtless, it helped to keep Pericard warm. Intent, however, now on the trick he meant to play, he felt no cold.

The old Jew salesman, who never *on principle* rejected the possible making of even a few sous, stopped to examine the shabby article. In deliberation as to its age, etc., he contrived also to feel the condition of its pockets. Instantly, as the boy hoped, he perceived the little piece of money. His greedy old face lit up. After thinking a moment, he offered one franc for the worthless garment.

Pericard could not part with it for a franc. Then he offered two. Pericard stuck out for three. He would give the greasy and ragged old coat for three francs. The Jew felt the pocket again. It was a large sum to risk for what in itself was not worth many sous; but, then, he might not have such a chance again. Finally, he made up his mind, and put three francs into Pericard's eager hand.

Instantly the old fellow pounced upon his hidden treasure. Behold! a solitary—a miserable centime. His rage knew no bounds! He called it an infamous robbery! He shouted to Pericard to take back his rags!

Whistling and laughing, the French boy exclaimed: "Pas si bete! " and then returned to the children.

The Children's Pilgrimage

Now, indeed, was Pericard happy. He nodded most vigorously to Cecile. He showed her his three francs. He tossed them in the air. He spun them before him on the dirty road. It seemed wonderful that he did not lose his treasures. Finally, after indulging in about six somersaults in succession, he deposited the coins in his mouth, and became grave after his own fashion again.

Now must he and the English children, for such he believed them, have the exquisite delight of spending this precious money. They turned into a street which resembled more an ordinary market than a street. Here were provisions in abundance; here were buyers and sellers; here was food of all descriptions. Each vender of food had his own particular stall, set up under his own particular awning. Pericard seemed to know the place well. Maurice screamed with delight at the sight of so much delicious food, and even patient Toby licked his chops, and owned to himself that their morning's breakfast had been very scanty.

Cecile alone—too intent on her mission to be hungry—felt little interest in the tempting stalls.

Pericard, however, began to lay in provisions judiciously. Here in this Rue de Sevres, were to be bought fruit, flowers, vegetables of all kinds, butter, cheese, cream, and even fish.

"Bonjour, Pere Bison, " said Pericard, who, feeling himself rich, made his choice with care and deliberation.

This old man sold turkey eggs, cream-cheese, and butter. Pericard purchased a tiny piece of deliciously fresh-looking butter, a small morsel of cream-cheese, and three turkey eggs; at another stall he bought some rolls; at a third a supply of fresh and rosy apples. Thus provided, he became an object of immense attraction to Toby, and, it must be owned, also to Maurice.

As they walked along, in enforced silence, Pericard indulged in delicious meditations. What a moment that would be when they sucked those turkeys eggs! how truly delightful to see his dainty little princess enjoying her morsel of cream-cheese!

At last, after what seemed an interminable time, they reached the faubourg dreamed of so vividly the night before by Cecile. It was a large place, and also a very poor neighborhood.

The Children's Pilgrimage

Having arrived at their destination. Pericard pointed to the name on a lamp-post, spreading out his arms with a significant gesture; then, letting them drop to his sides, stood still. His object was accomplished. He now waited impatiently for the moment when they might begin their feast.

Cecile felt a strange fluttering at her heart; the place was so large, the streets so interminable. Where, how, should she find the lady with the English name?

Pericard was now of no further use. He must follow where she led. She walked on, her steps flagging—despondency growing at her heart.

Was her dream then not real after all? Ah, yes! it must, it must be a Heaven-sent warning. Was not Joseph warned of God in a dream? Was he not told where to go and what to do? —just as Cecile herself had been told by the blessed Lord Himself. Only an angel had come to Joseph, but Jesus Himself had counseled Cecile. Yes, she was now in the faubourg—she must presently find the lady bearing the English name.

The Faubourg St. G—— was undoubtedly a poor suburb, but just even when Pericard's patience began to give way, the children saw a row of houses taller and better than any they had hitherto come across. The English lady must live there. Cecile again, with renewed hope and confidence, walked down the street. At the sixth house she stopped, and a cry of joy, of almost rapture, escaped her lips. Amid all the countless foreign words and names stood a modest English one on a neat door painted green. In the middle of a shining brass plate appeared two very simple, very common words—*"Miss Smith.*
"

The Children's Pilgrimage

CHAPTER XII.

THE WINSEY FROCK.

Her voice almost trembling with suppressed excitement, Cecile turned to her little brother.

"Maurice, Miss Smith lives here. She is an English lady. I must see her. You will stay outside with Pericard, Maurice; and Toby will take care of you. Don't go away. Just walk up and down. I shan't be long; and, Maurice, you won't go away? "

"No" answered Maurice, "I won't run away. I will eat some of that nice breakfast without waiting for you, Cecile; for I am hungry, but I won't run away. "

Then Maurice took Pericard's hand. Toby wagged his tail knowingly, and Cecile ran up the steps of Miss Smith's house. A young girl, with the round fresh face of old England, answered her modest summons.

"Yes, " she said, "Miss Smith was at home. " She would inquire if she could see the little girl from London. She invited Cecile to step into the hall; and a moment or two later showed her into a very small, neatly furnished parlor. This small room was quite in English fashion, and bore marks of extreme neatness, joined to extremely slender means.

Cecile stood by the round table in the center of the room. She had now taken her purse from the bosom of her dress, and when Miss Smith entered, she came up to her at once, holding it in her hand.

"If you please, " said Cecile, "Jesus the Guide says you will take care of this for me. He sent me to you, and said you would take great, great care of my money. 'Tis all quite right. Will you open the purse, please? 'Tis a Russia-leather purse, and there's forty pounds in it, and about eleven or twelve more, I think. I must have some to take me and Maurice and Toby down south. But Jesus says you will take great care of the rest. "

"Child, " said Miss Smith. She was a very little woman, with a white, thin, and worn face. She looked nearer fifty than forty. Her hair was scanty and gray. When Cecile offered her the purse she flushed painfully, stepped back a pace or two, and pushed it from her.

"Child, " she repeated, "are you mad, or is it Satan is sending you here? Pretty little girl, with the English tongue, do you know that I am starving? "

"Oh! " said Cecile. Her face showed compassion, but she did not attempt to take up her purse. On the contrary, she left it on the table close to Miss Smith, and retreated to the farther side herself.

"Starving means being very, very hungry, " said Cecile. "I know what that means, just a little. It is a bad feeling. I am sorry. There is a turkey egg waiting for me outside. I will fetch it for you in a moment. But you are quite wrong in saying it was Satan sent me to you. I don't know anything about Satan. It was the blessed, blessed Jesus the Guide sent me. He came last night in a dream. He told me to go to the Faubourg St. G—— and I should find an English lady, and she would take great care of my Russia-leather purse. It was a true warning, just as Joseph's dream was true. He was warned of God in a dream, just as I was last night. "

"And I am the only Englishwoman in the faubourg, " said Miss Smith. "I have lived here for ten years now, and I never heard of any other. I teach, or, rather, I did teach English in a Pension de Demoiselles close by, and I have been dismissed. I was thought too old-fashioned. I can't get any more employment, and I had just broken into my last franc piece when you came. I might have done without food, but Molly was *so* hungry. Molly is going to-morrow, and I shall be alone. Yes, little English girl, you do right to reprove me. I, too, have loved the Lord Jesus. Sit down! Sit down on that chair, and tell me, in my own dear tongue, the story of that purse. "

"I am not an English girl, " said Cecile; "I am French; I come from the south, from the Pyrenees; but my father brought me to England when I was two years old, and I don't know any French. My father died, and I had a stepmother; and my stepmother died, and when she was dying she gave me a charge. It was a great charge, and it weighs heavily on my heart, and makes me feel very old. My stepmother had a daughter who ran away from her when she married my father. My stepmother thinks she went to France, and got lost in France, and she gave me a purse of money—some to give to Lovedy, and some to spend in looking for her. I feel that Lovedy

The Children's Pilgrimage

has gone south, and I am going down south, too, to find her. I, and my little brother, and our dog, and a big, kind boy—we are all going south to find Lovedy. And last night Jesus the Guide came to me in a dream, and told me that my purse was in danger, and He told me to come to you. Satan had nothing at all to say to it. It was Jesus sent me to you. "

"I believe you, child, " said Miss Smith. "You bring the strangest tale, but I believe you. You bring a purse containing a lot of money to a starving woman. Well, I never was brought so low as not to be honest yet. How much money is in the purse, little girl? "

"There are four ten-pound notes—that makes forty pounds, " said Cecile—"that is Lovedy's money; there are about eleven pounds of the money I must spend. You must give me that eleven pounds, please, Miss Smith, and you must keep the forty pounds very, *very* safely until I come for it, or send for it. "

"What is your name, little girl? "

"Cecile D'Albert. "

"Well, Cecile, don't you think that if you had a dream about the forty pounds being in danger, that the eleven pounds will be in danger too? Someone must have guessed you had that money, little one, and and if they can't get hold of the forty pounds, they will take the eleven. "

Cecile felt herself growing a trifle pale.

"I never thought of that, " she said. "I cannot look for Lovedy without a little money. What shall I do, Miss Smith? "

"Let me think, " said Miss Smith.

She rested her chin on her hand and one or two puckers came into her brow, and she screwed up her shrewd little mouth. After a moment or two her face brightened.

"Is the money English money, little girl? " she said.

"Yes, " answered Cecile; "the captain on board the boat from England did change some, but all the French money is gone now. "

The Children's Pilgrimage

"That won't do at all, Cecile; you must have French money. Now, my dear, will you kindly take that eleven pounds out of your purse and reckon it before me? "

Cecile did so—eleven sovereigns lay glittering and tempting on Miss Smith's table.

"There, child, I am going to put on my bonnet and shawl, and I shall take that money out with me, and be back again in a few moments. You wait here, Cecile, I will bring back French money; you watch your purse until I return. "

While Miss Smith was out, there came a ring to the door bell, and the little fresh-colored English servant brought in a letter, and laid it beside the purse which Cecile stood near, but did not offer to touch.

In about twenty minutes Miss Smith reappeared. She looked excited, and even cheerful.

"It does me good to help one of the Lord's little ones, " she said, "and it does me good to hear the English tongue; except from Molly, I never hear it now, and Molly goes to-morrow. Well, never mind. Now, Cecile, listen to me. Do you see this bag? It is big, and heavy, it is full of your money; twenty-five francs for every sovereign—two hundred and seventy-five francs in all. You could not carry that heavy bag about with you; it would be discovered, and you would be robbed at once.

"But I have hit on a plan. See! I have brought in another parcel —this parcel contains cotton wool. I perceive that little frock you have on has three tucks in it. I am going to unpick those tucks, and line them softly with cotton wool, and lay the francs in the cotton wool. I will do it cleverly, and no one will guess that any money could be hidden in that common little winsey frock. Now, child, you slip it off, and I will put the money in, and I will give you a needle and thread and a nice little sharp scissors, and every night when folks are quite sound asleep, and you are sure no one is looking, you must unpick enough of one of the tucks to take out one franc, or two francs, according as you want them; only be sure you sew the tuck up again. The money will make the frock a trifle heavy, and you must never take it off your back whatever happens until you get to the English girl; but I can hit on no better plan, "

"I think it is a lovely, lovely plan, " said Cecile, and then she slipped off the little frock, and Miss Smith wrapped her carefully in an old shawl of her own; and the next two hours were spent in skillfully lining the tucks with their precious contents.

When this was finished Miss Smith got a hot iron, and ironed the tucks so skillfully that they looked as flat as they had done before. Some of the money, also, she inserted in the body of the frock, and thus enriched, it was once more put on by Cecile.

"Now, Cecile, " said Miss Smith, "I feel conceited, for I don't believe anyone will ever think of looking there for your money; and I am to keep the Russia-leather purse and the forty pounds and they are for an English girl called Lovedy. How shall I know her when she comes, or will you only return to fetch them yourself, little one? "

"I should like that best" said Cecile; "but I might die, or be very ill, and then Lovedy would never get her money. Miss Smith, perhaps you will write something on a little bit of paper, and then give the paper to me, and if I cannot come myself I will give the paper to Lovedy, or somebody else; when you see your own bit of paper again, then you will know that you are to give Lovedy's purse to the person who gives you the paper. "

"That is not a bad plan, " said Miss Smith; "at least, " she added, "I can think of no better. I will write something then for you, Cecile. "

She forthwith provided herself with a sheet of paper and a pen and wrote as follows:

"Received this day of Cecile D'Albert the sum of Forty Pounds, in four Bank of England notes, inclosed in a Russia-leather purse. Will return purse and money to the bearer of this paper whoever that person may be.

"So help me God. HANNAH SMITH. "

As Hannah Smith added those words, "So help me God, " a deep flush came to her pale face and the thin hand that held the pen trembled.

"There, Cecile, " she said, "you must keep that little piece of paper even more carefully than the money, for anyone who secured this might claim the money. I will sew it into your frock myself. " Which the good soul did; and then the old maid blessed the child, and she went away.

Long after Cecile had left her, Miss Smith sat on by the table—that purse untouched by her side.

"A sudden and sore temptation, " she said, at last, aloud. "But it did not last. So help me God, it will never return—SO HELP ME GOD. "

Then she fell on her knees and began to pray, and as she prayed she wept.

It was nearly an hour before the lonely Englishwoman rose from her knees. When she did so, she took up the purse to put it by. In doing this, she for the first time noticed the letter which had arrived when she was out. She opened it, read it hastily through. Then Miss Smith, suddenly dropping both purse and letter fell on her knees again.

The letter contained the offer of a much better situation as English teacher than the one she had been deprived of. Thus did God send both the temptation and the deliverance almost simultaneously.

CHAPTER XIII.

A MIDNIGHT SEARCH.

Anton had to wait a long time, until he felt both cross and impatient, and when at last Cecile and Maurice returned to the funny little attic in the Cite, Joe almost immediately followed them.

Joe told the children that he had made very exact inquiries, and that he believed they might start for the south the next day. He spoke, of course, in English, and, never supposing that Anton knew a word of that tongue was at no pains to refrain from discussing their plans in his presence.

Anton, apparently engaged in puffing a pipe in a corner of the room with his eyes half shut, looking stupid and half asleep, of course took in every word.

"They would start early the next morning. Oh, yes! they were more than welcome; they might go to the south, the farther from him the better, always provided that he secured the purse first. "

As he smoked, he laid his plans. He was quite sure that one of the children had the purse. He suspected the one to be Joe. But to make sure, he determined to search all three.

He must search the children that night. How should he accomplish his search?

He thought. Bad ideas came to him. He went out.

He went straight to a chemist's, and bought a small quantity of a certain powder. This powder, harmless in its after-effects, would cause very sound slumber. He brought in, and contrived, unseen by anyone, to mix it in the soup which the old grandmother was preparing for the evening meal. All—Pericard, Toby—all should partake of this soup. Then all would sleep soundly, and the field would be open for him; for he, Anton, would be careful not to touch any.

He had made arrangements before with the old grandmother to have a shake-down for the night in one of her rooms; from there it would be perfectly easy to step into the little attic occupied by the children, and secure the precious purse.

His plans were all laid to perfection, and when he saw six hungry people and a dog partaking eagerly of good Mme. Pericard's really nourishing soup, he became quite jocund in his glee.

An hour afterward the drugged food had taken effect. There was not a sound in the attics. Anton waited yet another hour, then, stepping softly in his stockinged feet, he entered the little room, where he felt sure the hidden treasure awaited him.

He examined Joe first. The lad was so tired, and the effect of the drug so potent, that Anton could even turn him over without disturbing his slumbers. But, alas! feel as he would, there was no purse about Joe—neither concealed about his person, nor hidden under his pillow, was any trace of what Anton hoped and longed to find. Half a franc he took, indeed, out of the lad's pocket—half a franc and a couple of centimes; but that was all.

Anton had to own to himself that whoever had the purse, Joe had it not.

He went over to the next bed, and examined little Maurice. He even turned Toby about.

Last of all, he approached where Cecile lay. Cecile, secure in her perfect trust in the heavenly Guide, sure of the righteousness of her great quest, was sleeping as such little ones sleep. Blessed dreams were filling her peaceful slumbers, and there is no doubt that angels were guarding her.

The purity of the white face on which the moon shone filled the bad man who approached her with a kind of awe. He did not call the feeling that possessed him by that name; nevertheless, he handled the child reverently.

He felt under the pillow, he felt in the little frock. Ah! good and clever Miss Smith! so thoroughly, so well had she done her work, that no touch of hard metal came to Anton's fingers, no suspicion of the money so close to him entered his head.

The Children's Pilgrimage

Having heard at Warren's Grove of a purse, it never occurred to him to expect money in any other way. No trace of that Russia-leather purse was to be found about Cecile. After nearly an hour spent in prowling about, he had to leave the children's room discomfited; discomfited truly, and also not wholly unpunished. For Toby, who had been a good deal satisfied with rolls and morsels of butter, in the feast made earlier in the day by Pericard, had taken so sparingly of the soup that he was very slightly drugged, and Anton's movements, becoming less cautious as he perceived how heavy was the sleep over the children, at last managed to wake the dog. What instinct was over Toby I know not. But he hated Anton. He now followed him unperceived from the room, and, just as he got into the passage outside, managed to insert his strong teeth deep into his leg. The pain was sharp and terrible, and the thief dared not scream. He hit Toby a blow, but not a very hard one, for the dog was exactly behind him. Toby held on for a moment or two, ascertained that the wound was both deep and painful, then retreated to take up his post by Cecile's pillow. Nor did the faithful creature close his eyes again that night. Anton, too, lay awake. Angry and burning were his revengeful thoughts. He was more determined than ever to find the purse, not to let his victims escape him. As to Toby, he would kill him if he could. There seemed little doubt now that the children had not the purse with them. Still Anton remembered Joe's confused manner when he had sounded him on the subject of money. Anton felt sure that Joe knew where the purse was. How could he force his secret from the lad? How could he make him declare where the gold was hidden? A specious, plausible man, Anton had, as I before said, made friends with Joe. Joe in a moment of ill-advised confidence had told to Anton his own sad history. Anton pondering over it now in the darkness, for there was no moon shining into *his* bedroom, felt that he could secure a very strong hold over the lad.

Joe had been apprenticed to a Frenchman, who taught him to dance and play the fiddle. Anton wondered what the law bound these apprentices to. He had a hazy idea that, if they ran away, the punishment was severe. He hoped that Joe had broken the law. Anton resolved to learn more about these apprentice laws. For this purpose he rose very early in the morning and went out. He was absent for about two hours. When he returned he had learned enough to make up a bad and frightening tale. Truly his old plans had been defeated in the night. But in the morning he had made even worse than these. He came in to find the children awakening from the effects of their long slumber, and Joe audibly lamenting that they were not already on their way.

"Not yet, " said Anton, suddenly dropping his French and speaking to the astonished children in English as good as their own, "I have a word to say about that same going away. You come out with me for a bit, my lad. "

Joe, still heavy from the drug, and too amazed to refuse, even if he wished to do so, stumbled to his feet and obeyed.

Cecile and Maurice chatted over the wonderful fact of Anton knowing English, and waited patiently. There was no Pericard to amuse them to-day; he had gone out long ago. They waited one hour—two hours—three hours, still no Joe appeared. At the end of about four hours there was a languid step on the stairs, and the lad who had gone away—God knows with how tranquil a heart—reappeared.

Where was his gayety? Where had the light in his dark eyes vanished to? His hands trembled. Fear was manifest on his face. He came straight up to Cecile, and clasping her little hands between both his own, which trembled violently, spoke.

"Oh, Cecile! he's a bad man. He's a bad, bad man, and I am ruined. We're all ruined, Cecile. Is there any place we can hide in—is there any place? I must speak to you, and he'll be back in half an hour. I must speak to you, Cecile, before he comes back. "

"Let's run away, " said Cecile promptly. "Let's run away at once before he comes again. There must be lots of hiding places in Paris. Oh! here's Pericard. Pericard, I know, is faithful. You ask Pericard to hide us, Joe. To hide us at once before Anton comes back. "

CHAPTER XIV.

A PLAN.

Cecile, impelled by some instinct, had said: "I know Pericard is faithful."

Joe, now turning to the French boy, repeated these few words in his best French:

"She says she knows you are faithful. We are in great danger—in great danger from that bad man Anton. Will you hide us and not betray us?"

To this appeal Cecile had added power by coming up and taking Pericard's hand. He gave a look of devotion to his little princess, nodded to Joe, and, bidding them all follow him, and quickly, left the room.

Down the stairs he took the children, down, down, down! at last they reached the cellars. The cellars, too, were full of human beings; but interested in their own most varied pursuits and callings, they took little notice of the children. They went through one set of cellars, then through another, then through a third. At the third Pericard stopped.

"You are safe here," he said. "These cellars have nothing to say to our house. No one lives in them. They are to be let next week. They are empty now. You will only have the company of the rats here. Don't be afraid of them. If you don't fight them they won't come nigh you, and, anyhow, Toby will keep 'em away. I'll be back when it grows dark. Don't stir till I return. Anton shan't find you here. Little Miss is right. Pericard will be faithful."

After having delivered this little speech in French, Pericard turned a rusty key in a lock behind the children, then let himself out by an underground passage directly into the street.

"Now, Joe," said Cecile, coming up at once to where the poor boy was standing, "we are safe here, safe for a little. What is the matter? What is wrong, dear Joe?"

The Children's Pilgrimage

"Maurice must not hear, " said Joe; "it will only make things still harder if little Maurice hears what I have got to say. "

"Maurice will not care to hear. See, how sleepy he looks? There is some straw in that corner, some nice clean straw; Maurice shall lie down on it, and go to sleep. I can't make out why we are all so sleepy; but Maurice shall have a good sleep, and then you can talk to me. Toby will stay close to Maurice. "

To this arrangement Maurice himself made no objection. He could scarcely keep his eyes open, and the moment he found himself on the bed of straw was sound asleep.

Toby, in obedience to Cecile's summons, sat down by his side, and then the little girl returned to Joe.

"No one can hear us now. What is wrong, Jography? "

"This is wrong, " said Joe, in a low, despairing voice: "I'm a ruined lad. Ef I don't rob you, and become a thief, I'm a quite ruined lad. I'll never, never see my mother nor my brother Jean. I'm quite ruined, Missie, dear. "

"But how, Joe. How? "

"Missie, that man wot come wid us all the way from Normandy, he's a spy and a thief. He wants yer purse, Missie, darling, and he says as he'll get it come what may. He wor at that farm in Kent when you was there, and he heard all about the purse, and he wor determined to get it. That wor why he tried to make friends wid us, and would not let out as he knew a word of English. Then last night he put some'ut in the soup to make us hall sleep sound, and he looked for the purse and he could not find it; and this morning he called me away, to say as he knows my old master wot I served in Lunnon, and that I wor apprenticed quite proper to him, and that by the law I could not run away without being punished. He said, Anton did, that he would lock me hup in prison this werry day, and then go and find Massenger, and give me back to him. I am never, never to see my old mother now. For I'm to go to prison if I don't give up yer purse to Anton, Missie. "

The Children's Pilgrimage

"But you would not take the Russia-leather purse that I was given to take care of for Lovedy? You would rather be shut up in prison than touch my purse or gold? " said Cecile.

It was nearly dark in the cellar; but the child's eyes shining with a steadfast light, were looking full at Joe. He returned their gaze as steadfastly.

"Missie, dear, 'tis a hard thing to give up seeking of yer own mother, and to go back to blows and starvation. But Joe 'ull do it. He once said, Missie Cecile, that he'd rayther be cut in pieces nor touch that purse o' gold. This is like being cut in pieces. But I'll stand up to wot I said. I'll go wid Anton when he comes back. But wot puzzles me is, how he'll get the purse from you, Missie? and how ere you two little mites ever to find Lovedy without your Joe to guide yer? "

"Yes, Joe, you shall guide us; for now I have got something to say — such a wonderful, wonderful thing, Joe dear. "

Then Cecile related all about her strange dream, all about Pericard taking them to the Faubourg St. G——, then of her finding Miss Smith, of her intrusting the purse to Miss Smith, and finally of the clever, clever manner in which Miss Smith had sewn the money that was necessary to take them to the south of France into her little winsey frock. All this did Cecile tell with glowing cheeks and eager voice, and only one mistake did she make. For, trusting Joe fully, she showed him the little piece of paper which anyone presenting to Miss Smith could obtain the purse in exchange.

Poor Joe! he bitterly rued that knowledge by and by, but now his feelings were all thankfulness.

"Then Anton can't get the purse: you ha'n't got it to give to him! "

"No; and if he comes and finds us, I will tell him so my own self; it won't do him no good putting you in prison, for he shan't never get Lovedy's purse. "

"Thank God, " said Joe, in a tone of deep and great relief. "Oh! Missie, that's a good, good guide o' your'n, and poor Joe 'ull love Him now. "

The Children's Pilgrimage

"Yes, Jography, was it not lovely, lovely of Him? I know He means you to go on taking care of us little children; and, Jography, I'm only quite a little girl, but I've got a plan in my head, and you must listen. My Aunt Lydia wanted to get the purse; and me and Maurice, we ran away from her and afterward we saw her again in London, and she wanted our purse we were sure, and then we ran away again. Now, Joe, could not we run away this time too? Why should we see that wicked, wicked Anton any more? "

"Yes, Missie, but he's werry clever; werry clever indeed, Anton is, and he 'ud foller of us; he knows 'tis down south we're going, and he'd come down south too. "

"Yes; but, Joe, perhaps south is a big place, as big as London or Paris, it might not be so easy for him to find us; you might get safe back to your old mother and your good brother Jean, and I might see Lovedy before Anton had found us again, then we should not care what he did; and, Jography, what I've been thinking is that as we're in great danger, it can't be wrong to spend just a franc or two out of my winsey frock on you, and when Pericard comes back this evening I'll ask him to direct us to some place where a train can take us all a good bit of the way. You don't know how fast the train took me and Maurice and Toby to London, and perhaps it would take us a good bit of the way south so that Anton could not find us; that is my plan, Joe, and you won't have to go to prison, Joe, dear. "

CHAPTER XV.

AN ESCAPE.

It was very late, in fact quite night, when Pericard returned. By this time the rats had come out in troops, and even Toby could scarcely keep them at bay. He barked, however, loudly, and ran about, and so kept them from absolutely attacking the children. By this, however, he exposed them to another danger, for his noise must soon have been heard in the street above, and it was well for them that the cellar in which they were hiding was not in the same house with Anton.

It was, as I said, quite late at night when Pericard arrived. He let himself in, not by the entrance through which he had come previously, but by the underground passage. He carried a dark lantern in one hand, and a neat little basket in the other. Never was knight of old more eagerly welcomed than was this French boy now by the poor little prisoners. They were all cold and hungry, and the rushing and scraping of the rats had filled their little hearts with most natural alarm.

Pericard came in softly, and laying down his dark lantern proceeded to unpack the contents of the basket. It contained cold sausages, broken bits of meat, and some rolls buttered and cut in two: there was also a pint bottle of *vin ordinaire*.

Pericard broke the neck of the bottle on the cellar wall. He then gave the children a drink by turns in a little tin mug.

"And now, " he said in French, "we must be off. Anton is in the house; he is waiting for you all; he is roaring with anger and rage; he would be out looking for you, but luckily—or you could not escape —he is lame. The brave good dog bit him severely in the leg, and now he cannot walk; and the grandmere has to poultice his leg. He thinks I have gone to fetch you, for I pretend to be on his side. You have just to-night to get away in; but I don't answer for the morning, for Anton is so dying to get hold of Joe there that he will use his leg, however he suffers, after to-night. You have just this one short night in which to make your escape. "

The Children's Pilgrimage

Then Joe told Cecile's plan to Pericard, and Pericard nodded, and said it was good—only he could not help opening his eyes very widely at the idea of three such little beggars, as he termed the children, being able to afford the luxury of going by train. As, however, it was impossible and, dangerous to confide in him any further, and as Cecile had already given Joe the number of francs they thought they should require out of her frock, he had to bear his curiosity in silence.

Pericard, who was well up to Paris, and knew not only every place of amusement, nearly every stall-owner, nearly every trade, and every possible way of securing a sou, but also had in his head a fund of odd knowledge with regard to railway stations, could now counsel the children what station to go to, and even what train to take on their way south.

He said they would probably be in time if they started at once to catch a midnight train to Orleans; that for not too large a sum they might travel third-class to Orleans, which city they would reach the next morning. It was a large place, and as it would be impossible for Anton to guess that they had gone by train at all, they would have such a good start of him that he would probably not be able to find them again.

Pericard also proposed that they should start at once, and as they had no money to spare for cabs or omnibuses, they must walk to the distant terminus from which they must start for the south. How strange they felt as they walked through the gayly-lighted streets! How tired was Maurice! how delighted Joe! how dreamy and yet calm and trustful, was Cecile. Since the vision about her purse, her absolute belief in her Guide knew no bounds.

As near and dear, as certain and present, was He now to Cecile as if in reality he was holding her little hand; as if in reality He was carrying tired Maurice. He was there, the Goal was certain, the End sure. When they got to the great big terminus she still felt dreamlike, allowing Joe and Pericard to get their tickets and make all arrangements. Then the children and dog found themselves in a third-class compartment. Toby was well and skillfully hidden under the seat, the whistle sounded, and Pericard came close and took Cecile's hand. She was only a little child, but she was his princess, the first sweet and lovely thing he had ever seen. Cecile raised her lips to kiss him.

The Children's Pilgrimage

"Good-by, Pericard—good Pericard—faithful Pericard. "

Then the train pulled slowly out of the station, and the children were carried into the unknown darkness, and Pericard went home. He never saw the children again. But all through his after-life he carried a memory about with him of them, and when he heard of the good God and the angels, this wild Paris lad would cross himself devoutly, and think of Cecile.

CHAPTER XVI.

CHILDREN'S ARCADIA.

It was early spring in the south of France—spring, and delicious, balmy weather. All that dreadful cold of Normandy seemed like a forgotten dream. It was almost impossible to believe that the limbs that ached under that freezing atmosphere could be the same that now felt the sun almost oppressive.

Little Maurice had the desire of his heart, for the sun shone all day long. He could pick flowers and smell sweet country air, and the boy born under these sunny skies revived like a tropical plant beneath their influence. It was a month now since the children had left Paris. They had remained for a day or so in Orleans, and then had wandered on, going farther and farther south, until at last they had passed the great seaport town of Bordeaux, and found themselves in the monotonous forests of the Landes. The scenery was not pretty here. The ground was flat, and for miles and miles around them swept an interminable growth of fir trees, each tall and straight, many having their bark pierced, and with small tin vessels fastened round their trunks to catch the turpentine which oozed slowly out. These trees, planted in long straight rows, and occupying whole leagues of country, would have been wearisome to eyes less occupied, to hearts less full, than those that looked out of the faces and beat in the breasts of the children who on foot still pursued their march. For in this forest Cecile's heart had revived. Before she reached Bordeaux she often had felt her hope fading. She had believed that her desire could never be accomplished, for, inquire as they would, they could get in none of the towns or villages they passed through any tidings of Lovedy. No one knew anything of an English girl in the least answering to her description. Many smiled almost pityingly on the eager little seekers, and thought the children a trifle mad to venture on so hopeless a search.

But here, in the Landes, were villages innumerable—small villages, sunny and peaceful, where simple and kind-hearted folks lived, and barndoor-fowl strutted about happily, and the goats browsed, and sheep fed; and the people in these tiny villages were very kind to the little pilgrims, and gave them food and shelter gladly and cheerfully, and answered all the questions which Cecile put through her interpreter, Joe, about Lovedy. Though there were no tidings of the

The Children's Pilgrimage

blue-eyed girl who had half-broken her mother's heart, Cecile felt that here surely, or in some such place as here, she should find Lovedy, for were not these exactly the villages her stepmother had described when she lay a-dying? So Cecile trudged on peacefully, and each day dawned with a fresh desire. Joe, too, was happy; he had lost his fear of Anton. Anton could never surely pursue him here. There was no danger now of his being forced back to that old dreadful life. The hardships, the cold, the beatings, the starvings, lay behind him; he was a French boy again. Soon someone would call him by his old forgotten name of Alphonse, and he should look into his mother's eyes, and then go out among the vineyards with his brother Jean. Yes, Joe was very happy, he was loved and he loved; he was useful, too, necessary indeed to the children; and every day brought him nearer to his beloved Pyrenees. Once amongst those mountains, he had a sort of idea that he soon should roll off that seven years of London cruelty and defilement, and become a happy and innocent child again.

Of course, Maurice was joyful in the Landes; he liked the south, it was sunny and good, and he liked the kind peasant-women, who all petted the pretty boy, and fed him on the freshest of eggs and richest of goat's milk. But, perhaps, of all the little pilgrims, Toby was now the happiest—the most absolutely contented. Not a cloud hung over Toby's sky, not a care lingered in his mind.

He was useful too—indeed he was almost the breadwinner of the little party. For Joe had at last taught Toby to dance, and to dance with skill quite remarkable in a dog of his age. No one knew what Toby suffered in learning that rather ponderous dance; how stiff his poor legs felt, how weak his back, how hard he had to struggle to keep his balance. But from the day that Joe had rescued the children in the snow, Toby had become so absolutely his friend, had so completely withdrawn the fear with which at first he had regarded him, that now, for very love of Joe, he would do what he told him. He learned to dance, and from the time the children left Bordeaux, he had really by this one accomplishment supported the little party.

In the villages of the Landes the people were simple and innocent, they cared very little about centimes, sous, or francs; but they cared a great deal about amusement; and when Joe played his fiddle and Toby danced, they were so delighted, and so thoroughly enjoyed the sport, that in return they gave supper, bed, and breakfast to the whole party free of charge.

Thus Cecile's winsey frock still contained a great many francs put away toward a rainy day; for, since they entered the Landes, the children not only spent nothing, but lived better than they had ever done before.

Thus the days went on, and it all seemed very Arcadian and very peaceful, and no one guessed that a serpent could possibly come into so fair and innocent an Eden.

CHAPTER XVII.

MAURICE TAKES THE MANAGEMENT OF AFFAIRS.

After many weeks of wandering about, the children found themselves in a little village, about three miles from the town of Arcachon. This village was in the midst of a forest covering many thousand acres of land. They had avoided the seaport town of Arcachon, dreading its fashionable appearance; but they hailed the little village with delight.

It was a pretty place, peaceful and sunny; and here the people cultivated their vines and fruit trees, and lived, the poorer folks quite in the village, the better-off inhabitants in neat farmhouses close by. These farmhouses were in the midst of fields, with cattle browsing in the meadows.

Altogether, the village was the most civilized-looking place the children had stopped at since they entered what had been a few years ago the dreary desert of the Landes. Strange to say, however, here, for the first time, the weary little pilgrims met with a cold reception. The people in the village of Moulleau did not care for boys who played the fiddle, and dogs that tried clumsily to accompany it. They looked with a fine lack of sympathy at Cecile's pathetic blue eyes, and Maurice was nothing more to them than a rather dirty little sunburnt boy.

One or two of the inns even refused the children a night's lodging for money, and so disagreeable did those that did take them in make themselves that after the first night Cecile and Joe determined to sleep in the forest close by. it was now April, the weather was delicious, and in the forest of pines and oak trees not a breath of wind ever seemed to enter. Joe, looking round, found an old tumbledown hut. In the hut was a pile of dry pine needles. These pine needles made a much snugger bed than they had found in a rather dirty inn in the village; and, still greater an advantage, they could use this pleasant accommodation free of all charge.

It was, indeed, necessary to economize, for the francs sewn into the winsey frock would come to an end by and by.

The Children's Pilgrimage

The children found to their dismay that they had by no means taken a direct road to the Pyrenees, but had wandered about, and had been misdirected many times.

There was one reason, however, which induced Cecile to stay for a few days in the forest close to the village of Moulleau.

This was the reason: Amongst the many sunny farms around, was one, the smallest there, but built on a slight eminence, and resembling in some slight and vague way, not so much its neighbors, as the low-roofed, many-thatched English farmhouse of Warren's Grove. Cecile felt fascinated by this farm with its English frontage. She could not explain either her hopes or her fears with regard to it. But an unaccountable desire was over her to remain in the forest for a short time before they proceeded on their journey.

"Let us rest here just one day longer, " she would plead in her gentle way; and Joe, though seeing no reason for what seemed like unnecessary delay, nevertheless yielded to her demand.

He was not idle himself. As neither fiddling nor dancing seemed to pay, he determined to earn money in some other manner; so, as there were quantities of fir cones in the forests, he collected great piles and took them into Arcachon for sale.

While Joe was away, sometimes accompanied by Maurice, sometimes alone, Cecile would yield to that queer fascination, which seemed unaccountable, and wander silently, and yet with a certain anxiety to the borders of that English-looking farm.

Never did she dare to venture within its precincts. But she would come to the edge of the paling which divided its rich meadows from the road, and watch the cattle browsing, and the cocks, and hens, and ducks and geese, going in and out, with wistful and longing eyes.

Once, from under the low and pretty porch, she saw a child run eagerly, with shouts of laughter. This child, aged about two, had golden hair and a fair skin. Cecile had seen no child like him in the village. He Looked like an English boy. How did he and that English-looking farm get into the sequestered forest of the Landes?

After seeing the child, Cecile went back to her hut, sat down on the pine needles, and began to think.

Never yet had she obtained the faintest clew to her search.

Looking everywhere for blue eyes and golden hair, it seemed to Cecile that such things had faded from the earth. And now! but no, what would bring the English girl Lovedy there?

Why should Lovedy be at Moulleau more than at any other village in the Landes? and in any case what had the English-looking child to say to Lovedy?

Cecile determined to put any vague hopes out of her head. They must leave Moulleau the next morning; that she had promised Joe. Whenever Lovedy did come across their path, she would come in very different guise. But still, try as she would, Cecile's thoughts returned over and over again to the golden-haired laddie, and these thoughts, which came almost against her will, might have led to results which would have quickly solved her difficulties, but for an event which occurred just then.

This event, terrible and anxious, put all remembrance of the English farm and English child far from her mind.

Joe had made rather a good day at Arcachon selling his pine cones; and Maurice, who had gone with him, and had tried in his baby fashion to help him, had returned to the hut very tired, and so sleepy that, after eating a little bread and fruit, he lay down on the pine needles and went sound asleep. Generally tired and healthy, little Maurice slept without moving until the morning. But this night, contrary to his wont, he found himself broad awake before Cecile or Joe had lain down. Joe, a lighted fir cone in his hand, which he carefully guarded from the dry pine needles, was sitting close to Cecile, who was reading aloud to him out of the Testament which Mrs. Moseley had given to her. Cecile read aloud to Joe every night, and this time her solemn little voice stumbled slowly over the words, "He that loveth father or mother more than Me is not worthy of Me."

"I think as that is a bit hard, " interrupted Joe. "I wonder ef Jesus could tell wot a hankering a feller has fur his mother when he ain't seen her fur seven years? Why, Miss Cecile, I'm real starved fur my mother. I dreams of her hevery night, and I feels as tho' we 'ud

The Children's Pilgrimage

never, never get back to the dear blue mountains again. No, " continued Joe, shaking his dark head, "I never, never could love Jesus better nor my mother. "

"I don't remember my mother, " said Cecile; "and I think I love Jesus the Guide even better than I love Maurice. But oh, Joe, I'm a selfish little girl. I ought not to stay on here when you want to see your mother so very badly. We will start to your mountains quite, quite early in the morning, Joe. "

"Thank yer, Missie, " said Joe, with a very bright smile; and then, having put the pine carefully out, the two children also lay down to sleep.

But little Maurice, who had heard every word, was still quite wide awake. Maurice, who loved his forest life, and who quite hated these long and enforced marches, felt very cross. Why should they begin to walk again? *He* had no interest in these long and interminable rambles. How often his feet used to ache! How blistered they often were! And now that the weather was so warm and sunny, little Maurice got tired even sooner than in the winter's cold. No; what he loved was lying about under the pine trees, and watching the turpentine trickling very slowly into the tin vessels fastened to their trunks; and then he liked to look at the squirrels darting merrily from bough to bough, and the rabbits running about, and the birds flying here and there. This was the life Maurice loved. This was south. Cecile had always told him they were going south. Well, was not this south, this pleasant, balmy forest-land. What did they want with anything further? Maurice reflected with dismay over the tidings that they were to leave quite early in the morning. He felt inclined to cry, to wake Cecile, to get her to promise not to go. Suddenly an idea, and what he considered quite a brilliant idea, entered his baby mind. Cecile and Joe had arranged to commence their march quite early in the morning. Suppose—suppose he, Maurice, slipped softly from the old hut and hid himself in the forest. Why, then, they would not go; they would never dream of leaving Maurice behind. He could come back to them when the sun was high in the heavens; and then Joe would pronounce it too hot to go on any journey that day. Thus he would secure another long day in his beloved woods.

CHAPTER XVIII.

AN OGRE IN THE WOOD.

Full of his idea, Maurice slept very little more that night. He tossed from side to side on the pine needles. But though he felt often drowsy, he was afraid to yield to the sensation; and early, very early in the morning, before the sun had risen, he got up. Going to the door of the hut, he stood there for a moment or so looking down into the forest. Just around the little hut there was a clearing of trees; but the forest itself looked dark. The trees cast long shadows, and Maurice felt rather nervous at the idea of venturing into their gloom. Suddenly, however, he heard a bird sing clear and sweet up into the sky, and the next moment two squirrels darted past his feet.

These two events decided him: the day was coming on apace, and soon Cecile and Joe would wake and begin to prepare for their journey. Without waiting to look around, he stepped into the dark shadows of the trees; and, in a moment, his little figure was lost in the gloom. To enable him to creep very quietly away—so quietly that even Toby should not awake—he had decided not to put on his shoes and stockings, and he now ran along the grass with his bare feet. He liked the sensation. The grass felt both cool and soft, and he began to wonder why he had ever troubled himself with such clumsy, tiresome things as shoes and stockings.

The sun had now risen, and the forest was no longer dark; and Maurice, looking back, saw that he had quite lost sight of the hut. He also, at the same moment, discovered, growing in great clusters, almost at his feet, dog violets, some as large as heart's-ease.

He gave a little cry of delight. He was very fond of flowers, and he decided to pick a great bunch to bring back to Cecile; in case she was a little vexed with him, she would be sure to be pacified by this offering.

He therefore sat down on the grass, and picked away at the violets until he had filled both his hands.

Then hearing, or fancying he heard, a little rustling in the grass, and thinking it might be Joe coming in search of him, he set off running again.

The Children's Pilgrimage

This time he was not so fortunate. A great thorn found its way into the little naked foot; the poor child gave a cry of pain, then sat plump down; he found that he could not walk another step. The day had now fully come, and the forest was alive with sights and sounds. Maurice was too young, too much of a baby to feel at all frightened. The idea of getting lost never even occurred to him. He said to himself that, as he could not possibly walk on his lame and swollen foot, he would wait quietly where he had planted himself, until Cecile or Joe or Toby found him out.

This quiet waiting resulted, as might have been expected, in the little fellow making up for the night's wakefulness, and soon he was sound asleep, his pretty head resting on his violets.

For several hours tired little Maurice slept. When at last he opened his eyes, a man was sitting by his side.

He looked at him for a moment sleepily and peacefully out of his velvet brown eyes; then sitting up, he exclaimed in a tone of joyful recognition:

"Anton! "

Anton—for it was indeed he—looked into the innocent face with his own guilty one, then nodded in the affirmative.

Maurice, having no idea of fearing Anton, knowing nothing about the purse of gold, and being on the whole rather prepossessed in his favor than otherwise, exclaimed:

"How did you come, Anton? did you find Cecile and Joe, and did they send you for me? and have I slept a long, long time, Anton? It is quite too late to begin a journey to-day? "

"'Tis about noon, lad, " replied Anton; "quite the hottest time of the day; and I have not seen no Joe, nor no Cecile, though I wants to see 'em; I ha' been a-looking fur 'em ever since they turned tail in that shabby way in Paris. I has a little debt to settle wid 'em two, and I'd like to see 'em again. "

"Oh! do you owe them money, and will you pay it? I am sure they'll be glad for that, for sometimes I hear Cecile say that she is afraid their money won't hold out, the journey is so very long. I am glad

The Children's Pilgrimage

you owe 'em money, Anton; and as it is past noon, and they won't start to-day, we may as well go back to the hut at once. Oh! won't they be surprised ta see you, Anton? "

Anton remained silent for a moment, his head buried in his hands. He was evidently thinking hard, and once he was heard to mutter, "a lucky chance; a rare and lucky chance. " Then he raised his head again and looked at Maurice.

"The others are in a hut, a hut in the forest, eh? "

"Oh, yes! quite a nice, snug little hut, and not so very far from here. We sleep on pine needles in the hut, and they are so soft and snug; and, Anton, I don't want to leave it. I like the forest, and I hate long, long walks; I'd rather stay in the hut, "

"How far away did you say it wor, lad? "

"Oh! not so very far away. I ran out quite early this morning, and I came down hill; and at last when I lost breath I stopped and gathered all these violets. Oh, they are withered—my poor violets! And then I ran a little bit and got this thorn into my foot, and after that I could walk no more. The hut can't be a great way off. Will you carry me back to it, Anton? "

Anton laughed.

"'Will I carry him? ' did he say? " he exclaimed in a tone of some derision. "Well, wot next? I ain't strong enough to carry sech a big chap as you, my lad. No, no; but I'll tell you wot I'll do: I'll take you over to a comrade o' mine as is waiting for me jest outside the forest, quite close by. He's a bit of a doctor, and he'll take the thorn out of your foot; and while he's doing it, I'll run down to the hut and bring that big Joe o' yourn back. He'll carry you fine—he ain't a weakly chap like me. "

"Poor Anton! " said little Maurice, "I forgot that you were weak. Yes, that's a very kind plan. " And he stretched out his arms for Anton to carry him just the little distance to his comrade at the other side of the forest.

CHAPTER XIX.

THREE PLANS.

It took Anton but a few strides to get out of the forest, at the other side away from the hut. Here, on a neatly-made road, stood a caravan; and by the side of the caravan two men. These men could not speak a word of English, and even their French was so mixed with dialect that little Maurice, who by this time knew many words of real French, did not understand a word they said. This, however, all the better suited Anton's purpose. He had a short but impressive conversation with the man who seemed to have the greatest authority. Maurice was then given over into this man's care. Anton assured him that he would return as quickly as possible with Joe. And then the bad man plunged once more into the depths of the forest.

Yes; Anton was most truly a bad man, and bad now were the schemes at work in his evil heart. He saw once more a hope of getting that money which he longed for. He would use any means to obtain this end. After the children had escaped from him in Paris, he had wandered about for nearly a week in that capital looking for them. Then he had agreed to join a traveling caravan which was going down south. Anton could assist in the entertainments given in the different small towns and villages they passed through; but this mode of proceeding was necessarily slow, and seemed all the more so as week after week went by and he never got a clew to the lost children; he was beginning to give it up as a bad job—to conclude that Cecile and her party had never gone south after all. He had indeed all but completed arrangements to return to Paris with another traveling party, when suddenly, wandering through the forest in the early morning, he came upon little Maurice D'Albert fast asleep—his crushed violets under his pretty head. Transfixed with joy and astonishment, the bad man stood still. His game was sure—it had not escaped him.

He sat down by the child. He did not care to wake him. While Maurice slept he made his plans.

And now, having given over Maurice to the owner of the caravan, with strict directions not to let him escape, he was hurrying through the forest to meet Joe. He wanted to see Joe alone. It would by no means answer his purpose to come across Cecile or even indeed at present to let Cecile know anything about his near vicinity.

Little Maurice's directions had been simple enough, and soon Anton came in sight of the hut. He did not want to come any nearer. He sat down behind an oak tree, and waited. From where he sat, he could watch the entrance to the hut, but could not himself be seen.

Presently he saw Cecile and Joe come out. Toby also stood at their heels. Cecile and Joe appeared to be consulting anxiously. At last they seemed to have come to a conclusion; Cecile and Toby went one way, and Joe another.

Anton saw with delight that everything was turning out according to his best hopes; Cecile and Toby were going toward the village, while Joe wandered in his direction. He waited only long enough to see the little girl and the dog out of sight, then, rising from the ground, he approached Joe.

The poor boy was walking along with his eyes fixed on the ground. He seemed anxious and preoccupied. In truth he was thinking with considerable alarm of little Maurice. Anton came very close, they were almost face to face before Joe saw him.

When at last their eyes did meet Anton perceived with delight that the boy's face went very white, that his lips twitched, and that he suddenly leant against a tree to support himself. These signs of fear were most agreeable to the wicked man. He felt that in a very short time the purse would be his.

"Anton, " said poor Joe, when he could force any words from his trembling lips.

"Aye, Anton, " echoed the man with a taunting laugh, "you seems mighty pleased to see Anton, old chap. You looks rare and gratified, eh? "

"No, Anton, I'm dreadful, dreadful pained to see you, " answered Joe. "I wor in great trouble a minute ago, but it ain't nothink to the trouble o' seeing you. "

Anton laughed again.

The Children's Pilgrimage

"You ere an unceevil lad, " he replied, "but strange as it may seem, I'm glad as you is sorry to see me, boy; it shows as you fears me; as you is guilty, as well you may think yerself, and you knows as Anton can bring yer to justice. You shall fear me more afore you has done, Master Joe. You 'scaped me afore, but there's no escape this time. We has a few words to say to each other, but the principal thing is as there's no escape this time, young master. "

"I know, " answered Joe, "I know as a man like you can have no mercy —never a bit. "

"There's no good a-hangering of me wid those speeches, Joe; I ha' found you, and I means to get wot I can out o' you. And now jest tell me afore we goes any further wot you was a-doing, and why you looked so misribble afore I spoke to you that time. "

"Oh! " said Joe, suddenly recalled to another anxiety by these words, "wot a fool I am to stay talking to you when there ain't a moment to spare. Little Maurice is lost. I'm terrible feared as little Maurice has quite strayed away and got lost, and here am I, a-standing talking to you when there ain't one moment to lose. Ef you won't leave me, you must come along wid me, fur I'm a-looking fur little Maurice. "

Joe now prepared to start forward, though his brain was still so perturbed at this sudden vision of his enemy that he scarcely knew where he was going, or in what direction to direct his steps. In a couple of strides Anton overtook him.

"You ha' no call to fash about the little chap, " he said; "and there ain't no use a-looking fur him, fur I have got him. "

"You have got little Maurice? " said Joe. "You have stole little Maurice away from Cecile and me? "

"I found little Maurice asleep in the wood. I have him safe. You can have him back whenever you pleases. "

"I must have little Maurice. Take me to him at once, " said Joe in a desperate tone.

"Softly, softly, lad! You shall have the little chap back. No harm shall happen to him. You and the little gal can have him again. Only one thing: I must have that ere purse first. "

The Children's Pilgrimage

"Oh! ain't you a wicked man? " said Joe, and now he flung himself full length on the grass, and burst into bitter lamentations. "Oh! ain't you the wickedest man in all the wide world, Anton? Cecile 'ull die ef she can't get little Maurice back again. Cecile 'ull die ef she loses that purse. "

Joe repeated these words over many times; in truth the poor boy was almost in a transport of grief and despair. Anton, however, made no reply whatever to this great burst of terrible sorrow, and waited quietly until the paroxysm had spent itself, then he too sat down on the grass.

"Listen, Joe, " he said. "'Tis no use a-blubbering afore me, or a-screaming hout afore me. Them things affects some folks, but they never takes no rises out o' me. I may be 'ard. Likely enough I am. Hanyhow hysterics don't go down with me. Joe Barnes—as that's the name wot you was known by in England—I'm *determined* to get that 'ere purse. Now listen. Wot I has to say is short; wot I has to say is plain; from wot I has now got to say—I'll never go back. I lay three plans afore you, Joe Barnes. You can choose wot one you like best. The first plan is this: as you and Cecile keeps the purse, and I takes Maurice away wid me; you never see Maurice, nor hears of him again; I sell him to yer old master whose address I has in my pocket. That's the first plan. The second plan is this: that Maurice comes back to his sister, and *you* comes wid me, Joe. I sells you once more to yer hold master, and he keeps yer *tight*, and you has no more chance of running away. This seems a sensible plan, and that 'ere little Cecile, as you sets sech store by, can keep her purse and her brother too. Ef you does this, Joe Barnes, there'll be no fear of Cecile dying—that's my second plan. But the third plan's the best of all. You can get that 'ere purse of gold. You get it, or tell me where to find it, and then you shall have Maurice back. Within one hour Maurice shall be with you, and you shall stay wid Cecile and Maurice, and I'll never, never trouble you no more. I calls the last the neatest plan of all, lad. Don't you? "

Joe said nothing; his head was buried in his hands. Anton, however, saw that he was listening.

"The last is the sensible plan, " he said; and he laid his hand on the lad's shoulder.

The Children's Pilgrimage

Joe started as though an adder had stung him. He threw off the defiling hand, and moved some paces away.

"There ere the others, " continued Anton. "There's the little chap a-being beat and starved in London, and his little heart being hall a-broken hup. Or *you* can go back to the hold life, Joe Barnes; you're elder, and can bear it better. Yer head is tough by now, I guess; a big blow on it won't hurt you much; and you'll never see yer old mother or yer brother—but never mind. Yer whole life will be spent in utter misery—still, never mind, that ere dirty purse is safe; never mind aught else. "

"We han't got the purse, " said Joe then, raising his haggard face. "'Tis the gospel truth as I'm telling you, Anton. Cecile took the purse to a lady in Paris to take care of fur her, and she is to keep it until someone gives her a bit of paper back which she writ herself. I can't give yer the purse, fur it ain't yere, Anton. "

"The bit o' paper 'ull do; the bit o' paper wid the address of the lady. "

Joe groaned.

"I can't do it, " he said. "I can't let Maurice go to sech a cruel life—I can't, I can't! I *can't* give hup the hope o' seeing my old mother. I must see my old mother once again. And I can't steal Cecile's purse. Oh! *wot shall I do*? "

"Look yere, lad, " said Anton, more slowly and in a kinder tone, "you think it hall well hover; one o' they three plans you must stick to. Now I'm a-going away, but I'll be back yere to-morrow morning at four o'clock fur my hanswer. You ha' it ready fur me then. "

So saying Anton rose from the grass, and when Joe raised his face his enemy was gone.

CHAPTER XX.

FOUR O'CLOCK IN THE MORNING.

It was night again, almost a summer's night, so still, so warm and balmy, and in the little hut in the forest of the Landes two children sat very close together; Cecile had bought a candle that day in the village, and this candle, now well sheltered from any possible breeze, was placed, lighted, in the broken-down door of the little hut. It was Cecile's own idea, for she said to Joe that Maurice might come back in the cool night-time, and this light would be sure to guide him. Joe had lit the candle for the little girl, and secured it against any possible overthrow. But as she did so he shook his head sorrowfully.

Seeing this Cecile reproved him.

"I know Maurice so well, " explained the little sister. "He will sleep for hours and hours, and then he will wake and gather flowers and think himself quite close to us all the time. He will never know how time passes, and then the night will come and he will be frightened and want to come back to me and Toby; and when he is frightened this light will guide him. "

Joe knowing the truth and seeing how impossible it would be for Maurice to return in the manner Cecile thought, could only groan under his breath, for he dared not tell the truth to Cecile; and this was one of the hardest parts of his present great trouble.

"Missie Cecile, " he said, when he had lit the candle and seen that it burned safely; "Missie, yer jest dead beat, you has never sat down, looking fur the little chap the whole, whole day. I'm a great strong fellow, I ain't tired a bit; but ef Missie 'ud lie down, maybe she'd sleep, and I'll stay outside and watch fur little Maurice and take care of the candle. "

"But I'd rather watch, too, outside with you, Joe. I'm trying hard, hard not to be anxious. But perhaps if I lie down the werry anxious feel may come. Just let me sit by you, and put my head on your shoulder; perhaps I shall rest so. "

"Werry well, Missie, " said Joe.

He seemed incapable of enforcing any arguments that night, and in a moment or two the children, with faithful Toby at their feet, were sitting just outside the hut, but where the light of the solitary candle could fall on them. Cecile's head was on Joe's breast, and Joe's strong arm encircled her.

After a long pause, he said in a husky voice:

"I'd like to hear that verse as Missie read to poor Joe last night. I'd like to hear it once again. "

"The last verse, Joe? " answered Cecile. "I think I know the last verse by heart. It is this: 'He that loveth father or mother more than Me, is not worthy of Me'"

"My poor old mother, " said Joe suddenly. "My poor, poor old mother. " Here he covered his face with his hands, and burst into tears.

"But, Joe, " said little Cecile in a voice of surprise, "you will soon see your mother now—very soon, I think and hope. As soon as we find Maurice we will go to the Pyrenees, and there we shall see Lovedy and your mother and your good brother Jean. Our little Maurice cannot stay much longer away, and then we will start at once for the Pyrenees. "

To this Joe made no answer, and Cecile, who had intended to remain awake all night, in a few moments was asleep, tired out, with her head now resting on Joe's knees.

He covered the pretty head tenderly with his great brown palm, and his black eyes were full of the tenderest love and sorrow as they looked at the little white face.

How could he protect the heart of the child he loved from a sorrow that must break it? Only by sacrificing himself; by sacrificing himself absolutely. Was he prepared to do this?

As he thought and Cecile slept, a great clock from the not far distant village struck twelve. Twelve o'clock! In four hours now Anton would return for his answer—what should it be?

The Children's Pilgrimage

To sacrifice Maurice—that would be impossible. Even for one instant to contemplate sending little baby, spoiled Maurice to endure the life he had led, to bear the blows, the cruel words, the starvations, the bad company that he had endured would be utterly impossible. No; he could not do that. He had long ago made up his mind that Maurice was to come back.

The question now lay between the Russia-leather purse and himself.

Should he give everything up—his mother, his brother, the happy, happy life that seemed so near—and go back to the old and dreadful fate? Should he show in this way that he loved Christ more than his mother? Was this the kind of sacrifice that Christ demanded at his hands? And oh! how Joe did love his mother! All the cruel, hard, weary of his captivity, his mother had lived green and fresh in his heart. Many and many a night had he wet his wretched pillow with the thought of how once he had lain in that mother's arms, and she had petted him and showered love upon him. The memory of her face, of her love, of her devotion, had kept him from doing the wrong things which the other boys in the company had done; and now, when he might so soon see her, must he give her up? He knew that if he once got back to his old master he would take good care to keep him from running away again; if he put himself at four o'clock in the morning into Anton's hands, *it would be for life*. He might, when he was quite old and broken down by misery and hardship, return to France; but what use would it be to him then, when he had only his mother's grave to visit? He could escape all that; he could go back to the Pyrenees; he could see his mother's face once more. How? Simply by taking from Cecile a little piece of paper; by taking it from her frock as she slept. And, after all, was this paper a matter of life and death? Was it worth destroying the entire happiness of a life? for Cecile might never find Lovedy. It was only a dream of the little girl's, that Lovedy waited for her in the Pyrenees; there might be no English girl hiding there! and even if there was, did she want that forty pounds so badly? Must he sacrifice his whole life for the sake of that forty pounds? Was it not a sacrifice too hard to expect of any boy? True, he had given his word! he had told Cecile that he would rather be cut in little bits than touch her purse of gold. Yes, yes; but this lifelong suffering was worse than being cut in pieces. "He that loveth father or mother more than Me, is not worthy of Me. " How could he love this unknown Christ better than the mother from whom he had been parted for seven long years?

The Children's Pilgrimage

After a time, worn out with his emotion, he dropped asleep. He had thought to stay awake all night; but before the village clock had again struck one, his head was dropped on his hands and he was sound asleep.

In his broken sleep he had one of those dreams which he dreaded. He saw his mother ill and calling for him, weeping for him. A voice, he did not know from where it sounded, kept repeating in his ear that his mother was dying of a broken heart because of him; because she so mourned the loss of her merry boy, she was passing into the silent grave. The voice told him to make haste and go to his mother, not to lose an instant away from her side. He awoke bathed in perspiration to hear the village clock strike four. The hour, the hour of his fate had come. Even now Anton waited for him. He had no time to lose, his dream had decided him. He would go back at any cost to his mother. Softly he put down his hand and removed the precious little bit of paper from the bosom of Cecile's frock, then, lifting her head tenderly from his knees, he carried her, still sleeping, into the hut, bade Toby watch by her, and flung himself into the silent gloom of the forest.

CHAPTER XXI.

HARD TIMES FOR LITTLE MAURICE.

All that long and sunny day Maurice sat contentedly on a little stool in the doorway of the traveling caravan. His foot, which had been very painful, was now nicely and skillfully dressed. The Frenchman, who did not know a word of English, had extracted a sharp and cruel thorn, and the little boy, in his delight at being free from pain, thanked him in the only way in his power. He gave him a very sweet baby kiss.

It so happened that the Frenchman had a wife and a little lad waiting for him in the Pyrenees. Maurice reminded him of his own dark-eyed boy, and this sudden kiss won his heart. He determined to be good to the child. So first providing him with an excellent bowl of soup and a fresh roll, for his breakfast and dinner combined, he then gave him a seat in the door of the caravan, for he judged that as he could not amuse the little fellow by talking to him, he might by letting him see what he could of what was going on outside.

For a long time Maurice sat still, then he grew impatient. He was no longer either in pain or sleepy, and he wanted to get home to Cecile; he wanted to tell her his adventures, and to show her the violets which he had gathered that morning, and which, though now quite dead and withered, he still held in his little hot hand. Why did not Anton return? What *was* keeping Joe? It was no distance at all back to the hut. Of this he was sure. Why, then, did not Joe come? He felt a little cross as the hours went on, but it never even occurred to his baby mind to be frightened.

It was late in the evening when Anton at last made his appearance, and alone. Little Maurice sprang off his stool to meet him.

"Oh, Anton, what a time you've been! And where's Joe? "

"Joe ain't coming to-night, young 'un, " said Anton roughly.

He entered the caravan with a weary step, and, throwing himself on a settle, demanded some supper in French of his companion.

The Children's Pilgrimage

Maurice, unaccustomed to this mode of treatment, stood quite still for a moment, then, brushing the tears from his big brown eyes, he went up to Anton and touched his arm.

"See, " he said, "I can walk now. Kind man there made my foot nearly well. You need not carry me, Anton. But will you come back with me to the hut after you've had some supper? "

"No, that I won't, " answered Anton. "Not a step 'ull you get me to stir again to-night. You sit down and don't bother. "

"Cross, nasty man, " replied Maurice passionately; "then I'll run away by myself, I will. I can walk now. "

He ran to the door of the caravan; of course it took Anton but a moment to overtake him, to catch him by his arm, and, shaking him violently, to lead him to an inner room, into which he flung the poor child, telling him roughly that he had better stay quiet and make no fuss, or it would be worse for him.

Little Maurice raised impotent hands, beating Anton with all his small might. Anton laughed derisively. He turned the key on the angry and aggrieved child and left him to his fate.

Poor little Maurice! It was his first real experience of the roughness of life. Hitherto Cecile had come between him and all hard times; hitherto, whatever hardships there were to bear, Cecile had borne them. It seemed to be the natural law of life to little Maurice that everyone should shield and shelter him.

He threw himself now on the dirty floor of the caravan and cried until he could cry no longer. Oh, how he longed for Cecile! How he repented of his foolish running away that morning! How he hated Anton! But in vain were his tears and lamentations; no one came near him, and at last from utter weariness he stopped.

It was dark now, quite dark in the tiny inner room where Anton had thrust him. Strange to say, the darkness did not frighten the little fellow; on the contrary, it soothed him. Night had really come. In the night it was natural to lie still and sleep; when people were asleep time passed quickly. Maurice would go to sleep, and then in the morning surely, surely Joe and Cecile would find him and bring him home.

The Children's Pilgrimage

He lay down, curling himself up like a little dog, but tired as he was he could not sleep—not at first. He was nothing but a baby boy, but he had quite a retrospect or panorama passing before his eyes as he lay on the dirty caravan floor. He saw the old court at home; he saw the pretty farm of Warren's Grove; he saw that tiring day in London when it seemed to both Cecile and himself that they should never anywhere get a lodging for the night; then he was back again with kind, with dear Mrs. Moseley, and she was telling to him and Cecile those lovely, those charming stories about heaven.

"I always, always said as heaven would suit me better than South, " sobbed the poor little boy. "I never did want to come South. I wished Jesus the Guide to take me to heaven. Oh, I do want to go to heaven! "

Over and over he repeated this wish aloud in the darkness, and its very utterance seemed to soothe him, for after a time he did really drop asleep.

He had not slept so very long when a hand touched him. The hand was gentle, the touch firm but quiet.

Maurice awoke without any start and sat up. The Frenchman was bending over him. He pointed to the open door of the room—to the open door of the caravan beyond.

"Run—run away, " he said. These were the only words of English he could master.

"Run away, " he repeated and now he carried the child to the open outer door. Maurice understood; his face brightened; first kissing his deliverer, he then glided from his arms, ran down the steps of the caravan, and disappeared.

CHAPTER XXII.

THE ENGLISH FARM.

Cecile had strange dreams that night. Her faith had hitherto been very simple, very strong, very fervent. Ever since that night at the meeting of the Salvation Army, when the earnest and longing child had given her heart to the One who knocked for admittance there, had she been faithful to her first love. She had found the Guide for whom her soul longed, and not all the troubles and anxieties of her long and weary journey—not all the perils of the way—had power to shake her confidence. Even in the great pain of yesterday Cecile was not greatly disturbed. Maurice was lost, but she had asked the good Guide Jesus so earnestly to bring back the little straying lamb, that she was quite sure he would soon be with them again. In this confidence she had gone to sleep. But whether it was the discomfort of her position in that sleep, or that Satan was in very truth come to buffet her; in that slumber came dreams so terrible, so real, that for the first time the directness of her confidence was shaken. In her dreams she thought she heard a voice saying to her over and over again: "There is no Guide—there is no Lord Jesus Christ. " She combated the wicked suggestion even in her sleep, and awoke to cast it from her with indignation.

It was daylight when the tired child opened her eyes. She was no longer lying against Joe's breast in the forest; no, she was in the shelter of the little hut, and Toby alone was keeping her company. Joe had vanished, and no Maurice had returned in the darkness as she had fondly hoped he would the night before. The candle had shed its tiny ray and burned itself out in vain. The little wanderer had not come back.

Cecile sat up with a weary sigh; her head ached, she felt cold and chilly. Then a queer fancy, joined to a trembling kind of hope, came over her. That farm with the English frontage; that fair child with the English face. Suppose those people were really English? Suppose she went to them and asked them to help her to look for Maurice, and suppose, while seeking for her little brother, she obtained a clew to another and more protracted search?

Cecile thought and thought, and though her temples throbbed with pain, and she trembled from cold and weariness, the longing to get as near as possible to this farm, where English people might dwell, became too great and strong to be resisted.

She rose somewhat languidly, and, calling Toby, went out into the forest. Here the fresher air revived her, and the exercise took off a growing sensation of heavy illness. She walked quickly, and as she did so her hopes became more defined.

The farm Cecile meant to reach lay about a mile from the village of Bolleau. It was situated on a pretty rise of ground to the very borders of the forest. Cecile, walking quickly, reached it before long; then she stood still, leaning over the paling and looking across the enchanted ground. This paling in itself was English, and the very strut of the barn-door fowl reminded her of Warren's Grove. How she wished that fair child to run out! How she hoped to hear even one word of the only language she understood! No matter her French origin, Cecile was all English at this moment. Toby stood by her side patiently enough.

Toby, too, was in great trouble and perplexity about Maurice, but his present strongest instinct was to get at a very fat fowl which, unconscious of danger, was scratching up worms at its leisure within almost reach of his nose.

Toby had a weakness, nay, a vice, in the direction of fowl; he liked to hunt them. He could not imagine why Cecile did not go in at that low gate which stood a little open close by. Where was the use of remaining still, in any case, so near temptation? The unwary fowl came close, very close. Toby could stand it no longer. He made a spring, a snap, and caught at its beak.

Then ensued a fuss and an uproar; every fowl in the place commenced to give voice in the cause of an injured comrade. Cackle, cackle, crow, crow, from, it seemed, hundreds of throats. Toby retired actually abashed, and out at the same moment, from under the rose-covered porch, came the pretty fair-haired boy. The child was instantly followed by an old woman, a regular Frenchwoman, upright, straight as a dart, with coal-black eyes and snowy hair tidily put away under a tall peasant's cap.

Cecile heard her utter a French exclamation, then chide pretty sharply the uproarious birds. Toby lying *perdu* behind the hedge, the fowl were naturally chided for much ado about nothing.

The Children's Pilgrimage

Just then the little boy, breaking from the restraining hand, ran gleefully into a field of waving corn.

"Suzanne, Suzanne!" shouted the Frenchwoman in shrill tones, and then out flew a much younger woman, a woman who seemed, even to the child Cecile, very young indeed. A tall, fair young woman, with a face as pink and white as the boy's, and a wealth of even more golden hair.

"Ah! you naughty little lad. Come here, Jean," she said in English; then catching the truant child to her bosom, she ran back with him into the house.

Cecile felt herself turning cold, almost faint. An impulse to run into that farmhouse, to address that fair-haired young woman, to drag her story, whatever it might be, from her lips, came over her almost too strongly to be resisted.

She might have yielded to it, she was indeed about to yield to it, when suddenly a voice at her elbow, calling her by her name, caused her to look round. There stood Joe, but Joe with a face so altered, so ghastly, so troubled, that Cecile scarcely knew him.

"Come, Cecile, come back to the hut; I have some'ut to tell yer," he said slowly and in hoarse tones.

And Cecile, too terrified by this fresh alarm even to remember the English folks who lived at the farm, followed him back into the forest without a word.

CHAPTER XXIII.

TELLING THE BAD NEWS.

All the way back to the forest not one word passed the lips of Joe. But when the two children, panting from their rapid run, reached the hut, he threw himself on the ground, covered his face for a brief instant, then asked Cecile to come to his side.

"For I've a story to tell yer, little Missie, " said Joe.

Cecile obeyed him at once. A great terror was over her, but this terror was partly assuaged by his first words.

"I ha' got some'ut to tell yer, Missie Cecile, " said Joe Barnes, "some'ut 'bout my old life, the kind o' way I used to live in Paris and Lunnon. "

At the words Cecile raised her little flower face with a sigh of relief; she was not going to hear of any fresh trouble; it was only an old, old woe, and Joe needed comfort.

"Dear Joe, " said the little girl, "yes, tell me about Paris and London. "

Joe felt himself shrinking away from the little caressing movement Cecile made. He looked at her for an instant out of two great hollow eyes, then began in a dull kind of voice.

"It don't make much real differ, " he said, "only I thought as I'd like fur yer to know as it wor a *werry* bitter temptation.

"I remember the last night as I slept along o' my mother, Missie Cecile, how she petted me, and fondled of me.

"Then I wor stolen away, and my master brought me to Paris. We lived in a werry low part o' Paris, high up in a garret. I wor taught to play the fiddle—I wor taught by blows; and when they did not do, I wor made real, desperate hungry. I used to be given jest one meal a day, and when the others as did better nor me wor eating, I had to stand by and wait on 'em. Then, when I knew enough, I wor sent into the streets to play, and when I did not bring in enough money, I

The Children's Pilgrimage

wor beat worse nor ever. One day my master sold me to an Englishman. Talk o' slaves! well, this man give my master a lot o' money fur me. I seed the money, and they told me as I wor apprenticed to him, and that I could not run away, for ef I did, the law 'ud bring me back. My new master tuk me to England. He tuk me to Lunnon. It wor bad in Paris, but in Lunnon it wor worse. I wor farther from my mother. I wor out o' my own country, and I did not know a word of English.

"Oh! I did find out wot hunger and cold and misery wor in London. Nobody—nobody give me even a kind word, except one poor lad worse off nor myself. He belonged to hour company, and he broke his leg. My master would not send him to 'orspitle, and he died. But afore he died he taught me a bit of English, and I picked up more by and by. I grew bigger, and the years went on. Oh! it wor a dreadful life. I did nothink but long for my mother and pine for the old home, and once I tried to run away. I wor found the first time, and kep' in a dark cellar on bread and water for a week arter.

"Then I seed you and Maurice at the night-school. I heerd you say you wor goin' to France, and when I heerd sech plucky words from sech a little mite as you, Missie, why I thought as I'd try to run away again; and the second time, no matter how, I succeeded. I had wot I called real luck, and I got to France, and there, jest outside Calais, I met you two, and I thought as I wor made. Oh, Missie Cecile, but for the purse o' gold—but for the purse o' gold, I might ha' been made. "

Here Joe paused, again covered his face, and groaned most bitterly.

"The purse of gold is quite safe with Miss Smith in Paris, " said Cecile, in a tone of surprise. "Dear Joe, I don't quite understand you. Those were dreadful days, but they are over. You will soon see your old mother again. All the dreadful days are over, Joe dear. "

"Ah! Missie, but that's jest wot they ain't. But I likes to hear you say 'dear Joe' once again, for soon, when you know all, you'll hate me. "

"Then may I kiss you before I know all? and I don't think I *could* hate you, Jography. "

"Ah! yes, " said Joe, receiving the little kiss with almost apathy, "you has a werry tender heart, Missie Cecile, you always seems to me like an angel, but even you'll hate Joe Barnes arter you know all. Well,

The Children's Pilgrimage

yesterday, you remember how we lost little Maurice. We missed him when we woke in the morning. We thought as he had strayed in the forest, and would soon be back, and you went one way to look for him, and I went another. I had not gone a hundred yards when jest behind our hut I saw Anton! Yes, Missie, our old enemy Anton had come back again.

"'Anton' I said; and then, Missie, oh! my dear, dear little Missie Cecile, I must jest tell it in few words. He said as he had stole little Maurice, that he had him safe, and that we should never, never get him back unless I give him—Anton—the purse of gold. I said as I had not it—that neither of us had it. But he drew out o' me about the little bit o' paper and he said as the paper 'ud do as well as the purse. He said that ef he did not get the bit o' paper, Maurice should go back and be sold to my dreadful old master. Either that, or, ef I liked it better, Maurice might come back to you, and I should be sold. He gave me till four o'clock this morning to think on it. Maurice was to go away to the dreadful life, or I was to go back to the dreadful life, or he was to get the paper that 'ud make Miss Smith give up the Russia-leather purse. Missie, I said once that I'd rayther be cut in little bits nor touch that purse of gold. I meant wot I said. But, Missie Cecile, last night the temptation wor too strong fur me, much too strong. Maurice must not go to sech a life, nor could I; never to see my mother no more; always, always to be a slave, and worse nor a slave; all hope gone. Oh, Missie Cecile! I did love my old mother more nor Christ. I ain't worthy of your Christ Jesus. In the morning I tuk the piece of paper out o' yer frock, darlin'. As the clock in the village struck four I did it. I ran away then, and I found Anton waiting for me where he said as he 'ud wait. "

"And Maurice? " asked Cecile. She was sitting strangely, unnaturally quiet, and when she was told that the paper was stolen she did not even start.

"Ah, Missie! that's the worst, the worst of all; fur I did it—the cruel, the bad thing—for nothink. For when Anton and I went back to a caravan by the roadside to get Maurice (for Anton had hid him there), he wor gone. A man wot had charge of the caravan and horses said he must have run away in the night. I ha' stole yer money, and I ain't brought back Maurice. That's my news, Missie. "

"Yes, " said Cecile vaguely, "that's the news. " She was still quiet—so quiet that one would suppose she scarcely felt. This was true; the

The Children's Pilgrimage

blow was so sudden and sharp that it produced no pain as yet, but her usually sweet and tranquil blue eyes had a dazed and startled look, and her hands were locked tightly together.

Joe, frightened more by a calm so unnatural than he would be by any exclamation, threw himself on the ground at her feet.

"Oh, Miss Cecile—my little lady, my little princess, who I love—I know I ha' broke yer heart; I know it bitter well. But don't, don't look like that. I know I ha' broke yer heart, and you can never, never forgive me—but oh! don't, don't look like that. "

"Yes, Jography, I do forgive you, " answered Cecile. "It was a dreadful temptation; it was too strong for you, poor Jography. Yes, perhaps my heart is broken; but I quite forgive you. I have not much pain. All the bad news does not hurt as it ought. I have a weight here, " pointing to her breast, "and my head is very light, and something is singing in my ears; but I know quite well what has happened: little Maurice is gone! Little, little darling Maurice is quite and really lost! and Lovedy's purse is stolen away! And—I think perhaps the dream is right—and there is—no—*Jesus Christ*. Oh, Joe, Joe—the—singing—in my head! "

Here the tightly folded hands relaxed their strained tension, the blue eyes closed, and Cecile lay unconscious at Joe's feet.

CHAPTER XXIV.

"A CONSIDERING-CAP. "

When Cecile sank down in a swoon in the hut, Toby, who had been lying on the ground apparently half asleep, had risen impatiently. Things were by no means to this dog's liking; in fact, things had come to such a pass that he could no longer bear them quietly. Maurice gone; Joe quite wild and distracted; and Cecile lying like one dead. Toby had an instinct quite through his honest heart that the time had come for *him* to act and with a wild howl he rushed into the forest.

Neither of the two he left behind noticed him; both were too absorbed in the world into which they had entered—Cecile was lying in the borderland between life and death, and Joe's poor feet had strayed to the edge of that darker country where dwells despair.

The dog said to himself: "Neither of them can act, and immediate steps must be taken. Maurice must be found; I, Toby, must not rest until I bring Maurice back. "

He ran into the forest, he sniffed the air, for a few moments he rushed hither and thither; then, blaming himself for not putting his wits into requisition, he sat down on his haunches. There, in the forest of the Landes, Toby might have been seen putting on his considering-cap. Let no one laugh at him. This dog had been given brains by his Maker; he would use these brains now for the benefit of the creatures he loved. Maurice had strayed into the forest; he must bring him back. Now, this particular part of the forest was very large, covering indeed thousands of leagues. There was no saying how far the helpless child might have strayed, not being blessed with that peculiar sense which would have guided Toby back to the hut from any distance, He might have wandered now many leagues away; still Toby, the dog who had watched over his infancy, would not return until he found him again. The dog thought now in his own solemn fashion, What did Maurice like best? Ah! wise Toby knew well: the pretty things, the soft things, the good things of life were little Maurice's desires; plenty of nice food, plenty of warmth and sunshine, plenty of pretty things to see, to touch. In the forest what could Maurice get? Food? No, not without money; and Toby knew that Cecile always kept those little magic coins, which meant so much to them all, in her own safe keeping. No, Maurice could not have food in the forest, but he could have flowers. Toby therefore would seek for the straying child where the flowers grew. He found whole beds of hyacinths, of anemones, of blue-bells, of violets; wherever these grew, there Toby poked his sagacious nose; there he endeavored to take up the lost child's scent. At last he was successful; he found a clew. There was a trampled-down bed of violets; there were withered violets scattered about. How like Maurice to fill his hands with these treasures, and then throw them away. Clever Toby, sniffing the ground, presently caught the scent he desired. This scent carried him to the main road, to the place where the caravan had stood. He saw the mark of wheels, the trampling of horses' feet, but here also the scent he was following ended; the caravan itself had absolutely disappeared. Toby reflected for a minute, threw his head in the air, uttered a cry and then once more rushed back into the forest. Here for a long, long time he searched in vain for any fresh scent; here, too, he met with one or two adventures. A man with a gun chased him, and Toby's days might have been numbered, had he not hidden cleverly under some brushwood until the enemy had disappeared. Then he himself yielded to a canine weakness, and chased a rabbit, but only to the entrance of its burrow; but it was here also that he again took up the clew, for there were just by this rabbit's burrow one or two violets lying dead where no other violets were growing. Toby sniffed at them, gave a glad and joyful cry, and then was off like a shot in quite the contrary direction from where he had come. On and on, the scent sometimes growing very faint, sometimes almost dying out, the dog ran; on and on, he himself getting very tired at last, his tongue hanging out, feeling as if he must almost drop in his longing for water; on and still on, until he found his reward; for at last, under a wide-spreading oak tree, fast asleep, with a tear-begrimed and pale face, lay the little wanderer.

Was ever dog so wild with delight as Toby? He danced about, he capered, he ran, he barked, he licked the little pale face, and when little Maurice awoke, his delight was nearly as great as the dog's; perhaps it was greater, for Maurice, with his arms tight round Toby, cried long and heartily for joy.

"Toby, take me home; take me back to Cecile and Joe, " said the boy.

Toby looked intelligent and complying, but, alas! there were limits even to his devotion. Back he and his little charge could not go until he had stretched his weary limbs on that soft grass, until he too had indulged in a short slumber. So the child and the dog both lay side by side, and both slept.

God's creatures both, and surely his unprotected creatures they seemed, lying there all alone in so vast a solitude. But it was only seeming, it was not so in reality, for round them guardian angels spread protecting wings, and the great Father encircled them both with his love. Two sparrows are not sold for a farthing without his loving knowledge, and Maurice and Toby were therefore as safe as possible.

In the cool of the evening the two awoke, very hungry, it is true, but still refreshed, and then the dog led the lost child home.

CHAPTER XXV.

ALPHONSE.

But in vain Maurice lay down by Cecile's side and pressed his little cool lips to hers. He had returned to her again, but Cecile did not know him. Maurice was quite safe once more; the danger for him was over; but to Cecile he was still a lost child. She was groping for him, she would never find him again. The child her dying father had given into her tender care; the purse her stepmother had set such store by, both were gone, and gone forever. She had been faithless to her trust, and, cruelest of all, her heavenly Guide had not proved true.

Poor Cecile! she pushed away the soft baby face of her little brother. She cried, and wrung her hands, and turned from side to side. Maurice was frightened, and turned tearfully to Joe. What had come to Cecile? How hot she looked! How red were her cheeks! How strange her words and manner!

Joe replied to the frightened little boy that Cecile was very ill, and that it was his fault; in truth, Joe was right. The blow dealt suddenly, and without any previous warning, was too much for Cecile. Coming upon a frame already weakened by fatigue and anxiety she succumbed at once, and long before Toby had brought Maurice home, poor little Cecile was in a burning fever.

All day long had Joe watched by her side, listening to her piteous wailings, to her bitter and reproachful cries. I think in that long and dreadful day poor Joe reaped the wages of his weakness and sin of the night before. Alone, with neither Toby nor Maurice, he dared not leave the sick child. He did not know what to do for her; be could only kneel by her side in a kind of dull pain and despair. Again and again he asked for her forgiveness. He could not guess that his passionate words were falling on quite unconscious ears.

In his long misery Joe had really forgotten little Maurice, but when he saw him enter the hut with Toby he felt a kind of relief. Ignorant truly of illness, an instinct told him that Cecile was very ill. Sick people saw doctors, and doctors had made them well. He could therefore now run off to the village, try to find a doctor, get him to come to Cecile, and then, when he saw that there was a chance of her

The Children's Pilgrimage

wants being attended to rush off himself to do what he had made up his mind to accomplish some time earlier in the day. This was to find Anton, and getting back the little piece of paper, then give himself up to his old life of hardship and slavery.

"You set there, Maurice, " he said, now addressing the bewildered little boy; "Cecile is ill; and you must not leave her. You set quite close to her, and when she asks for it, let her have a drink of water; and, Toby, you take care on them both. "

"But, Joe, I'm *starving* hungry, " said Maurice; "and why must I stay alone when Cecile is so queer, and not a bit glad to see me, though she is calling for me all the time? Why are you going away? I think 'tis very nasty of you, Joe. "

"I must go, Maurice; I must find a doctor for Cecile; the reason Cecile goes on like that is because she is so dreadful ill. Ef I don't get a doctor, why she'll die like my little comrade died when his leg wor broke. You set nigh her, Maurice, and yere's a bit of bread. "

Then Joe, going up to the sick child and kneeling down by her, took one of the burning hands in his.

"Missie, Missie, dear, " he said, "I know as yer desperate ill, and you can't understand me. But still I'd like fur to say as I give hup my old mother, Missie. I wor starving fur my mother, and I thought as I'd see her soon, soon. But it worn't fur to be. I'm goin' back to my master and the old life, and you shall have the purse o' gold. I did bitter, bitter wrong; but I'll do right now. So good-by, my darling darlin' little Missie Cecile. "

As the poor boy spoke he stooped down and kissed the burning hands, and looked longingly at the strangely flushed and altered face; then he went out into the forest. Any action was a relief to his oppressed and overstrained heart, and he knew he had not a moment to lose in trying to find a doctor for Cecile.

He went straight to the village and inquired if such a person dwelt there.

"Yes, " an old peasant woman told him; "certainly they had a doctor, but he was out just now; he was with Mme. Chillon up at a farm a mile away. There was no use in going to the doctor's house, but if the boy would follow him there, to the said farm, he might catch him before he went farther away, for there were to be festivities that night, and their good doctor was always in requisition as the best dancer in the place. "

So Joe followed the doctor to the farm a mile away, and was so fortunate as to find him just before he was about to ride off to the fete mentioned by the old peasant.

Joe, owing to his long residence in England, could only speak broken French, but his agitation, his great earnestness, what little French he could muster, were so far eloquent as to induce the young doctor, instead of postponing his visit to the hut in the forest until the morning, to decide to give up his dance and go with the boy instead.

Joe's intention was to direct the doctor to the hut, and then, without returning thither himself, set off at once on his search for Anton. This, however, the medical man would not permit. He was not acquainted with the forest; he would not go there at so late an hour on any consideration without a guide, so Joe had to change his mind and go with him.

They walked along rapidly, the doctor wondering if there was any chance of his still being in time for his promised dance, the boy too unhappy, too plunged in gloom, to be able to utter a word. It was nearly dark in the forest shade when at last they reached the little tumbledown hut.

But what was the matter? The place Joe had left so still, so utterly without any sound except that made by one weak and wandering voice, seemed suddenly alive. When the doctor and the boy entered, voices, more than one, were speaking eagerly. There was life, color, and movement in the deserted little place.

Bending over the sick child, and tenderly placing a cool handkerchief dipped in cold water on her brow, was a young woman of noble height and proportions. Her face was sunshiny and beautiful, and even in the gathering darkness Joe could see that her head was crowned with a great wealth of golden hair. This young woman, having laid the handkerchief on Cecile's forehead, raised her then tenderly in her arms. As she did so, she turned to address some words in rather broken French to a tall, dark-eyed old woman who stood at the foot of the bed of pine needles.

The Children's Pilgrimage

Both women turned when the boy and the man came in, and at sight of the doctor, whom they evidently knew well, they uttered many exclamations of pleasure.

The young doctor went over at once to his little patient, but Joe, suddenly putting his hand to his heart, stood still in the door of the hut.

Who was that old woman who held Maurice in her arms—that old woman with the upright figure, French from the crown of her head to the sole of her feet? Of what did she remind the boy as she stood holding the tired little child in her kind and motherly clasp?

Ah! he knew, he knew. Almost at the second glance his senses seemed cleared, his memory became vivid, almost too vivid to be borne. He saw those same arms, that same kind, dear, and motherly face, only the arms held another child, and the eyes looked into other eyes, and that child was her own child, and they were in the pretty cottage in the Pyrenees, and brother Jean was coming in from his day's work of tying up the vines.

Yes, Joe knew that he was looking at his mother; once again he had seen her. Though he must not stay with her, though he must give her up, though he must go back to the old dreadful life, still for this one blessed glimpse he would all the rest of his life acknowledge that God was good.

For a moment he stood still, almost swaying from side to side in the wonderful gladness that came over him, then with a low cry the poor boy rushed forward; he flung his arms round the old woman's neck; he strained her to his heart.

"Ah, my mother!" he sobbed, speaking in this sudden excitement in the dear Bearnais of his childhood, "I am Alphonse. Do you not know your little lost son Alphonse?"

CHAPTER XXVI.

LAND OF BEULAH.

The whole scene had changed. She had closed her eyes in a deserted hut lying on a bed of pine needles. She had closed her eyes to the consciousness of Maurice gone, of everything lost and over in her life. It seemed but a moment, but the working of an ugly dream, and she opened them again. Where was she? The hut was gone, the pine-needle bed had vanished; instead she found herself in a pretty room, with dimity curtains hanging before latticed windows; she felt soft white sheets under her, and knew that she was lying in a little bed, in the prettiest child's cot, with dimity curtains fastened back from it also. The room in its freshness and whiteness and purity looked something like an English room, and from the open windows came in a soft, sweet scent of roses.

Had Cecile then gone back to England, and, if so, what English home had received her?

She was too tired, too peaceful, to think much just then. She closed her languid eyes, only knowing that she was comfortable and happy, and feeling that she did not care much about anything if only she might rest on forever in that delicious white bed.

Then, for she was still very weak, she found herself with her thoughts wandering. She was back in England, she was in London. Kind Mrs. Moseley had taken her in; kind Mrs. Moseley was taking great care of Maurice and of her. Then she fancied herself in a vast place of worship where everybody sang, and she heard the words of a very loud and joyful refrain:

"The angels stand on the hallelujah strand,
And sing their welcome home. "

Had she then got home? Was this happy, restful place not even England? Was all the dull and weary wandering over, and had she got home—to the best home—the home where Jesus dwelt? She really thought it must be so, and this would account for the softness of this little bed, and the delicious purity of the beautiful room. Yes, she heard the singing very distinctly; "welcome home" came over and over again to her ears. She opened her eyes. Yes, surely this was heaven, and those were the angels singing. How soft and full and rich their voices sounded.

She tried to raise her head off her pillow, but this she found she could not manage. Where she lay, however, she could see all over the small room. She was alone, with just the faint, sweet breath of roses fanning her cheeks, and that delicious music in the distance. Yes, she certainly must be in the home of Jesus, and soon He would come to see her, and she would talk with Him face to face.

She remembered in a dim kind of way that she had gone to sleep in great trouble and perplexity. But there was no trouble lying on her heart now. She was in the home where no one had any trouble; and when she told Jesus all her story, he would make everything right. Just then a voice, singing the same sweet refrain, came along the passage. As it got near, the music ceased, the door softly opened, and a young woman with golden hair and the brightest of bright faces came softly in. Seeing Cecile with her eyes open, she went gladly up to the bed, and, bending over her, said in a full but gentle voice:

"Ah! dear English little one, how glad I am that you are better! "

"Yes, I'm quite well, " answered Cecile, in her feeble tone. Then she added, looking up wistfully: "Please, how soon may I see Jesus? "

At these words the pleased expression vanished from the young woman's face. She looked at Cecile in pity and alarm, and saying softly to herself, "Ah! she isn't better, then, " turned away with a sigh; but Cecile lifted a feeble hand to detain her.

"Please, I'm much better. I'm quite well, " she said. "This is heaven, isn't it? "

"No, " answered the young woman. She was less alarmed now, and she turned and gazed hard at the child. "No, " she said, "we thought you were going to heaven. But I do believe you really are better. No, my dear little girl! this is very different from heaven. This is only a French farm; a farm in the Landes—pretty enough! but still very different from heaven. You have been very ill, and have been lying on that little bed for the last fortnight, and we did fear that you'd die. We brought you here, and, thanks to my good mother-in-law and our doctor, we have, I do trust, brought you through, and now you must sleep and not talk any more. "

The Children's Pilgrimage

"But please, ma'am, if this is a French farm, how do you speak English? "

"I am English by birth, child; though 'tis a long time now since I have seen my native land. Not that I feel very English, for my good Jean's country is my country, and I only spoke English to you because you don't know French. Now, little girl, lie very still. I shall be back in a minute. "

The young woman did come back in a minute, holding, of all people in the world, Maurice by the hand.

Maurice then, who Cecile thought was quite lost, was back again, and Cecile looked into his dear brown eyes, and got a kiss from his sweet baby lips. A grave, grave kiss from lips that trembled, and a grave look from eyes full of tears; for to little Maurice his Cecile was sadly changed; but the young woman with the bright hair would not allow him to linger now. She held a cup of some delicious cooling drink to the sick child's lips, and then sat down by her side until she slept, and this was the beginning of a gentle but slow recovery.

Pretty young Mme. Malet sat most of the day in Cecile's room, and Maurice came in and out, and now and then an old woman, with an upright figure and French face, came and stood by the bedside and spoke softly and lovingly, but in a tone Cecile could not understand, and a lovely little boy was brought in once a day by his proud young mother, and suffered to give Cecile one kiss before he was taken away again. And the kindest care and the most nourishing food were always at hand for the poor little pilgrim, who lay herself in a very land of Beulah of rest and thankfulness.

Her memory was still very faint; her lost purse did not trouble her; even Lovedy became but a distant possibility; all was rest and peace, and that dreadful day when she thought her heavenly Guide had forsaken her had vanished forever from her gentle heart.

One afternoon, however, when Mme. Malet sat by the open window quietly knitting a long stocking, a disturbing thought came to Cecile; not very disturbing, but still enough for her to start and ask anxiously:

"Why doesn't Joe ever come to see me? "

The Children's Pilgrimage

At these words a shade came over the bright face of the young wife and mother; she hesitated for a moment, then said, a trifle uneasily:

"I wouldn't trouble about Joe just now, deary. "

"Oh! but I must, " answered Cecile. "How is it that I never missed him before? I do love Joe. Oh! don't tell me that anything bad has happened to my dear, dear Joe. "

"I don't know that anything bad has happened to him, dear. I trust not. I will tell you all I know. The night my mother-in-law and I found you in that little hut I saw a tall dark boy. He had gone to fetch the doctor for you, and he stood in the gloom, for we had very little light just then. All on a sudden he gave a cry, and ran to my mother-in-law, and threw his arms round her neck, and said strange words to her. But before she could answer him, or say one single sentence in reply, he just ran out of the hut and disappeared. Then we brought you and Maurice and Toby home, and we have not heard one word of Joe since, dear. "

CHAPTER XXVII.

REVELATIONS.

After this little conversation with Mme. Malet Cecile's sojourn in the land of Beulah seemed to come to an end. Not that she was really unhappy, but the peace which gave a kind of unreal sweetness to this time of convalescence had departed; her memory, hitherto so weak, came back fully and vividly, she remembered all that dreadful conversation with Joe, she knew again and felt it through and through her sensitive heart that *her* Joe had proved unfaithful. He had stolen the piece of paper with the precious address, he had given over the purse of gold into the hands of the enemy. Not lightly had he done this thing, not lightly had he told her of his wrongdoing. Could she ever forget the agony in his eyes or the horror in his poor voice as he told her of the life from which he had thus freed himself. No, all through her illness she had seen that troubled face of Joe's, and now even she could scarcely bear to dwell upon it. Joe had been sorely tempted, and he had fallen. Poor Joe! No, she could not, she would not blame Joe, but all the same her own life seemed ended; God had been very good. The dear Guide Jesus, when He restored to her little Maurice, had assuredly not forsaken her; but still, all the same, *she* had been faithless. Her dying stepmother had put into her hands a sacred trust, and she never now could fulfill that trust.

"Though I tried to do my best—I did try to do my very, very best, " sighed the poor little girl, wiping the tears from her eyes.

Cecile was now sufficiently recovered to leave her pretty and bowery bedroom and come down to the general living room. This room, half kitchen, half parlor, again in an undefined way reminded her of the old English farmhouse where she and Maurice had been both happy and unhappy not so long ago. Here Cecile saw for the first time young Mme. Malet's husband. He was a big and handsome fellow, very dark—as dark as Joe; he had a certain look of Joe which rather puzzled Cecile and caused her look at him a great deal. Watching him, she also noticed something else. That handsome young matron, Mme. Malet, that much idolized wife and mother, was not quite happy. She had high spirits; she laughed a full, rich laugh often through the day; she ran briskly about; she sang at her work; but for all that, when for a few moments she was quiet, a shadow would steal over her bright face. When no one appeared to

The Children's Pilgrimage

notice, sighs would fall from her cherry lips. As she sat by the open lattice window, always busy, making or mending, she would begin an English song, then stop, perhaps to change it for a gay French one, perhaps to wipe away a hasty tear. Once when she and Cecile were alone, and the little girl began talking innocently of the country where she had been brought up, she interrupted her almost petulantly:

"Stop, " she said, "tell me nothing about England. I was born there, but I don't love it; France is my country now. "

Then seeing her husband in the distance, she ran out to meet him, and presently came in leaning on his arm, but her blue eyes were wet with sudden tears.

These things puzzled Cecile. Why should Mme. Malet dislike England? Why was Mme. Malet sad?

But the young matron was not the only one who had a sad face in this pretty French farm just now; the elderly woman, the tall and upright old Frenchwoman, Cecile saw one day crying bitterly by the fire. This old woman had from the first been most kind to Cecile, and had petted Maurice, often rocking him to sleep in her arms, but as she did not know even one word of English, she left the real care of the children to her daughter-in-law Suzanne. Consequently Cecile had seen very little of her while she stayed in her own room, but when she came downstairs she noticed her sad old face, and when she heard her bitter sobs, the loving heart of the child became so full she could scarcely bear her own feelings. She ran up to the old Frenchwoman and threw her arms round her neck, and said "Don't cry; ah, don't cry! " and the Frenchwoman answered "*La pauvre petite*! " to her, and though neither of them understood one word that the other said, yet they mingled their tears together, and in some way the sore heart of the elder was comforted.

That evening, that very same evening, Cecile, sitting in the porch by the young Mme. Malet's side, ventured to ask her why her mother-in-law looked so sorry.

"My poor mother-in-law, " answered Suzanne readily, "she has known great trouble, Cecile. My Jean was not her only child. My mother-in-law is mourning for another child. "

"Another child, " replied Cecile; "had old Mme. Malet another child? and did he die? "

"No, he didn't die. He was lost long, long ago. One day he ran away, it was when they lived, my good Jean and his mother, in the Pyrenees, and little Alphonse ran out, and they fear someone stole him, for they never got tidings of him since. He was a bright little lad, and, being her youngest, he was quite a Benjamin to my poor mother-in-law.

"Oh! she did fret for him bitterly hard, and they—she and my good Jean—spent all the money they had, looking for him. But this happened years ago and I think my mother-in-law was beginning to take comfort in my little son, our bonnie young Jean, when, Cecile, that boy you call Joe upset her again. He could not have been her son, for if he was, he'd never have run away. Besides, he did not resemble the little lad with black curls she used to talk to me about. But he ran up to her, doubtless mistaking her for someone else, and called her his mother, and said he was her lost Alphonse.

"Then before she could open her lips to reply to him, he darted out of the little hut, and was lost in the darkness, and not a trace of him have we come across since, and I tell my poor mother-in-law that he isn't her child. But she doesn't believe me, Cecile, and 'tis about him she is so sad all day. "

"But he is her child, he is indeed her child, " answered Cecile, who had listened breathless to this tale. "Oh! I know why he ran away. Oh, yes, Mme. Malet is indeed his mother. I always thought his mother lived in the Pyrenees. I never looked to find her here. Oh! my poor, poor dear Joe! Oh, Mme. Suzanne, you don't know how my poor Joe did hunger for his mother! "

"But, Cecile, Cecile, " began young Mme. Malet excitedly. So far she had got when the words, eager and important as they were, were stayed on her lips.

There was a commotion outside. A woman was heard to shriek, and then to fall heavily; a lad was heard to speak comforting words, choked with great sobs; and then, strangest of all, above this tumult came a very quiet English voice, demanding water—water to pour on the lips and face of a fainting woman.

The Children's Pilgrimage

Suzanne rushed round to the side from whence these sounds came. Cecile, being still weak, tried to follow, but felt her legs tottering. She was too late to go, but not too late to see; for the next instant big strong Jean Malet appeared, carrying in his fainting old mother, and immediately behind him and his wife came not only Cecile's own lost Joe, but that English lady, Miss Smith.

CHAPTER XXVIII.

THE STORY AND ITS LISTENERS.

It was neither at the fainting mother nor at Joe that Cecile now looked. With eyes opening wide with astonishment and hope, she ran forward, caught Miss Smith's two hands in her own, and exclaimed in a voice rendered unsteady with agitation:

"Oh! have you got my purse? Is Lovedy's Russia-leather purse quite, quite safe? "

Busy as young Mme. Malet was at that moment, at the word "Lovedy" she started and turned round. But Cecile was too absorbed in Miss Smith's answer to notice anyone else.

"Is Lovedy's purse quite, quite safe? " asked her trembling lips.

"The purse is safe, " answered Miss Smith; and then Joe, who had as yet not even glanced at Cecile, also raised his head and added:

"Yes, Cecile, the Russia-leather purse is safe. "

"Then I must thank Jesus now at once, " said Cecile.

With her weak and tottering steps she managed to leave the room to gain her own little chamber, where, if ever a full heart offered itself up to the God of Mercy, this child's did that night.

It was a long time before Cecile reappeared, and when she did so order was restored to the Malet's parlor. Old Mme. Malet was seated in her own easy-chair by the fire; one trembling hand rested on Joe's neck; Joe knelt at her feet, and the eyes of this long-divided mother and son seemed literally to drink in love and blessing the one from the other.

All the anxiety, all the sorrow seemed to have left the fine old face of the Frenchwoman. She sat almost motionless, in that calm which only comes of utter and absolute content.

Miss Smith was sitting by the round table in the center of the room, partaking of a cup of English tea. Big brother Jean was bustling in

The Children's Pilgrimage

and out, now and then laying a great and loving hand on his old mother's head, now and then looking at the lost Alphonse with a gaze of almost incredulous wonder.

Young Mme. Malet had retired to put her child to bed, but when Cecile entered she too came back to the room.

Had anyone had time at such a moment to particularly notice this young woman, they would have seen that her face now alone of all that group retained its pain. Such happiness beamed on every other face that the little cloud on hers must have been observed, though she tried hard to hide it.

As she came into the room now, her husband came forward and put his arm round her waist.

"You are just in time, Suzanne, " he said; the English lady is going to tell the story of the purse, and you shall translate it to the mother and me. "

"Yes, Cecile, " said Miss Smith, taking the little girl's hand and seating her by her side, "if I had been the shrewd old English body I am, you would never have seen your purse again; but here it is at last, and I am not sorry to part with it. "

Here Miss Smith laid the Russia-leather purse on the table by Cecile's side.

At sight of this old-fashioned and worn purse, young Mme. Malet started so violently that her husband said: "What ails thee, dear heart? "

With a strong effort she controlled herself, and with her hands locked tightly together, with a tension that surely meant pain.

"The day before yesterday, " continued Miss Smith, "I was sitting in my little parlor, in the very house where you found me out, Cecile; I was sitting there and, strange to say, thinking of you, and of the purse of gold you intrusted to me, a perfect stranger, when there came a ring to my hall door. In a moment in came Molly and said that a man wanted to see me on very particular business. She said the man spoke English. That was the reason I consented to see him, my dear; for I must say that, present company excepted, I do hate foreigners. However, I said I would see the man, and Molly showed him in, a seedy-looking fellow he was, with a great cut over his eye. I knew at a glance he was not English-born and I wished I had refused to see him; he had, however, a plausible tongue, and was quite quiet and *well-behaved.

"How astonished I was when he asked for your purse of gold, Cecile, and showed me the little bit of paper, in my own writing, promising to resign the purse at any time to bearer.

"I was puzzled, I can tell you. I thoroughly distrusted the man, but I scarcely knew how to get out of my own promise. He had his tale, too, all ready enough. You had found the girl you were looking for: she was in great poverty, and very ill; you were also ill, and could not come to fetch the purse; you therefore had sent him, and he must go back to the south of France without delay to you. He said he had been kept on the road by an accident which had caused that cut over his eye.

"I don't know that I should have given him the purse, —I don't believe I should, —but, at any rate, before I had made up my mind to any line of action, again Molly put in an appearance, saying that a ragged boy seemed in great distress outside, and wanted to see me immediately; 'and he too can speak English, ' she continued with a smile.

"I saw the man start and look uneasy when the ragged boy was mentioned, and I instantly resolved to see him, and in the man's presence.

"'Show him in, ' I said to my little servant.

"The next instant in came your poor Joe, Cecile. Oh! how wild and pitiful he looked.

"'You have not given him the purse, ' he said, flying to my side, 'you have not given up the purse? Oh! not yet, not yet! Anton, ' he added, 'I have followed you all the way; I could not catch you up before. Anton, I have changed my mind, I want you to give me the bit of paper, and I will go back to my old life. My heart is broken. I have seen my mother, and I will give her up. Anton, I must have the bit of paper for Cecile. Cecile is dying for want of it. I will go back to my

The Children's Pilgrimage

old master and the dreadful life. I am quite ready. I am quite ready at last'

"There was no doubt as to the truth of this boy's tale, no doubt as to the reality of his agitation. Even had I been inclined to doubt it, one look at the discomfited and savage face of the man would have convinced me.

"'Tis a lie, ' he managed to get out. 'Madame, that young rogue never spoke a word of truth in his life. He is a runaway and a thief. Mine is the true tale. Give me the purse, and let me take it to the little girl.'

"'Whether this boy is a rogue or not,' I said, 'I shall listen to his tale as well as yours.'

"Then I managed to quiet the poor boy, and when he was a little calmer I got him to tell, even in the presence of his enemy, his most bitter and painful history.

"When Joe had finished speaking, I turned to the villain who was trying if possible to scare the poor lad's reason away.

"'The threat you hold over this boy is worthless' I said. 'You have no power to deliver him up to his old master. I believe it can be very clearly proved that he was stolen, and in that case the man who stole him is liable to heavy punishment. So much I know. You cannot touch the lad, and you shall not with my leave. Now as to the rest of the tale, there is an easy way of finding out which of you is speaking the truth. I shall adopt that easy plan. I shall give the purse to neither of you, but take it myself to the little girl who intrusted it to me. I can go to her by train to-morrow morning. I had meant to give myself a holiday, and this trip will just suit me to perfection. If the boy likes to accompany me to his mother, I will pay his fare third-class. Should the old woman turn out not to be his mother and his story prove false, I shall have nothing more to say to him. As to you, Anton, if that is your name, I don't think I need have any further words with you. If you like to go back to the little girl, you can find your own way back to her. I shall certainly give to neither of you the purse.

"My dear, " continued Miss Smith, "after this, and seeing that he was completely foiled, and that his little game was hopeless, that bad man, Anton, took it upon him to abuse me a good deal, and he might, it is just possible, he *might* have proceeded to worse, had not this same Joe taken him quietly by the shoulders and put him not only out of the room, but out of the door. Joe seemed suddenly to have lost all fear of him, and as he is quite double Anton's size, the feat was easy enough. I think that is all, my dear. I have done, I feel, a good deed in restoring a son to a mother. Joe's story is quite true. And now, my dear, perhaps you will take care of that purse yourself in future. "

"And oh, Cecile! now—now at last can you quite, quite forgive me? " said Joe. He came forward, and knelt at her feet.

"Poor Joe! Dear, dear Joe! " answered Cecile, "I always forgave you. I always loved you. "

"Then perhaps the Lord Christ can forgive me too? "

"Oh, yes! "

"That's as queer a story as I ever heard, " here interrupted Jean Malet. "But I can't go to bed, or rest, without hearing more. How did a little maiden like her yonder come by a purse full of gold? "

"I can tell that part, " said Joe suddenly. "I can tell that in French, so that my mother and my brother can understand. There is no harm in telling it now, Cecile, for everything seems so wonderful, we must find Lovedy soon. "

"But is it not late—is it not late to hear the story to-night? " said Suzanne Malet in a faint voice.

"No, no, my love! What has come to thee, my dear one? " said her husband tenderly. "Most times thou wouldst be eaten up with curiosity. No, no; no bed for me to-night until I get at the meaning of that purse. "

Thus encouraged, Joe did tell Cecile's story; he told it well, and with pathos—all about that step-mother and her lost child; all about her solemn dying charge; and then of how he met the children, and their adventures and escapes; and of how in vain they looked for the English girl with the golden hair and eyes of blue, but still of how their faith never failed them; and of how they hoped to see Lovedy in some village in the Pyrenees. All this and more did Joe tell, until his old mother wept over the touching story, and good brother Jean wiped the tears from his own eyes, and everyone seemed moved except Suzanne, who sat with cheeks now flushed—now pale, but motionless and rigid almost as if she did not hear. Afterward she said her boy wanted her, and left the room.

"Suzanne is not well" remarked her husband.

"The sad, sad tale is too much for her, dear impulsive child, " remarked the old mother.

But honest Jean Malet shook his head, and owned to himself that for the first time he quite failed to understand his wife.

CHAPTER XXIX.

THE WORTH OF THE JOURNEY.

That same night, just when Cecile had laid her tired head on her pillow, there came a soft tap to her door, and young Mme. Malet, holding a lamp in her hand, came in.

"Ah, Madame, " said Cecile, "I am so glad to see you. Has it not been wonderful, wonderful, what has happened to day? Has not Jesus the Guide been more than good? Yes. I do feel now that He will hear my prayer to the very end; I do feel that I shall very soon find Lovedy. "

"Cecile" said Mme. Malet, kneeling down by the child's bed, and holding the lamp so that its light fell full on her own fair face, "what kind was this Lovedy Joy? "

"What kind? " exclaimed Cecile. "Ah, dear Mme. Suzanne, how well I know her face! I can see it as her mother told me about it-blue eyes, golden hair, teeth white and like little pearls, rosy, cherry lips. A beautiful English girl! No-I never could mistake Lovedy. "

"Cecile, " continued Mme. Malet, "you say you would know this Lovedy when you saw her. See! Look well at me—the light is shining on my face. What kind of face have I got, Cecile? "

"Fair, " answered Cecile—"very fair and very beautiful. Your eyes, they are blue as the sky; and your lips, how red they are, and how they can smile! And your teeth are very white; and then your hair, it is like gold when the sun makes it all dazzling. And—and— —"

"And I am English-an English girl, " continued Madame.

"An English girl! " repeated Cecile, "you—are—like *her*—then! "

"Cecile, I am her—*I am Lovedy Joy*! "

"You! you! " repeated Cecile. "You Lovedy! But no, no; you are Suzanne—you are Mme. Malet. "

"Nevertheless I was—I am Lovedy Joy. I am that wicked girl who broke her mother's heart; I am that wicked girl who left her. Cecile, I

The Children's Pilgrimage

am she whom you seek; you have no further search to make—poor, brave, dear little sister—I am she. "

Then Lovedy put her arms round Cecile, and they mingled their tears together. The woman wept from a strong sense of remorse and pain, but the child's tears were all delight.

"And you are the Susie about whom Mammie Moseley used to fret? Oh, it seems *too* good, too wonderful! " said Cecile at last.

"Yes, Cecile, I left Mammie Moseley too; I did everything that was heartless and bad. Oh, but I have been unhappy. Surrounded by mercies as I have been, there has been such a weight, so heavy, so dreadful, ever on my heart. "

Cecile did not reply to this. She was looking hard at the Lovedy she had come so many miles to seek—for whom she had encountered so many dangers. It seemed hard to realize that her search was accomplished, her goal won, her prize at her feet.

"Yes, Lovedy, your mother was right, you are very beautiful, " she said slowly.

"Oh, Cecile! tell me about my mother, " said Lovedy then. "All these years I have never dared speak of my mother. But that has not prevented my starving for her, something as poor Joe must have starved for his. Tell me all you can about my mother—-more than Alphonse told downstairs tonight. "

So Cecile told the old story. Over and over again she dwelt upon that deathbed scene, upon that poor mother's piteous longing for her child, and Lovedy listened and wept as if her heart would break.

At last this tale, so sad, so bitter for the woman who was now a mother herself, came to an end, and then Lovedy, wiping her eyes, spoke:

"Cecile, I must tell you a little about myself. You know the day my mother married your father, I ran away. I had loved my mother most passionately; but I was jealous. I was exacting. I was proud. I could not bear that my mother should put anyone in my place. I ran away. I went to my Aunt Fanny. She was a vain and silly woman. She praised me for running away. She said I had spirit. She took me to Paris.

"For the first week I got on pretty well. The new life helped to divert my thoughts, and I tried to believe I could do well without my mother. But then the knowledge that I had done wrong, joined to a desperate mother-hunger, I can call it by no other word, took possession of me. I got to hate my aunt, who led a gay life. At last I could bear it no longer. I ran away.

"I had just enough money in my pocket to take me to London; I had not one penny more. But I felt easy enough; I thought, I will go to our old home, and make it up with mother, and then it will be all right. So I spent my last, my very last shilling in a cab fare, and I gave the driver the old address.

"As I got near the house, I began to wish I had not come. I was such an odd mixture; all made up of love and that terrible pride. However, my pride was to get a shock I little expected.

"Strangers were in the old rooms; strangers who knew nothing whatever about my mother. I found that I had so set my heart against this marriage, that I had not even cared to inquire the name of the man my mother had married; so I had no clew to give anyone, no one could help me. I was only a child then, and I wandered away without one farthing, absolutely alone in the great world of London.

"It drove me nearly wild to remember that my mother was really in the very same London, and I could not find her, and when I had got as far as a great bridge—-I knew it was a bridge, for I saw the water running under it—-I could bear my feelings no longer, and I just cried out like any little baby for my Mammie.

"It was then, Cecile, that Mrs. Moseley found me. Oh! how good she was to me! She took me home and she gave me love, and my poor starved heart was a little satisfied.

"Perhaps she and her husband could have helped me to find my mother. But again that demon pride got over me. I would not tell them my tale. I would acknowledge to no one that my mother had put another in my place; so all the time that I was really starving for one kiss from my own mother, I made believe that I did not care.

The Children's Pilgrimage

"I used to go out every day and look for her as well as I could by myself, but of course I never got the slightest clew to where she lived; and I doubt then, that even if I had known, so contrary was I, that I would have gone to her.

"Well, one day, who should come up to me, quite unexpectedly, but Aunt Fanny again. Oh! she was a bad, cruel woman, and she had a strange power over me. She talked very gently, and not a bit crossly, and she soon came around a poor, weak young thing like me; she praised my pretty face, and she roused my vanity and my pride, and at last she so worked on me, that she got me to do a mean and shameful thing—I was to go back to Paris with her, without ever even bidding the Moseleys good-by.

"Well, Cecile, I did go—-I hate myself when I think of it, but I did go back to Paris that very night with Aunt Fanny. I soon found out what she was up to, she wanted to make money by me. She took me to a stage-manager, and he said he would prepare me for the stage— I had a voice, as well as a face and figure, he said. And he prophesied that I should be a great success. Then I began the most dreadful life. I heard horrible things, bad things.

"Perhaps the thought of all the triumphs that were before me might have reconciled me to my fate, but I had always in my heart the knowledge that I had done wrong: however, Aunt Fanny ruled me with a tight hand, and I had no chance of running away. I was so unhappy that I wrote to the Moseleys begging them to forgive and help me, but I think now Aunt Fanny must have stopped the letters, for I never got any answer.

"Well, Cecile, she died rather suddenly, and the manager said I was his property, and I must come and live in his house.

"I could not stand that. I just made up my mind; I ran away again. It was night, and I wandered alone in the Paris streets. I had two francs in my pocket. God only knows what my fate would have been, but *He* took care of me. As I was walking down a long boulevard I heard a woman say aloud and very bitterly:

"'God above help me; shall I ever see my child again?'

"She spoke in French, but I understood French very well then. Her words arrested me; I turned to look at her.

"'Oh, my dear! you are too young to be out alone at night like this, " she said.

"Oh! but she had the kindest heart. Cecile, that woman was Mme. Malet; she had come up to Paris to look for her lost Alphonse; she took me home with her to the South; and a year after, I married my dear, my good Jean. Cecile, I have the best husband, I have the sweetest child; but I have never been quite happy — often I have been miserable; I could not tell about my mother, even to my Jean. He often asked me, but I always said:

"'I hate England; ask me nothing about England if you love me.'"

"But you will tell him to-night; you will tell him all to-night? " asked Cecile.

"Yes, dear little one, I am going to him; there shall never be a secret between us again; and now God reward, God bless thee, dear little sister. "

CHAPTER XXX.

THE END CROWNS ALL.

Summer! summer, not in the lovely country, but in the scorching East End. Such heated air! such scorching pavements! Oh! how the poor were suffering! How pale the little children looked, as too tired, and perhaps too weak to play, they crept about the baking streets. Benevolent people did all they could for these poor babies. Hard-working East End clergymen got subscriptions on foot, and planned days in the country, and, where it was possible, sent some away for longer periods. But try as they would, the lives of the children had to be spent with their parents in this region, which truly seems to know the two extremes, both the winter's cold and the summer's heat. It was the first week in August, and the Moseleys' little room, still as neat as possible, felt very hot and close. It was in vain to open their dormer windows. The air outside seemed hotter than that within. The pair were having some bread and butter and cold tea, but both looked flushed and tired. They had, in truth, just returned from a long pleasure excursion under their good clergyman, Mr. Danvers, into the country. Mrs. Moseley had entire charge of about twenty children, her husband of as many more; so no wonder they looked fagged. But no amount of either heat or fatigue could take the loving sparkle out of Mammie Moseley's eyes, and she was now expatiating on the delights of the little ones in the grass and flowers.

"There was one dear little toddle, John, " she said; "she seemed fairly to lose her head with delight; to see that child rolling over in the grass and clutching at the daisies would do any heart good. Eh! but they all did have a blessed day. The sin and shame of it is to bring them back to their stifling homes to-night. "

"I tell you what, wife, " said John Moseley, "the sight of the country fairly made a kitten of yerself. I haven't seen yer so young and so sprightly since we lost our bit of a Charlie. And I ha' made up my mind, and this is wot I'll do: We has two or three pounds put by, and I'll spend enough of it to give thee a real holiday, old girl. You shall go into Kent for a fortnight. There! "

"No, no, John, nothink of the kind; I'm as strong and hearty as possible. I feels the 'eat, no doubt; but Lor'! I ha' strength to bear it. No, John, my man, ef we can spare a couple o' pounds, let's give it to

The Children's Pilgrimage

Mr. Danvers' fund for the poor little orphans and other children as he wants to send into the country for three weeks each."

"But that'll do thee no good, " expostulated John Moseley, in a discontented voice.

"Oh! yes, but it will, John, dear; and ef you don't like to do it for me, you do it for Charlie. Whenever I exercises a bit of self-denial, I thinks: well, I'll do it for the dear dead lamb. I thinks o' him in the arms of Jesus, and nothink seems too hard to give up for the sake of the blessed One as takes such care of my darling."

"I guess as that's why you're so good to 'strays,'" said John Moseley. "Eh! but, Moll, wot 'as come o' yer word, as you'd take no more notice o' them, since them two little orphans runned away last winter?"

"There's no manner o' use in twitting at me, John. A stray child allers reminds me so desp'rate hard o' Charlie, and then I'm jest done for. 'Twill be so to the end. Hany stray 'ud do wot it liked wid Mammie Moseley. But eh! I do wonder wot has come to my poor little orphans, them and Susie! I lies awake at night often and often and thinks it all hover. How they all vanished from us seems past belief."

"Well, there seems a power o' 'strays' coming hup the stairs now, " said John Moseley, "to judge by the noise as they makes. Sakes alive! wife, they're coming hup yere. Maybe 'tis Mr. Danvers and his good lady. They said they might call round. Jest set the table tidy."

But before Mrs. Moseley could do anything of the kind, the rope which lifted the boards was pulled by a hand which knew its tricks well, and the next instant bounded into the room a shabby-looking dog with a knowing face. He sprang upon John Moseley with a bark of delight; licked Mammie Moseley's hands; then, seeing the cat in her accustomed corner, he ran and lay down by her side. The moment Toby saw the cat it occurred to him that a life of ease was returning to him, and he was not slow to avail himself of it. But there was no time to notice Toby, nor to think of Toby, for instantly he was followed by Maurice and Cecile and, immediately after them, a dark-eyed boy, and then a great big man, and last, but not least, a fair-haired and beautiful young woman.

The Children's Pilgrimage

It was at this young woman Mammie Moseley stared even more intently than at Cecile. But the young woman, taking Cecile's hand, came over and knelt on the ground, and, raising eyes brimful of tears, said:

"Mammie, mammie, I am Susie! and Cecile has brought me back to you!"

* * * * *

Over the confusion that ensued—the perfect Babel of voices—the endless exclamation—the laughter and the tears—it might be best to draw a veil.

Suffice it to say, that this story of a brave endeavor, of a long pilgrimage, of a constant purpose, is nearly ended. Lovedy and her party spent a few days in London, and then they went down into Kent and found good faithful Jane Parsons, now happily married to the very night-guard who had befriended Cecile and Maurice when they were sent flying from Aunt Lydia to London. Even Aunt Lydia, as her mother's sister, did repentant Lovedy find out; and, seeing her now reduced to absolute poverty, she helped her as best she could. Nothing could make Lydia Purcell really grateful; but even she was a little softened by Lovedy's beauty and bewitching ways. She even kissed Cecile when she bade her good-by, and Cecile, in consequence, could think of her without fear in her distant home.

Yes, Cecile's ultimate destination was France. In that pretty farmhouse on the borders of the Landes, she and Maurice grew up as happy and blessed as children could be. No longer orphans—for had they not a mother in old Mme. Malet, a sister in Lovedy, while Joe must always remain as the dearest of dear brothers? Were you to ask Cecile, she would tell you she had just one dream still unfulfilled. She hopes some day to welcome Mammie Moseley to her happy home in France. The last thing that good woman said to the child, as she clung with arms tightly folded round her neck, was this:

"The Guide Jesus was most wonderful kind to you, Cecile, my lamb! He took you safely a fearsome and perilous journey. You'll let Him guide you still all the rest of the way?"

"All the rest of the way," answered Cecile in a low and solemn voice. "Oh, Mammie Moseley I could not live without Him."

Just two things more... Anton is dead. Miss Smith has ever remained a faithful friend to Cecile; and Cecile writes to her once a year.

Copyright © 2021 Esprios Digital Publishing. All Rights Reserved.